The Purrfect Romance

By

Sheryl Letzgus McGinnis

READING ENTERTAINMENT FOR THE ENTIRE FAMILY

Editor: Kase J. Reed

Line Editor: Topaz Publishing

ISBN: TPEB000000031

ISBN-13: 978-0615742748

ISBN-10: 0615742742

WC: 69,205

Genre: Topaz Holiday ~ Sweet, Christian & Inspirational Romance

Topaz Publishing, LLC

USA

www.topazpublishingllc.com

Topaz Publishing, LLC

Thank you for buying a product of Topaz Publishing
Quality Reading for the Entire Family

Book Blurb

The Purrfect Romance

A Catalyst for Love

Lacey Belle Robertson is a beautiful southern gal from Charleston, South Carolina. When both parents die within a year of each other, she finds herself alone with no real purpose in life. She cared for her parents during their illness, and now she was orphaned. Her life is suddenly changed when she meets the handsome and wealthy attorney, Steve Schmidt. Steve introduces Lacey to a lavish lifestyle, and adorns her with jewels, couture clothing, and fine dining. It isn't long before Lacey realizes she's nothing more than eye candy to Steve; someone he can show off to his friends. Steve is controlling, and has a frightening temper—a fact she discovers when she doesn't yield to his wishes.

Lacey flees to Vermont where she has just inherited a mansion. Until her recent death, the home belonged to her Nana. To decide whether or not she'll return to South Carolina Lacey needs space from Steve. Fate intervenes, and Lacey meets a gorgeous Australian named, Jake Anderson. Jake's dark past colors the way he treats people. He antagonizes Lacey with his strange Australian expressions, and his apparent dislike of her. Bewildered by his odd behavior, Lacey wonders why she's treated with such disdain.

A Tuxedo Cat with healing powers also enters her life. Jingles is the companion of Jake's uncle, Alex. Before the year is out, Jingles intervenes with hilarious results. The lovable, but ornery cat works his magic on everyone. Can Jingles bring Jake and Lacey together, by healing their wounds?

ACKNOWLEDGMENTS

For my beloved husband, Jack, my sons, Dale and Scott, and my wonderful Australian family. This book is also dedicated to all the terrific cats and dogs I've been privileged to have in my life. They're all bonzer!

CHAPTER ONE

"Well, Lacey Belle Robertson, you have a big decision to make now. Do you phone Steve and tell him you're not coming back to him, or do you go back home and give him another chance?"

Lacey's thoughts flew through her head faster than fat cells could multiply on her thighs. She screamed her most dreaded word, "Decision!" She was good at a lot of things, but making decisions was not one of them. The irony of the thought amused her.

"I'm such a coward. I should have discussed this matter before I left." Lacey sighed, and pushed thoughts of Steve out of her head. Her indecision notwithstanding, she simply didn't feel up to doing anything right now. "C*ould there be such a thing as delayed jet lag?"*

Nana's spacious country kitchen had a brick tiled floor, and a generous food island. Sandwiched between two huge windows were walls of richly polished oak cabinets adorned with hunter green and white checked curtains. Large bows added a special touch to the windows. A maple table with six matching chairs occupied one-half of the oversized kitchen. Columns of gleaming copper pots hung from a heavy burnished metal rack waiting like silent sentries. An array of colorful dried peppers hung from one end of the rack and complemented an equally long length of aromatic cinnamon sticks and spice sachets on the opposite end.

Lacey closed her eyes, evoking the aromas of

Nana's scrumptious cheese and tomato omelets with sides of potatoes. Onions, bacon and steaming hot coffee also came to mind. Memories of many happy breakfasts brought a smile to her face, and warmth to her heart.

Needing to share her feelings, Lacey picked up her cell phone then called her best friend, Summer. The phone rang several times while Lace waited patiently. "What took you so long, Summer? Were you in the shower?" Before Summer could answer, Lace prattled on. "I'm standing in Nana's kitchen. My emotions are all jumbled up. I miss you really bad. Help."

"Slow down. You're much too excited. And, I miss you more. I was just about to call you. Your vibes arrived in Charleston in record time. Seriously. Now, take a deep breath, then tell me what's going on."

"Okay." Lacey forced a smile. By the end of their conversation, Summer would no doubt bring a true smile to her face. "I have quite an adjustment to make, and Nana's kitchen is bringing back so many memories."

"Of course it is, hon."

"There's so much to tell you. You know me, I get started and I can't stop."

"Let me sit down, Lacey Belle. Do you think you'll feel at home there?"

"Absolutely, Summer. Nana has a dining room; a

dining hall is more like it. The table is grand enough to comfortably seat 16 people. I'd feel like I was hosting a state dinner if I served food in there.

"Nana doesn't put on airs. She said the dining room was used to accommodate people when the kitchen table wouldn't suffice. It was convenient and functional to Nana's way of thinking. Summer, she really loved her home. And, when you come for a visit, you will too."

"Go on, Lacey. So far, it sounds delightful. When I come to visit, I expect to be served at that table, okay?" Lacey was a jeans and tee shirt girl, formalities didn't interest her. Already she was beginning to feel less stressed. "Did I tell you the story of Nana, and her sweet cat, Taffy? "

"No. Not yet."

Lacey could feel the warmth in Summer's voice. Of course, Summer would let her talk as long as she needed. "Taffy would perch himself smack dab in the middle of the dining room table. He hated to leave when guests arrived."

"Sounds like a typical cat, Lacey. What's so unusual about that?"

"Nana didn't mind Taffy curling up on the table. It was the one-time exuberant leap onto the highly polished table that Nana didn't like. He went sliding down the length of it, scattering expensive crystal goblets and causing Aunt Jean to squeal with fright. Well, even Nana couldn't tolerate that. She said, henceforth he was confined to her bedroom during dinner parties. A fate worse than death, judging by Taffy's loud protestations. I'm glad I remembered that story. I feel a bit better already."

"Cats are funny. Tell me more about the place so I'll feel like I belong there when I come up to see you."

"Well, of course you'll belong here. I've selected the perfect bedroom for you. Did I tell you this place has 6 bedrooms?"

"Yeah, you did. It would make a perfect B&B with you as the charming innkeeper."

"I've had the same thought, Summer. Maybe, one day. But, continuing the grand tour, there's an old-fashioned hutch and dry sink built by Gramps. There's also a huge wood and wrought iron chandelier holding a dozen electric candles. It's suspended from thick, sturdy black coated chains watching over the table. It casts a warm glow at night. I do remember that. Wow, I really am waxing poetic aren't I?"

"I wouldn't expect anything less from you, Lacey. Continue. I'm picturing myself there already. Maybe you should write travel brochures."

"I'll grant you that. This place certainly is worthy of a travel brochure. The view from the dining room during the day is magnificent, looking out onto the woodland with a lovely small lake. Right now it's a bit gloomy though."

"But you'll brighten it up, sweetie. Just you wait."

"I hope so. I'm so impatient. You know me, instant gratification isn't quick enough."

"The kitchen is the heart of the home." Nana's words echoed in Lacey's mind as she cast her eyes around the room. "Well, that pretty much describes the inside. The outside is incredible too."

"I'm sure it is. Vermont is a beautiful state—all those mountains. I love Charleston, but if I could have a mountain or two here, I'd be ecstatic."

"You've got that right, Summer. If I could have a beach or an ocean here, I'd be ecstatic. We should be happy with what we've got, right?"

"Yep. We do have a lot, Lace. I count my blessings every day. You have ten acres, right?"

"No, Summer, I have ten *wondrous* acres and sitting on them is a three-story Vermont fieldstone Victorian style home. The property is almost all woods. Everything is so green, even in winter. To reach my home you have to drive down a long, straight driveway. Then it ends in a circular drive in front where you'll be welcomed through two massive front doors."

Summer let out an audible gasp. "You're kidding me. But I'm going to come up there and see you standing in front of a storage shed, right?"

Lacey hadn't realized she'd been pacing while she was describing her home until she stopped. Her anxiety had dissipated, and now she had Summer to thank for that. A laugh broke out of her throat as she compared her home to a storage shed. "Hardly, my dear friend. The place is indeed huge and some might even call it a mansion. It all depends on how you view things, and what kind of house you were brought up in, I suppose."

Summer agreed. "I'm sure it's just marvelous, even if it is a storage shed. I'm not so sure you aren't pulling my leg. We'll see about that when we set up Skype. Ah! Did you think of that?"

"You're too much, you know that? It would serve you right if I did rent a storage shed and put you in there."

"We'd have fun anywhere and you know it. Are you feeling better now?"

Lacey looked out the kitchen window and back into the kitchen again, smiling broadly. She was pleased with all she surveyed. "Thank you, Summer. You're better than any medicine. Thanks for allowing me to describe this place. I think I appreciate it even more now. Maybe one day, I will write a travel guide. This little town, Ascot Vale, is like taking a step back in time. I feel safe and comfortable here."

"I'm pleased to hear that. Lacey, should we talk about the elephant in the room now? If you don't want to, that's okay."

Lacey felt her chest constrict at the mere thought of that elephant. Steve. "There's really not much to talk about. I came here to think, to get some perspective. The truth is, I think I already know the answer to my dilemma. I can't go back to him, Summer. I feel free here, no more knots in my chest, if I don't do what he wants, or dress how he wants me to. I feel like a bird that's been freed from its cage, and I want to keep on flying."

"I hear ya, Lacey. Although, I didn't want you to leave Charleston, I knew it would be best for you. Steve doesn't deserve you, and frankly, he scares me."

"Me, too. But I'm going to put that all behind me as of right now. Just call me, Freebird. I'll call you again soon and let's seriously get Skype going, okay?"

"Absolutely. Enjoy your newfound freedom. I love you, bye."

"Love you too." She cringed. *"Come on Lacey, concentrate. Like it or not you do have decisions to make even if you don't feel up to it. Decide. Delay. Procrastinate. Do something, even if it's wrong!"*

Lacey always anticipated her summers, and the Christmas breaks which allowed her to spend time with her grandparents. She loved New England, which was so different from where she'd grown up in Charleston, South Carolina.

Charleston, she had lived there with her parents, Iris and Jack. They were the two best parents any girl could ask for. Now gone, but always alive in her heart. The beautiful Southern town was where Lacey attended school. Later she graduated with a degree in journalism at the College of Charleston. Charleston College was where she met her beau, Steve. Steve received his law degree from the University of South Carolina. He was a much sought after graduate, and could have joined just about any law firm he desired. But, after passing the bar, he moved from Columbia to Charleston, which was more prestigious. There, he joined the most successful law firm in Charleston. Soon Steve was making more money than he'd ever imagined.

Steve Schmidt, bon vivant, man about town, handsome and smart, with a bit of an edge. Most thought he was cocky, but Lacey thought his attitude was more one of confidence. She liked his take-charge personality. After the death of her parents from illness, within a year of each other, Lacey was floundering. Now, she appreciated his guidance and support.

Steve introduced Lacy to a lifestyle of whirlwind parties, fine wines, and dining, as well as expensive trips to exotic places. He even hired a personal dresser who coaxed her out of casual attire and into an elegantly dressed woman. With Steve and the dresser's help, she would be welcomed in any upper echelon social setting. *"All he had to do was give me elocution lessons and I'd be a modern day Eliza Doolittle,"* Lacey reflected.

Lately though, Lacey couldn't explain the nagging feeling, which grew the more she got to know Steve. It was a feeling that bubbled to the surface like a slow simmering pot of water. When you're not watching, suddenly it spills over.

If the jewelry she selected to wear with a certain outfit didn't please Steve, he would remove it, and buy her something more suitable; at least, more suitable in his eyes. He wanted her to look absolutely perfect at all times. If she chose a green dress, when he wanted her in something red, he'd get angry. She could never make the proper selection anymore; and it seemed he'd ridicule her for her lack of taste.

It was true that Steve had never laid a hand on her, but his temper was escalating. Now, Lacy worried that it was just a matter of time. If only he'd shown this side of himself when they first began dating, she could have saved herself a lot of grief. Instead, Steve was the proverbial wolf in sheep's clothing.

Standing in her Nana and Gramps's kitchen, Lacey knew she had to be strong. There were tough decisions to make. Being away from Steve had given her clarity of vision. She chided herself for being so shallow—for being so impressed with Steve's wealth and stature. Lacy was also disappointed for needing him, or more accurately, for needing anyone who could offer her comfort after her parents died.

Steve was good at spoiling her, but over time, she was beginning to feel more like an object, another one of Steve's possessions. She was coming to the realization that the gifts Steve bought for her were more for his benefit. They were nice things to adorn his prize; to make him look even better in the eyes of his friends and associates.

But, the main reason Lacey was hesitant to return to Steve was his foreboding temper, and possessiveness. His lack of compassion for animals was a huge drawback, too.

The thought turned over, and over in Lacey's head. That was then, this is now. Gramps had been gone for many years. Nana had recently passed on, leaving the enormous home to Lacy, along with a goodly sum of money.

Now, she had to make a decision. That word again. She'd come here to sign the papers, and decide which of Nana's belongings she wanted, and which she would donate to charities.

Underneath, Lacey knew she'd left her comfort zone to give her space. She needed to look at her relationship with Steve, in a different light. He was an emotional abuser; loving and kind one moment, and then, mean and cruel the next. Still reeling from the deaths of her loving parents, Lacy thought she needed him.

Lacey was beginning to feel much like Scarlett O'Hara. *"I can't think about that right now. If I do, I'll go crazy. I'll think about that tomorrow."* She could so relate to Scarlett.

The ringing of her cell phone startled her; she dreaded answering it.

CHAPTER TWO

"Hello, Steve."

"Hi, Lacey. It's so good to hear your voice, honey. I know you left only six days ago, but it seems like you've been gone forever. I need you to come back as soon as you can. Have you made any progress, yet?"

"Not really, Steve. I think I've got a delayed reaction to jet lag, or something. I'm very tired and don't feel like doing a darn thing. I'm sure I'll feel better tomorrow."

"Sounds good, Lacey Belle. Take a nap. Wrap up your business there, and get on the first plane home. I have an important dinner with some very influential clients scheduled for next week. I need my eye candy by my side. You know how to charm people, honey, and boy do these clients need to be charmed. My charisma won't be enough to get them to sign on with the firm. It'll take both barrels to win them over, so I'm really counting on you. I know you can do it, and I know you won't let me down."

"Of course I won't, Steve—let you down that is. But don't you want me to come home, just to be with me?"

"I'm sorry honey," Steve interrupted. "See what I mean? I need to take a refresher course in Charm 101. Of course, I want you here—just to be with you, to kiss those gorgeous lips. Then I want to take you out on the town. I need to show you off, and remind everyone how lucky Steve Schmidt is to have such a beautiful woman. Lacey, you truly are the most beautiful woman I've ever known. One blue eye, and one green eye and that mane of thick red hair all drive me crazy. Not to mention that gorgeous figure. All the guys in the office envy me, but you're mine, baby. All mine."

"Steve. Oh, never mind."

"What is it Lacey? Did I say something wrong, again? If so, I apologize. I just miss you, and I have a ton of work to do. Plus, I'm tired; didn't get much sleep last night."

"I'm sorry. Did Mrs. Archer's dog bark all night, again?"

"Of course it did. That damn dog. These condo walls are paper thin, I swear. As soon as my lease is up, I'm out of here. I'm moving to a place that doesn't allow barking, whining pets."

"Steve. I spoke with Mrs. Archer before I left, and she told me that Rusty is sick. He won't be around much longer. From the sound of it, last night, may have been his last. She said she wouldn't let him suffer. I wouldn't be surprised if she hasn't already taken him to the vet to have him put down."

"Okay, okay, you're right. It's not the dog's fault, if he's sick. I guess."

"You guess?"

"But it's not my fault either. I need my sleep to be at the top of my game in the courtroom. Speaking of the courtroom, guess who I had the bad luck to draw as judge on this case? Just found out today."

"I don't know, Steve. Who?"

"I'm too tired to care right now."

"Old hang 'em high, Harry. That's who. He probably believes his own mother is guilty of something sinister."

"Yeah, probably guilty of birthing a son like you."

"Lacey. You there?"

"Oh, sorry. I really think I'm coming down with something. In fact, I'm sure I am. I'm feeling hot and flushed. Icky, for lack of a better word."

"All the more reason for you to rush home to me, sweetheart. I'll make sure you're up and running, after a short rest in bed; if you catch my drift. Okay? Lacey? Earth to Lacey."

"Yes, okay. I just can't seem to concentrate, and I have a pretty big deal freelance story due next week."

"Well. Listen, honey, just take care of yourself. Get plenty of rest. I'll call you tomorrow, if I have time." Steve paused. "It's going to be a busy day, and I have a lot of prep work to do. Without much sleep last night, I'll be one sleepy puppy tonight."

Steve laughed at the irony of his jest. Of course, Steve always laughed at his own jokes. However, Lacey was not amused.

Lacey plopped onto the comfortable sofa, too

tired to stand.

"Okay, Steve. I have to go now. My throat is beginning to feel tickly, and I feel warm with no energy. Take care, and maybe we'll talk tomorrow."

"Or, maybe not."

"You take good care of yourself, Lacey Belle. Gargle with some salt water or something, then go to bed. I want you looking your usual fabulous self when we meet with these clients. Okay? Wait until you see the outfit I bought you. It'll knock your socks off, and dazzle the prospective clients."

"Sure. Okay, Steve. I'll dazzle them."

"That's my girl! I know I can always depend on you. Bye, Lacey. Love you. Hurry home."

"Bye."

"I never said 'love you too. ' Did he even notice? He didn't even ask about my freelance job. Gargle? That's the extent of his concern for my health? Has he always been this shallow and neglectful?"

Lacey realized with absolute certainty, that Steve had indeed been abusing her emotionally. Notwithstanding, he kept her off-balance with kindness and lavish gifts one day, and then treating her like, *a thing* the next.

Lacey hit *End* on her cell, and went to make a cup of tea. Suddenly, she was overcome with ennui. No, it was more than that. It was exhaustion and perhaps even a low-grade temperature. She'd have to search Nana's medicine cabinet for a thermometer, but later. Right now, she just wanted rest.

It was 6:00 p. m., and already dark outside. November in Vermont, what did she expect?

CHAPTER THREE

"This is so unlike me. I usually have more energy than a Bengal cat. Right now, even a sloth would put me to shame. This is not mere jet lag."

Fighting to keep her eyelids open, Lacey marveled at the objects outside the living room windows. Swirling before her tired eyes were pristine snowflakes. Beautiful, delicate snowflakes.

"You're not in Kansas anymore, Dorothy. You're not in South Carolina, for sure."

Lacey sat back, mesmerized, with childhood memories. They whirled inside her head, dancing in time with the falling snowflakes outside the large casement windows. She was reminded of Christmas breaks with Nana and Gramps. There were square dances in Pop Jones's barn, and old-fashioned sleigh rides. Currier and Ives couldn't have portrayed a more picturesque portrait of her childhood, if they'd tried. In fact, she was certain Nana and Gramps's magnificent home was exactly the image the printmakers had in mind when they produced their heartwarming lithographs.

With her shoes off, Lacey curled up on the sofa. She tugged at the light eiderdown comforter draped across the back of the sofa, then she snuggled in. After getting comfortable, Lacey again stared out the window and watched the falling snow. At first, it was just a light dusting, but rapidly it increased, covering the bushes and trees. Comfy on Nana's sofa, Lacy decided she'd get a cup of tea later. For now, sleep was calling her.

*****

The sound of an insistent, *"mroww, mroww,"* grew more impatient by the second. A demanding scratch on the front door, catapulted Lacey into an upright position.

An ornate grandfather clock against the far wall revealed she'd been asleep for a couple of hours. *"What the heck was that noise?"*

Struggling to open her eyes, Lacey wondered if perhaps she'd dreamed the loud sounds. But no, there it was again. She managed to rise from the sofa, steadying herself by holding onto the sofa arm. All the while, her head was pounding and she felt weak.

"Who's there?" Lacey called as strongly as she could. Even speaking hurt. Her question was met by a louder, *"mroww, mroww."* This time, the scratching was more furious.

Lacey shuffled to the door and looked through the peephole, but saw no one. Not sure if she was hallucinating, and against her better judgment, she hesitatingly opened the door. What she perceived nearly bowled her over. Either it was an extra-large skunk, or a very small pony. Whatever it was, it was big.

The cold air swarmed in, and just as quickly, the critter skittered into the room. Promptly, it leaped upon the sofa, then patted the sofa cushion as if beckoning Lacey to join him, or her.

Lacey accepted the cat's invitation with an amused smile. Slowly, she made her way back to the sofa, relieved to sit down and rest. Even more, she was glad there was a cat at the door, and not the bogeyman.

This time, the loud *mroww* was replaced with a gentle purring sound. The cat looked at Lacey with its mesmerizingly brilliant, blue-green eyes.

"Well, who have we here? You sure know how to make yourself at home, don't you?"

"Mroww, purr purr."

"Let's get a good look at you." She checked the Tuxedo cat's neck, and noted there was indeed a collar. A careful examination, revealed only a partial phone number; the last two digits being blurred.

"So, you look well fed. Someone cared enough to put a flea collar on you. But, without a complete phone number I don't know who you belong to."

"Meow?"

"Are you hungry big guy? I'll find something for you, and then you can go on your way. You'd better appreciate this monumental effort, kitty. I wouldn't do this for just any cat. But, something tells me you're special."

Lacey summoned her last bit of strength, and trudged into the kitchen. The Tuxedo cat barreled in front of her, nearly toppling Lacey in her weakened state.

"Okay, kitty. Slow down, will you? Nana should have some tuna in the pantry. That will have to do until you go home and get your regular food. Surely, someone must be missing you right now."

"Meow?"

"If the temperature keeps dropping, and the snow comes down any harder, I wouldn't feel right putting you out without feeding you. You can spend the night if you'd like, and something tells me, you'd like."

While searching for the tuna, Lacey noticed the kitty pawing at the bottom shelf and meowing.

"Whoa!" Now that's really strange, kitty. How did you know there was regular cat food in here?" She opened the cabinet and got a bowl. *"I've heard that cats are psychic, hmmm."*

"Mroww, mroww, purr, purr."

"My energy is depleted, kitty. I'll give you some food and a bowl of water, and that's it. I have to lie down, before I fall down."

"Meow?"

"What now? What? Oh. You're right. You need a litter box. I'm sorry, big guy. I'll try to find a box for you, but I don't see any litter. Anyway, what would Nana be doing with cat litter? Or cat food for that matter. Hmmm, very strange. Nana's sweet little Taffy died two years ago."

With his tail held high and proud, kitty turned from Lacey and headed in the direction of the pantry. Once again, she had a clear view of his hindquarters. "Wait, where are you going?" He was indeed a male, she noted, but apparently a neutered male.

"Well, that's good. No contributing to the pet overpopulation for you, eh? So, somebody really does love you. That's nice to know. And what's not to love about you? You're gorgeous."

The cat took a few steps farther into the large walk-in pantry, turned right, and then halted in front of a plastic container. Lacey was stunned. Not only did Tuxedo Cat know where the litter box was, he was also pawing at a box of cat litter.

"This is insane. Something tells me you've been here before. Have you?"

"Mroww, meow."

"Well, I just happen to be a writer, and I think I'm going to make you the topic of my next article. Of course I'd have to submit it in the fiction category because nobody would believe you're real."

The tuxedo cat did a little dance around Lacey's legs, purring like a well-tuned engine.

With great effort, Lacey took two more bowls from the kitchen cabinet. She filled one with the contents of a small can of cat food, the other with the dry kibble, and the other with water. Her final task, before she could get off her feet and rest, was to fill the litter box.

"There you go, big guy. I believe all your needs are met, so if you'll excuse me, the couch is waiting."

Lacey made her way back to the great room on wobbly legs, while Tuxedo Cat had no such problem. He bolted past Lacey and headed straight for the sofa. With ballerina-like grace, he jumped onto the sofa waiting for Lacey to join him.

"Amazing. For such a big cat, you're so lithe and agile." Lacey settled in on the couch. Much too tired to go to her bedroom, she really wanted to crash on the couch. At home, this was her usual habit. Former home, she corrected herself. She'd stay up late writing, and then, fall asleep in place.

Lacey laid back and pulled the eiderdown over her. The Tuxedo Cat seemed impatient to get on her chest. Lacey stroked the cat as he lay on her chest purring. His head was quite large. There was nothing little about this beauty.

"Um. Your fur is so soft and silky, but inside you must be made of lead weights. You're so heavy! You know what? You're making me feel better already." Lacey felt herself growing sleepier by the second. She wondered why the cat didn't remain in the pantry to eat, seeming to prefer staying by her side.

"Ok, sweetie, you can stay here tonight. If I'm feeling better tomorrow, I'll try to find out where you live. In the meantime, let's get some shut-eye."

CHAPTER FOUR

The brilliance of the sun shining through the great room's expansive windows cajoled Lacey from her deep sleep. She'd been sleeping on her back, and apparently snoring, because her throat felt quite sore.

When she tried to roll onto her side, she was met with an indignant *mroww,* from the black and white fur bundle on her tummy.

"Oh, I'm sorry. I wondered why I felt so heavy. Such a big weight, you are. Have you been here all night?"

"Meow, purr, purr."

The cat sat up and then began kneading Lacey's belly. Purring, it looked at her through sleepy, slitted eyes.

"I can't even sit up, kitty. I feel so sick. I don't think snoring is the cause of my sore throat. And now, I'm coughing and sneezing. Well, I'm sure you don't want to hear about it. I just want to go back to sleep."

The melodious purring of her furry new friend lulled Lacy back to sleep. Dutifully, he licked her exposed hand. As sleep overtook her, she felt peaceful, despite being so sick.

At approximately 7:00 p. m., Lacey awoke disoriented and totally in the dark. Reaching for the lamp switch took tremendous effort. She turned the light on, and then noted that the cat was not with her.

As though bidden by some unseen force, a black and white streak whizzed into the room. It seemed the cat was alerted by Lacey's waking movement and felt she needed his attention. The cat jumped on the sofa. Gingerly padding his way toward Lacey's head, he purred softly, and began licking Lacey's face. She was amazed by how much better she was beginning to feel. No doubt, she was still sick, but oddly, she was comforted by this seemingly caring creature.

Lacey noted that kitty's breath had a distinct fishy odor, which made her realize her stomach was growling. She wasn't hungry, but knew she had to eat something.

"So that's where you were, kitty. Having a bit of supper, were you? Too bad you can't make me something to eat."

"Meow?"

"Well, okay. If you insist, I'll have a cup of chicken soup, and a few crackers." She paused. *"Get a grip Lacey. Now you're ordering food from a cat. I'll bet he'd bring me soup if he could though."*

Slowly removing the eiderdown from her hot and tired body, Lacey sat up, and then placed her feet on the floor. She stood up, pleased that she didn't fall back down. "I'm going to try to make it to the kitchen. If I'm not back in ten minutes, come looking for me, okay."

Lacey needn't have worried about the cat looking for her; she quickly discovered he wasn't going to leave her side. So, she ambled toward the kitchen. The tuxedo kitty pranced happily by her side, his motor going full tilt.

The ringing of her cell intruded on Lacey's peace and quiet. She didn't want to be bothered by anyone right now. All she wanted was a little bit of soup, some more sleep, and her new friend cuddling next to her.

Reluctantly, Lacey pulled her cell from her pocket, gave into a coughing spasm, and then meekly rasped, "Hello."

CHAPTER FIVE

"Hey, Lace. It's your lovin' man. I miss you."

"Oh. Hey, Steve."

"What's up, babe? You sound strange."

Seized by another fit of coughing, Lacey moved the phone from her mouth. After several seconds, she said, "Excuse me, Steve. I know that sounded awful."

"What's wrong, Lace? Are you still feeling sick? You're not too sick to get on a plane are you? I sure hope not. I need you here with me."

Lacey stifled a groan and a sarcastic remark. She was too sick to put up with Steve's selfish ways. "Yes, I'm definitely sick. I don't know if it's the flu or what, but I'm feeling really punk right now, and I need a lot of rest."

Kitty stood on his hind legs. Angling for her attention, the cat reached up to paw Lacey, then he let out a loud meow.

There was silence on the other end of the phone, although brief. "Is that a cat I just heard?" Steve exclaimed. "Don't tell me you've got a cat." Like a thunderbolt, Lacey realized she didn't have to make any decision. Steve had just unwittingly made it for her. She wasn't returning to South Carolina. But, telling him would wait for a later time.

"Well. Yes, and no, Steve. He showed up yesterday and it's really snowing. I didn't have the heart to turn him away. He has a collar, so obviously he belongs to someone. Maybe he's lost, I don't know yet, and I've been too sick to find out."

"Well, do you think you'll be better in a couple of days, hon?"

"Oh, please. Enough of the phony 'hon' endearment."

Lacey took a deep breath and tried not to cough. "I'll let you know. It's too soon to even think about traveling." She thought she'd break it to him, in bits and pieces. "I may have to stay a little longer. Just until I'm over whatever this crud is. All I know is that I'm as weak as a kitten."

On cue, the big cat let out a couple of sympathetic meows. Did he know she was speaking of his species? At least, that's how Lacey chose to interpret his vocalizations. She looked at the cat. Inside she knew if anyone in the world understood her, it was this beautiful, loving, ball of fur.

Reaching down to pet his head, she immediately knew that wasn't a smart move. Waves of dizziness overtook her, and she slowly straightened up, but not before TC, gave her a couple of drooling licks on her hand.

"I think I love you, big guy." Lacey actually mouthed the words aloud, and into the phone, no less.

"Well, that sounds more like my girl. I love you too, Lace. I'll hang on another day. I'm sure you'll be better by then, and you can come home. Rest a day or two, and then you'll be ready to meet the new clients. At least, I hope they'll be the new clients." Lacey heard Steve draw in a breath. "You'll dazzle them with your charm and beauty. Then they'll be begging me to sign them on."

Lacey looked around the kitchen savoring all the sights and memories. She didn't need to hop on a plane to get home; she *was* home. It felt so right. Judging from his purring and alternating cat noises, TC seemed to think so too.

"Lacey. Say something please. And, quiet that stupid cat. I'm trying to talk to you, not that mangy animal."

TC must have intuited that the voice on the phone spoke disparagingly of him. He expelled a growl and a hiss.

"Ha! You tell him, TC. You're one strange cat. I swear you understand human. I'll have to learn 'cat'. But, even I understood that!"

"Look, Steve. I really have to get this chicken soup in me, followed by some more sleep. I'll call you later. TC, that's what I've named the cat, and I, are going back to the sofa, to lie down."

"Now, that'll frost 'em for sure. The devil made me say it, or was it you, TC?" Lacey laughed silently, then gave TC a sly smile. Oddly, she was quite certain the cat returned her smile.

"Alright, Lacey. This is getting us nowhere. I

think your sickness, or whatever it is, is responsible for your current attitude. Eat your soup and get your rest. By the way, I wouldn't be surprised if that cat is not responsible for your condition. You know they carry all kinds of germs and fleas. You're your own worst enemy, Lacey. But, you've never listened to me about this subject before. I don't know why I expect you to now." Steve let out an exasperated sigh. "Feel better. Talk later. Bye."

Lacey was gratified. Her arrow had hit the mark. Now, his curt responses didn't bother her. Finding a can of chicken soup, she opened it, and then placed it in a pot on Nana's large stove. After finding some crackers, she ate them with the soup, and managed to get half of it down. Then, she poured herself a glass of water and took a large gulp.

"Shall we go now, TC?" Had the new feline become her nurse/companion? She was definitely not feeling as bad as she normally felt with such a horrendous cold. TC was positively wonderful.

Padding along with tail erect, TC purred while dutifully leading the little parade of two back into the great room. Leaping onto the sofa, he then began dancing back and forth seeming impatient for Lacey to join him.

"Hold your horses, big guy. I'm coming, I'm coming. Just a little slow right now." Lacey shuffled along, heading to the sofa. "We can rest tonight. Tomorrow, I'm sorry to say, we have to see if we can find your owner. That is, if I'm feeling better. I really don't want you to leave. I think we'd make a great team, you and me."

"Meow? Purr, purr," TC assented very agreeably.

CHAPTER SIX

Lacey and TC spent a lovely night on the sofa once again. By morning, she was feeling better, and yearned for the luxury of sleeping in her big four-poster bed. Every time she came to stay with Nana and Gramps, this was her coveted bed—her bed; and now, her home. For the first time in several days, Lacey felt renewed strength, a feeling of optimism, and a hope for her future. She knew there would be no turning back.

The only obstacle to Lacey's future happiness was how to tell Steve she wasn't going back to South Carolina. Well, there was one other obstacle; a big one. How could she give up TC? She had to make a serious effort to find his owner. After all, if TC were her cat, she would want someone to make the effort to return him.

Lacey showered, and shampooed her hair, dreading what she would have to do next. Actually, she would need to call Steve, then walk into town to make inquiries about TC. How incredibly quickly she had bonded with the cat. Now, she was hopelessly attached and didn't want to give him up. She felt so much better when he was around.

"I think you have magical properties, TC. It's like, I know I'm sick, yet oddly enough, I feel good—comforted. But, I'll bet you know that, don't you? In fact, you're the one who should meet Steve's clients. You would charm them off their feet, wouldn't you?"

"Mroww, mroww."

"What? No purr? I hear ya, TC." Lacey giggled. "Don't worry big boy. You're never going to meet Steve. I wouldn't do that to you."

Finding TC's owner bothered her more than breaking Steve's heart. Or, more accurately, ruining his precious plans. Yes, she'd made the right choice to stay here, in Ascot Vale.

Her musings were interrupted by the black and white ball of fur, winding around her legs, and vibrating. "You sure do have a loud purrer, TC." Lacey laughed as she reached down and picked him up for a cuddle.

TC arched his head for Lacey to chuck him under the chin. In doing so, she exposed a black, almost perfect heart-shaped spot on his white chin fur. "You know what, TC? I'm going to write a story about you. To insure that "*Crazy About Cats*" magazine picks it up, I'll have Summer photograph you. She's a professional photographer and her specialty is pet pictures. Plus, she's my BFF. Oh, that's my *Best Friend Forever,* to you. Now, I'll just have to get her up here. Knowing Summer, she'll be thrilled to do it."

Lacey opened her luggage, which had been lying on the bed. Save for the clean underwear and toiletries she'd been using, Lacy had been too ill to unpack. She picked out a favorite lavender cashmere sweater, her best skinny jeans, and her leather knee boots.

"Thank you, Steve. You may have been a royal pain, but you did treat me well in some areas. But that's not

what I wanted. I only wanted to be loved – truly loved for who I am. Treated as an equal, or at least as a human. Was that asking too much?"

Lacey's cell rang, interrupting her pity party. Her heart dropped. She wasn't ready for the confrontation with Steve. Well, she'd never be ready for that, but it was inevitable. With trepidation, and shaking hands she answered her phone.

Her voice shook as she squeaked out a weak, *"Hello."*

"Hey, girlfriend, what's up? Are you feeling less anxious since we last talked?" Summer's voice was like a breath of fresh air, ironically, as inviting as a summer breeze.

Lacey fell back on the bed, and nearly landed on TC, who seemed determined to never be more than a cat's whisker away. "Summer, I was just telling TC about you, and then you call. How strange is that? I need you to come up here as soon as you can. That is if you wouldn't mind. Well, actually sooner than that if you can."

Summer's voice teetered between concern and amusement. "Lacey, slow down. What's going on? Why do you need me up there? And, who is TC? You've only been gone a few days, and already you've got a new fish on the line? Well, now you've got *me* hooked. You know I'll be on the first plane out of here."

Lacey stroked TC's back. He rewarded her with

extra loud purrs. Holding the cell to TC's chest for a few seconds, she then spoke. "Summer, did you hear that?"

"Lacey we may be a couple of thousand miles apart, but I'm not deaf. That was a cat purring. And from the sound of it, I'd say it's a mighty big cat."

"Did you hear that TC? I think Summer likes you already. But what's not to like? You're special. Sorry 'bout that, Summer. You're right, TC is a wonderful cat. He showed up here at Nana's. Hey, listen. I'll tell you all about him, and my plans, when you get here."

"Great, but actually *you* don't sound too good. Cold?"

"A cold, indeed," Lacey admitted, trying to stifle a cough. "But not to worry. I have a great little nurse here, so I'll be as fit as a fiddle in no time. Plus, your visit will help a lot!"

Lacey ended their call with Summer promising to make the flight arrangements post-haste.

Lacey turned toward the cat. "Now, I have to go out for a while. Be good. I'll be back before you know it." Knowing her little jaunt to the town square might culminate in the discovery of TC's owner, she tried to sound upbeat. In her heart, she knew it was the right thing to do. Perhaps his owner or owners would allow her to visit him from time to time.

CHAPTER SEVEN

Lacey grabbed her jacket and headed out the door. The brisk air invigorated her as she walked down the long driveway from Nana's home—no, now it was *her* home. The snow had stopped, and the brilliant sunlight made the snow-covered trees and bushes glisten like stars. Lacey was still tired, and a bit run down, but she knew the walk would do her good.

She walked along Hawthorn, a dead end street situated in front of her home. It wasn't just the fresh air that invigorated her. Seeing the quaint little shops that surrounded the central square brought back memories from her childhood. The happiest days of her life included snowball fights with her friend, Abby, and Abby's raucous brothers. Together they'd skated on Miller's pond, and built bonfires by the frozen lake. Summertime was equally enjoyable. There was swimming in Miller's pond, picnics in the park, movies at the outdoor theater, and roller-blading with her friends.

In the center of the square there were wrought iron benches sitting on a well-manicured green space. But, the focal point of the park was the World War II commemorative monolith. It held the names of young men and women who served their country during World War II. Gramps's name was there; Lacey rubbed the plaque in silent tribute.

Shops with Early American style fronts surrounded the square on all four sides. Shooting off from the square in all four corners were streets lined with beautiful trees. Pagoda dogwoods, Hawthorns, and American Mountain Ash, attracted an abundance of birds in the summer and fall.

As she grew older, Lacey hadn't been able to visit her grandparents as much as she would have liked. College, and then an apprenticeship in journalism at the local newspaper, demanded most of her time. Her parents had both become ill, her dad with heart disease, and her mother with PSP, a rare neurological disorder. Lacey was devoted to taking care of them. Sadly, within the space of a year Lacey had lost both parents, leaving her alone and bereft.

For a while, she floundered. Through her grieving, she was very vulnerable. She was an only child, and her parents had doted on her. However, she wasn't spoiled; just well loved. That's when Steve came into her life. Looking back, Lacey realized she just needed someone to love, someone to take care of her, and someone for her to take care of.

Lacey was amazed at the number of new shops that had opened since her last visit. One shop in particular, caught her eye. Aunt Lois's Hearth and Home. The façade was certainly inviting. There were big windows with deep red country curtains behind them. A red door was adorned with one of the prettiest grape vine wreaths Lacey had ever seen. It was decorated with orange and red bows. Miniature pumpkins understated the elegance of the trimming.

Peeking in the window, Lacy discovered a large room with cozy seating spread throughout. Coffee tables were surrounded by love seats and oversized chairs. A long diner style counter lined the wall, while beneath the counter there were a dozen or so wooden bar stools with padded cushions. The walls behind the counter were decorated with what appeared to be family pictures. Shelves held candles, knick knacks, and everything you might see in someone's home; not a place of business.

The central feature of the room was a castle-size fireplace with a huge stone mantel. It was laden with greenery, and Thanksgiving decorations. This was the hearth of all hearths! Immediately, Lacey felt drawn to this place.

When she walked inside her senses were filled with the delightful scent of patchouli incense. The delicious aromas of pumpkin pie spice also grabbed her attention along with other sweet confections.

Lacey's eyes were rewarded by a visual potpourri of all things country. From grapevine wreaths, cinnamon scented straw brooms, to elegantly crafted local pottery, there were various types of fall paraphernalia. Lacey was soothed by the lovely music in the background.

Enthralled by her surroundings, Lacey found Aunt Lois's Hearth and Home an absolute delight; she hadn't even been seated, or sampled the food.

"I thought I'd let you admire the view before you sit down." A tall, very attractive woman with silvery-white hair appeared before her. With her hair pulled into a chic bun, her smile was as warm and inviting as the room. Deep blue eyes were set in an almost unlined face, making it difficult to estimate her age. She could be anywhere from fifty to seventy, Lacey mused. Whatever her age, she was beautiful and Lacey sensed that she was very kind. Immediately, she liked her.

"Thank you." Lacey returned her smile. "And, you're right. I was definitely admiring everything in here. I hope my mouth wasn't hanging open. I love the ambience. Early American, *Just Right,* is how I'd describe it. Lacey Robertson," she said, extending her hand.

"Welcome to Aunt Lois's Hearth and Home, Lacey. If you haven't already guessed, I'm Lois Lindsey. Everybody calls me, Aunt Lois. Well, almost everybody," she said enigmatically. "I'd be pleased if you would call me Aunt Lois, too."

Aunt Lois placed her other hand atop the hand that was clasping Lacey's. "Lacey Robertson. Welcome. I know you're Lacey Belle Robertson, Nana Robertson's granddaughter."

"No secrets here, right? Same small town I remember." Lacey said with warmth. "I'm sorry to admit this, but I don't remember you, Lois. I mean, Aunt Lois. It's been a few years since I've been here."

Aunt Lois took Lacey by the arm and led her to a quiet table near the hearth. She nodded to everyone and called them by name. Choruses of, "Hello, Aunt Lois, who's your beautiful friend?" followed them through-out the room.

After Lacey removed her jacket, she placed it on the chair beside her, and sat down. Much to her surprise Aunt Lois sat down opposite her.

"I hope you don't mind me sitting here, Lacey. I won't be long, but I wanted to talk to you about your Nana and your grandfather. I was friendliest with your Nana. Your Gramps was usually busy in his workshop; making lovely furniture for their home." Seemingly, she smiled at the thought. "Your Nana was always talking about how proud she was of you. She was a lovely woman and I miss her."

"Thank you. I'm sorry I couldn't be here these last few years, but I know she understood. We did talk on the phone—all the time, but still, that isn't the same as seeing her in person. How I'd love being on the receiving end of one of her big hugs. I miss her so much. I hope she knew how very much I loved her."

"Indeed, she did Lacey. By the way, did you happen to notice her picture on the wall behind the counter? I put all of my favorite people's pictures on that wall, both the two-legged and four-legged variety."

"Speaking of four-legged creatures, I noticed you have a picture of a black and white cat on the wall. It looks a bit like my cat. Well, he's not actually *my* cat, but I'm hoping I'll be able to keep him. He showed up at Nana's home. Sorry. My home. That's hard to get used to saying. I call him, TC. Do you mind if I take a closer look at the picture? Cats look so much alike that it's difficult to tell one from the other."

"Not at all. But first, let me ask you something, Lacey. Have you been sick since you arrived in Ascot Vale?"

"Yes. Actually, I have been ill. Still am, but I'm recovering. Why do you ask? Oh, I must look an awful mess. I must be terribly pale." She pinched her cheek.

A pleasant look crossed Aunt Lois's face. "Oh no, dear, you look quite lovely. Go to the counter and take a look at the pictures. Especially, the ones with the cat in them. Let me know what you think."

Lacey curled her lips into a smile as she walked toward the counter. In response to soft whistles, she waved and gave a friendly smile to the men sitting at the next table.

What she saw, stopped her in her tracks; she couldn't believe her eyes. It wasn't the lovely picture of Nana with Aunt Lois that grabbed her attention. There were eight pictures of different people, all posing with a black and white tuxedo cat. *Her* cat. TC.

"Eight people. How can this be?" She frowned. *"TC. Who the devil are you?"*

CHAPTER EIGHT

His name wasn't TC. The pictures were autographed with the names of various town's peoples. Each picture had a different name for the cherished pussycat. The most prominent picture was of the cat being held by a handsome, kind looking, elderly gentleman. The picture was signed, *'Alex and Jingles. '* Next, there was a photograph of Aunt Lois cuddling the very same cat. The inscription read *'Aunt Lois and Tuffy'*. The next was, *John and Ellie with Lucky*, then *Esther and Boo Boo, Grand mom Jane, with Trigger, Jack and T. O. B. Y. (Tobias Orville Beauregard Yancy) Cat, Mary Rose and Kit Kat, Dr. and Mrs. James, with Hippocrates.*

Making her way back to her table, Lacey's mind was in a haze. Was she a victim of a con? Plopping in the chair, she felt numb. Was she swindled, or duped?

"It figures. He's a male. The cheating little rascal." Lacey found herself grinning in spite of herself.

"So," Aunt Lois raised a brow. "Is it TC? Don't bother answering. Of course, it's TC."

Lacey's curiosity was getting the better of her. "How did you know TC came to the house? Although, I suspect you know everything that goes on here, don't you?"

Aunt Lois took a sip of the coffee that had been served by her head waitress, Marianne. "Well, maybe not everything, just the important things."

"In such a small place, everything is important."

Lacey agreed.

Aunt Lois obviously liked Lacey. She appeared self-assured, confident, and very kind. "Have you ever heard of the nursing home cat? The cat that senses when patients are dying? He comes into their room and stays with them until the end?"

Lacey drew a sharp breath, nearly spilling her coffee. "Are you saying what I think you're saying?"

"No. No, Lacey. Quite the opposite." Aunt Lois chuckled. "Whereas that cat seemed to presage death, TC, or whatever we want to call him, visits sick people. He comforts them until they recover. Actually, he's quite a celebrity. The local TV news featured him in their *'Pets and People'* segment. Newspaper articles have been written about him."

"But who owns him?" Lacey asked, trying to determine whether, or not Aunt Lois was pulling her leg.

"You don't know much about cats, do you?" Aunt Lois had commented without a trace of sarcasm. "Honey, nobody owns cats. They allow us to merely be their guardians. They let us *think* we own them. Someone once said that thousands of years ago, cats were worshipped as gods. Cats have never forgotten this."

Knowing that what Aunt Lois had said was true, Lacey laughed. She had been owned by several cats in her lifetime. "But surely, he has a guardian. I can't bear the thought of him being homeless and wandering from house to house."

"Alex. Alex Kelly is his main guardian, or a servant; which is more like it." Alex found him years ago on Christmas Eve. He'd apparently been abandoned in the woods near Alex's house. He was a scrawny little kitten, fighting to survive on his own. Alex took him in, fed him, and made sure he got the best veterinary care."

Lacey smiled, but her heart was a little heavy. It was just good luck that Alex came along. TC didn't suffer the fate of so many strays and unwanted pets.

"Evidently, Alex is a very kind man, but I'm surprised he lets TC roam the neighborhood. There are too many dangers out there. I'd be worried sick about him. He's been at my place for a couple of days now. Alex must be worried about him. I need to get in touch with him right away.

Aunt Lois reached across the table, and patted Lacey's arm. "Don't worry, Lacey. Ascot Vale is a small town. Everybody knows Jingles, and watches out for him. The first couple of times Jingles, or TC as you call him, took off, Alex was indeed concerned. But soon, he came to appreciate TC's unique gift. I think that's when Alex first came to the understanding that no one owns cats." Aunt Lois chuckled.

They chatted for quite a bit, exchanging stories and feeling an inexplicable bond. Finally, Aunt Lois stood, and picked up her empty coffee mug. "Look honey. I'll call Alex right now, and let him know that

TC's been visiting you. He'll want to meet you; that's for sure. Alex is very sociable. He likes to meet everyone TC adopts, so to speak."

Immediately, Lacey's spirits lifted. TC had a good home, but conversely she was dispirited knowing she couldn't have him. She'd felt such a strange bond with this special cat. He'd helped her feel better after being so sick.

"Marianne," Aunt Lois called, "please bring a menu for Lacey. I'm sure she's more than a bit peckish right now." Aunt Lois looked at Lacey. "I'll make that phone call to Alex, now. You can sit here and enjoy your meal. Personally, I recommend my secret recipe—Maple flavored breakfast patty. If I must say so myself, all the food is delicious. Don't let the name fool you; these patties are good for breakfast *and* lunch. They make a perfect late night snack, too. Take your time and relax. It's good to have you here, Lacey."

CHAPTER NINE

When Aunt Lois turned to walk away, she nearly collided with a man. Actually, the best-looking man Lacey had *ever* seen. Period. She inhaled, but couldn't stop staring.

Beneath a sexy wide-brimmed hat, wavy, jet black hair fell below his ears, and half way to his shoulders. The word *rakish* came to mind. She didn't want to be caught staring, but a quick look into his eyes revealed they were vivid blue. They were as blue as the former movie star, Paul Newman, who was known for his beautiful baby blues. A surreptitious look revealed the most kissable looking lips she'd ever seen. *"He's tall, very tall. About 6'1" give or take,"* she thought. *"Lean but muscular. Oh, my god, I'm looking at the cover model for a 'bodice ripper' romantic novel. Close your mouth, Lacey Belle."*

"Excuse me, Aunt Lois," the Adonis muttered. "I wasn't looking where I was going. Sorry." He walked over to the counter, picked up a brown paper bag, and folded it neatly.

"Not a problem, Jake," Aunt Lois replied. "Enjoy your lunch."

"Have you decided what you'd like to eat?" Marianne inquired of Lacey.

"Oh yeah, I'd like him!" Naughty thoughts, raced through Lacey's head; she felt her cheeks flush. She'd never had such a reaction to a man before. Not even to Steve when she first met him. This Jake was a

vision in tight jeans, but not vulgarly tight, just right, she decided. He wore a deep blue shirt, which emphasized the brilliance of his eyes. Long, black lashes appeared almost feminine against his rugged good looks.

"This is so unfair. No man should be that beautiful."

Jake wore his shirt tucked inside his waistband. The sleeves were rolled up show-casing muscular forearms, with a nice gold watch on his left wrist. There was something sexy about a man who wore a watch. Lacey couldn't explain why. She just liked it.

"Miss, Lacey?" Marianne inquired.

"Oh, I'm sorry. I was daydreaming," Lacy sputtered trying to regain her composure. "Yes, I'm Lacey, Lacey Robertson. Aunt Lois suggested her secret recipe maple patty, so that's what I'll have, and another cup of coffee, please."

"Coming right up," Marianne said as she picked up the menu. Giving Lacey a knowing smile, she said, "His name is Jake. Jake Anderson and he's single. Don't look now, but he's coming this way."

Before Lacey could deny that she'd been looking at Jake, he walked right past her table, offering her the slightest smile.

"Oh yeah, they're definitely Paul Newman blue." She smiled at him, with her most engaging smile. Then, Lacey felt her heart flutter in her chest; she actually felt a bit weak. After another slight smile, Jake

inclining his head toward her. He walked past her, retrieved his coat from a hook, and then strolled out of the door.

Marianne leaned close to Lacey, and whispered, "At least, he sort of smiled at you. That's something. It's more than he gives most people."

Still surprised by the reaction this man evoked in her, Lacey chuckled nervously. "It isn't every day you see a Greek God walking right toward you, Marianne. He is seriously good looking. I'm sure he can have the pick of the litter, though," Lacey commented with a smile.

"Yes, indeed." Marianne agreed. I'll put your order in now."

A nice, elderly couple stopped by Lacey's table on their way out. "Hello. I'm John Stuyvesant, and this is my wife, Ellie. I hope you don't mind us intruding. We noticed you looking at the pictures of the town cat. We call him, Lucky. That's the three of us there, the fourth photo on the right," John said, as he pointed to their picture.

Lacey reached out and shook hands with them. "No, you're not intruding at all. I'm Lacey Belle Robertson, and I call him TC, for Tuxedo Cat."

"So, Lacey, have you been sick, too? My Ellie here was sick for several days. Lucky came to visit, and stayed until Ellie was fully recovered. It's just the strangest thing. That cat is uncanny. As soon as Ellie recovered, Lucky said goodbye and left. Well, he twined himself around our legs, and then scratched the front door to get out. We'd like to think he was saying goodbye." John chuckled.

"Well, you'll be glad to see him leave, because that'll mean you're completely better. Alex will be glad to get his cat back, again." Ellie interjected.

"Oh, no, I don't want him to go," Lacey blurted. "I'm actually taking him back to Alex tonight, as soon as Aunt Lois lets him know I'm coming. It's the right thing to do, and it's also a hard thing to do."

Ellie patted Lacey on the shoulder, a warm, grandmotherly smile on her face. "Join the crowd, Lacey. Everyone in town loves that cat, especially those of us who have been blessed by his healing presence. But don't worry, you'll see him often. Alex brings him in here about once a month, so everyone can revisit with him, usually on a Sunday afternoon. Jingles. That's his *real* name, thrives on the attention. He just soaks it right up, like the little celebrity he is."

"I'll be here for sure, with bells on, jingle bells!" Lacey beamed, as John and Ellie smiled.

John tugged his ear. "Will you be staying in Ascot Vale, Lacey? Or, are you just visiting?"

"Yes." Lacy brightened. "I'll be living here now." She folded her arms with satisfaction. *"That has such a lovely ring, indeed."*

"I used to visit my grandparents here every Christmas, and during the summer. Perhaps you knew them? Elise and Roy Robertson. They lived at the end of Hawthorn."

"Yes," Ellie admitted, "in the beautiful gray stone mansion. It's quite the landmark here in Ascot Vale. I've often thought it would make a perfect B & B, a very large B & B, but an elegant one."

Lacey tingled with enthusiasm. "Funny. I've had the same thought, but I'm only in the thinking stage. Actually, I've got a long way to go."

John extended his hand. "We wish you luck, Lacey. Welcome back to Ascot Vale."

"Bye, Lacey. Don't forget to have your picture taken with Jingles. Aunt Lois will put it on the wall. You won't have to coax him either. He's quite the ham," Ellie said, as the couple strolled away.

In no hurry to return TC to Alex, Lacey walked home in slow motion. Aunt Lois had called Alex. He told her he was looking forward to having Jingles back home. Now, Alex was eagerly anticipating their meeting.

Alex's house was within walking distance from Lacey's home. A beautiful two- story saltbox house, with Federal blue siding, and Mineral red trim, was framed by well-tended shrubbery that extended along both sides of the slate walkway.

A split rail fence ran across the front of the property. The white mailbox on the west side of the driveway displayed a painting of a black and white cat. The numbers 705, and the name, Kelly, marked the entrance to the residence.

Lacey carried TC in a makeshift silk sling which hung around her neck. After removing the sling, she put TC down by the front door. She knew he'd probably walk beside her if she let him, but she didn't want to take any chances.

Taking a deep breath, and then letting it out slowly, Lacey whispered to TC, "Well, you're home now, big guy. And you know it too, don't you? Look at that little dance you're doing."

"Meow, meow."

Lacey rang the doorbell expectantly, waiting for Alex to greet her. She heard a shout of, "Coming, don't get your knickers in a knot."

"What?"

The door opened and Lacey couldn't believe her eyes.

CHAPTER TEN

Standing before her with a quizzical look on his handsome face, was the Greek God.

"Do I have the wrong house? Did I take a wrong turn and land in heaven?"

Before Lacey had a chance to say hello, TC bolted through the front door, kicking his back legs out sideways. Obviously, he was happy to be back home. Another patient, under his care, no longer needed his services.

"Welcome home, Jingles," a male voice called from somewhere behind the Greek god. "Saved another life did you? Jump into daddy's arms. That's a good boy!"

"Come on in," the Greek god said rather gruffly. "We're not heating all of Ascot Vale, you know. You can hang your coat up there." He indicated an intricately carved hall tree.

"Ah! There it is. Buyer beware. A beautiful exterior with an ugly interior."

As the Greek god stepped aside, Lacey hurried past him. She was anxious to get clear of the cold chill, and not from the weather, but from him. What a difference a few hours makes.

"You must be Lacey, of course," Alex said, joyfully. "Pay no attention to Jake. He's Australian." As if that explained his behavior.

"Hi, Alex. I'm so pleased to meet you," Lacey said. She gave Alex a hug which also encompassed, TC who was now happily ensconced in Alex's arms. "I'm glad you're home where you belong, Jingles."

"Boofhead! That's a better name for him," Jake, who was still standing just inside the door, said sardonically. "That's what I call him."

Lacey smiled softly. She suspected that Jake was not as surly as he appeared. "Why do you call him Boofhead, if you don't mind my asking? Is that an Australian term?"

"Do you need glasses, woman? Have you not noticed the size of his head? It's bloody huge, like a wombat's. And yes, that's an Aussie name. I'm from Oz, as Uncle Alex has already told you. And, before you ask, Oz is another name for Australia."

Alex put Jingles down. Immediately, he twined himself around Lacey's legs, his engine running on high.

"Oh TC, I mean Jingles. I'm really going to miss you."

Alex took Lacey by the arm, ushering her into the rustic, well-appointed living room. A fire was blazing in a large brick fireplace. "There's no reason to miss him, Lacey. You can visit him anytime. Jake and I will both enjoy your company. Won't we Jake? Jake!"

"What? Oh. Sorry, the size of Boofhead's head was distracting me."

A slight smile on Jake's face lit up his impossibly gorgeous blue eyes.

"As I said," Alex remarked. "He's Australian. No further explanation necessary. I didn't properly introduce you either. Jake, this is Lacey. Lacey, meet Jake. Now, shake hands and make nice."

Lacey decided she'd disarm this Greek god, this arrogant, but maybe not really so arrogant, Jake Anderson. She did something very un-Lacey-like. She gave him a hug, and noticed a half-hearted attempt to return the hug. It was obvious he was uncomfortable doing so.

She smiled sweetly, hoping Jake had a sense of humor. "So nice to meet you Jake; your being from Oz, notwithstanding." Next to kindness, a sense of humor was very important to Lacey.

She'd been shy all of her life. When she was a cheerleader in high school, she didn't often take the initiative. People commented on her looks, but she never thought of herself as beautiful. But, something about this Jake—his smugness, his rudeness some might say, actually tugged at her heartstrings. Being a shy person herself, she knew how her diffidence had often been misinterpreted as rudeness or downright snobbishness.

Jake surprised her by breaking into a big smile, from which he quickly recovered, and then instantly adopted his stone-faced persona.

"Yeah. Nice to meet you too, your being a Seppo

and a Sheila notwithstanding," Jake said with an implied *Figure that one out.*

"Believe it or not," Alex said, "he's showing his best side tonight, Lacey. He actually smiled; and he didn't really insult you. A Seppo is Aussie slang for an American, and a Sheila is just another name for a woman. It's not used much these days. Jake likes the old ways. He can be very old-fashioned."

Jake's response was merely a lazy half smile and a shrug of his masculine shoulders—shoulders that Lacey wanted to shake, to shake the arrogance out of him.

Alex showed Lacey to a comfortable armchair by the fireplace. Jake settled in a recliner, stretching his long, muscular legs, which formed a perfect lap for Jingles to hop onto, which he promptly did.

"Get out of here, Boofhead," Jake said sternly; making a half-hearted attempt to move him.

"Jingles 1, Jake 0." Lacey looked bemused. She was becoming sure that Jake wasn't the ogre he pretended to be, or at least thought he should portray himself to the public. She perceived an inner kindness. He must have a sense of humor, because he didn't seem to take offense at her remark about his Aussie heritage.

Alex headed toward the kitchen. "Now, who would like a cup of coffee, or some hot chocolate?"

Lacey seized the opportunity to prolong her stay, not only to know Jake and Alex, but to spend time with TC. If she were honest, she'd admit that mainly she wanted to get to know the enigma known as, Jake.

"I'd love some hot chocolate, Alex, thank you. Your home is so warm and inviting. I'd like to stay for a little while, if you don't mind. That way, I can get to know you, and spend some time with TC. I'm sorry, I can't get used to calling him Jingles. I suppose he'll always be TC to me."

Alex laughed a deep, hearty laugh. "No worries, Lacey. He's called many different names, by many different people. It doesn't matter what you call him, he won't respond anyway unless he feels like it. He's a cat!"

Jake stormed, "He's a bludger, a bludgering cat. And yes Lacey, that is…"

"Another Aussie term," Lacey admitted. "Yes, I get that, Jake, but what exactly does it mean?"

"He's a sponge in other words. Doesn't work, and bludges off us."

"So, you're saying he's an Australian cat?" Alex's booming laugh could be heard from the kitchen. Lacey laughed too, shocked at her own temerity, but also wondering if she'd gone too far by joking with this taciturn hunk.

"Ha! He wishes," was all Jake offered.

"Mroww," Jingles vocalized as he stood and turned around on Jake's lap. He settled down once

again, curling his tail around his head, which he rested on his pillows of paws. The sonorous sounds of sweet purring soon filled the room.

Alex came back into the room, and asked Lacey if she'd like a sweet to go with her hot chocolate. "He understands English, you know. Be careful what you say around him," he said with a smile in his voice.

"Jingles? Or, Jake? Oh, sorry, Alex, you meant Jingles, of course. Jake doesn't speak English, he speaks Australian."

Alex high-fived Lacey as they both enjoyed a laugh at Jake's expense.

"Well, now, aren't you two the comedians?" Jake grumbled. "At least I don't speak American. I'm sorry, Uncle Alex." Jake quickly apologized. "You know I don't mean anything by that. After all, I'm an Australian," he said with a sheepish grin.

Alex shrugged and then shook his head. Now, Lacey, would you care for one of Jake's delicious lamingtons? They're delicious Aussie desserts—a small sponge cake with raspberry or lemon filling, chocolate icing, and coconut. And, before you decline, they might have a few calories in them, but if you don't mind me saying so, you don't have to worry about that."

Not waiting for an answer, Alex left the room again. In a flash, he was back with a tray laden with lamingtons, and three mugs—hot chocolate for Lacey, and coffee for Alex and Jake.

"They should be called, Jingles cakes," Jake said gruffly.

Lacey opened her mouth to say something. Alex held up his hand in a staying manner. "Don't encourage him. He means lamingtons are sponge cakes."

"No worries, Alex," Lacey added. "I get the implication they're sponge cakes. Bludger cakes. Jingles cakes. Duly understood. Not appreciated, but understood."

"Well. No worries, Lacey," Jake said, with a bite to his voice. His statement was accompanied by another half-smile. "You Yanks wish you were Aussies, I think. You're stealing our expressions, *No worries,* and *Bob's your uncle.* Next you'll be saying, *happy as Larry*. It's just a matter of time.

"First, I would love to have one of Jake's lamingtons, Alex. I suspect they'll make me *happy as Larry,*" Lacey said, as she smiled at Alex. She was certain she'd used the expression appropriately.

Jake re-crossed his legs, which elicited a meow from Jingles who shifted his big body a tad, and then began purring. "So yes, Lacey, you used the term correctly and now for the burning question. Let's see if you know the origin of, *happy as Larry,* and just who Larry is. He cocked his head, raised a brow, and waited for her answer. Taking a sip of his coffee, he seemed to conceal his amusement.

She cursed herself for not having an iPOD; she

might be able to surreptitiously google the answer. That would wipe the smug look off that gorgeous face.

Before she could embarrass herself by hazarding a stupid guess, or have to admit her lack of knowledge to this arrogant Aussie, he kindly spared her the discomfort. But, not before letting her stew for an hour. At least, that's what it seemed like to Lacey. It was merely a few moments.

"You can relax, Lacey. I'll tell you the answer. Actually, there is no answer. No one knows for sure who Larry is, and why he's so bloody happy."

"So I could have guessed, and you wouldn't have been able to disprove what I said?"

Alex passed a small plate to Lacy with a delicious looking lamington on it. He took one for himself, and then settled down on what Lacey presumed was his favorite chair.

"Good thing you didn't pretend you knew the answer," Alex said, after taking a bite of the lamington. Nodding his head toward Jake he said, "There are two theories, and Jake knows them both. I do too, and now so will you."

Jake lifted Jingles off his lap, muttering, "Get out of here Boof," and then depositing him on the floor. Despite his gruff manner, Lacey noticed he did so with a gentle hand. Jake brushed his hands, picked up one of his lamingtons, took a large bite, chewed, and swallowed. Then he turned his attention to Lacey.

"One theory is—a famous Australian boxer from the 1800s, who had never lost a fight, won a lot of money. His name was Larry Foley. He was presumably very happy, as one could imagine. Another theory is that it derives from the Aussie/Kiwi term *larrikin,*" in other words, a hooligan. But my money's on the first theory. The second one doesn't make sense to me. And now, having learned something today, you too can be as happy as Larry, yes?"

Lacey didn't know whether she wanted to smack him, or throw a shoe at him. However, he irritated and intrigued her.

Jingles pranced happily over to Lacey. Jumping onto her lap, he then pawed at her face with soft paws. Lacey's heart melted. She had been terribly agitated with Jake, and now, TC was working his magic; making her feel better again.

"Oh. I learned a lot today, Jake—especially about Australians. Thank you for the lesson. Very interesting. I'll remember it when I visit Australia one day. I'd love to see kangaroos and koala bears, up close."

Alex nearly spilled his coffee as he broke into convulsions of laughter. Lacey wondered what would cause such a reaction to her simple comment. She wouldn't have long to wait.

"Don't you Yanks know anything about Australia?" Jake growled, throwing up his hands in mock exasperation." Bloody oath, mate. Think about it, just give it some thought. Is a bear a marsupial?"

"No," she replied, shaking her head, "of course not. Does a bear, well, never mind. No, a bear is definitely not a marsupial. What's your point? And, I know you have one," Lacey joked.

"I bloody well do. Tell me, is a koala a marsupial?"

"Yes. Again, what's your point?"

Jake grinned as if savoring the moment, and preparing to pounce. Lacey's breath was taken away. If she thought he was gorgeous before, he looked even more so when he really smiled. She actually went weak in the knees.

"So. If a bear is not a marsupial, and a koala *is*, tell me why you call a koala, a koala *bear*? Riddle me that, Lacey."

"He uses my name constantly, and it never sounded so good. What a larrikin! But a handsome, larrikin."

"Cat got your tongue, eh Lacey?"

"The best way to end an argument is to agree with the other person. Of all the things I'd like to do, arguing with Jake isn't one of them. I'd better stop thinking about those other possibilities before I really do embarrass myself."

He was really teasing her now, and she had no smart retort. "Well, I always hear people calling them koala *bears*. I just never gave it any thought."

"You're right, of course," Lacey said with a

treacly smile. "How stupid of me not to have realized that."

Alex laughed and clapped his hands. "Lois was right in her estimation of you, Lacey. I believe you two are a good match, or should I say, you're worthy opponents?"

Recalling the line from Prince Hal in Shakespeare's Henry IV, Lacey agreed with the premise, *'the better part of valor is discretion,'* so she opted for a smile, instead of a barb.

"So, Lacey," Alex teased, "I'll bet you'll never forget that a koala is not a bear, will you?"

"No, Alex. I won't," Lacey replied, with her eyes fixed on Jake. A sly grin formed across her face. "I've also learned that some grizzly bears are not quite as scary as they'd have us believe."

"At least they know they aren't marsupials." Jake actually laughed at his snide comment, while seeming to search Lacey's face for a reaction.

Before she could, answer her cell rang. "S*teve!*"

CHAPTER ELEVEN

There was a time when Lacey would have been thrilled to hear Steve's voice. That seemed so long ago now. Of all the people she didn't want to hear from, Steve was at the top of her list.

"Excuse me," Lacey said, as she stood. "I really have to take this call."

"You can take it in there," Alex said, motioning toward the kitchen.

"Lacey heard Jake sputter as she left the room, "Just like a Sheila, can't stay off the bloody phone for more than five minutes."

Saved by the bell, Lacey thought, or by the cell. She knew she had no clever response to Jake's maddening comments. "Steve. What's up?"

"I just wanted to confirm that you're coming back home soon. Emphasis on the soon! Have you gotten your ticket, yet?"

A comforting tail swished against Lacey's legs. She knew TC was coming to her rescue, once again. Yes, she needed courage to let Steve know she'd decided not to go back to South Carolina, or back to him.

The decision had been made to stay here; and she was proud of herself. Now, she didn't call South Carolina home. Vermont was definitely her home. Vermont with its beautiful scenery, four seasons, friendly people, an incredible cat, and one prickly pear.

Even prickly pears, though beautiful on the outside, are delicious on the inside, once you manage to carefully peel away the skin. Preferably, she'd need kid gloves when dealing with the likes of Jake.

Lacey picked up TC for extra comfort and courage. He purred loudly as if he knew Steve would hear him. Lacey wasn't so sure that that wasn't the cat's motive. She knew how intuitive TC was.

"Mroww, mroww, purr, purr."

"Lacey, do you still have that darn cat? I can't talk to you with that distraction. Put him down, will you? We need to talk about your coming home. I need to set a definite date to take my potential clients to dinner. It has to be soon."

Lacey took a deep breath. "Is tomorrow soon enough for you Steve?"

"Not at all. That's terrific, Lace. Let me know what time you'll be at the airport and I'll have a limo sent for you."

Lacey put TC down, and then lifted her hair from her neck. She was hot and getting clammy. Her hands were shaking, a typical reaction to her stress.

"Steve, why couldn't you have asked how I'm feeling? But, now I'm glad you didn't. Although, this won't be easy, you're making it less hard."

"Don't bother with a limo, Steve. I won't need it."

"I insist, Lace. We want to show these clients that we're first class. We'll be using the same limo to pick them up. That'll knock their socks off, along with an expensive dinner at Magnolias. I'll book a private dining room on the Upper Level Gallery. Then, they'll know they're not dealing with just any law firm. This will mean millions for the firm, and a big payday for *us*."

"Steve, there's no easy way to say this, so I'll just come out and say it. I'm not coming back to South Carolina. Not now, or anytime."

"I know you're kidding, Lacey. It isn't funny."

"No, Steve. I'm not kidding. I've decided to make my home here. It's where I belong. I didn't want to tell you over the phone, but there's no other way. I'm sorry. Really and truly, sorry."

"You're wrong, Lacey! You belong here. You belong with me! I won't stand for this."

Lacey waited patiently for Steve to run out of steam. She'd been on the receiving end of his bad temper before, but he'd always manage to calm down. Of late, he was getting worse; much worse.

"How can you do this to me, Lacey? After all I've done for you—all the expensive gifts I've bought you, all the places I've taken you. I've treated you like a queen for god's sake. And, this is what I get for it? You turn your back on me?"

"Yes, Steve. You've certainly been very good to

me. Your gifts have been extravagant; even when I told you I wasn't interested in material things. I just wanted to be loved and..."

Steve interrupted her with an exasperated shout. "Didn't I show my love for you by doing all these things? What more could I have done? You're acting like a spoiled child who has everything she wants, and still wants more."

"I thought you did those things because you love me, Steve. I didn't realize it was quid pro quo. Sometimes love is 50/50, but sometimes it's 70/30, or even 90/10. I don't have money, but I gave you my love. I gave you me. I gave you everything and didn't expect anything in return, other than your love and respect."

"Lacey! Listen to yourself. You're not making any sense and you're beginning to really tick me off. You need to..."

"No, Steve," Lacey interrupted, "I don't *need* to do anything other than hang up and let you calm down. Look, I'm visiting someone right now, and I'm being rude by talking on the phone. Let me go, and I'll call you in about an hour."

"What? You're worried about being rude to strangers? What about how rude you're being to me?"

"Mrowwwwwww," TC chimed in.

"Damn it, Lacey! I can't talk to you with that

damn cat howling. I thought you said you were visiting someone? What do you do, take that cat with you everywhere you go? Really, Lacey? I swear you love that cat more than me."

Picking up TC, and tucking him under her arm, comforted Lacey. "Steve, I really do have to go now. I'll call you when I get home; in an hour or so."

After saying a terse good-bye to Steve, she snapped her cell phone shut. She gave TC a kiss on his boofhead, as Jake liked to say. Immediately, she was rewarded with extra loud purring. Was it her imagination or did TC actually smile at her?

TC's purr was extra loud as Lacey carried him back into the living room. He enjoyed being carried like the little prince he apparently thinks he is.

Immediately, she was greeted by that now familiar gruff voice. "Well, you've decided to play nice and rejoin us. What a bloody cheek. But I guess that's typical Seppo behavior."

Alex waved his arm holding an imaginary white flag. "Now, now, Jake. Truce! Lacey is not the enemy. She's a guest and deserves to be treated with respect. How could you subject her to your ill temper? And, just remember, nephew, before you continue maligning us Seppos, you might do well to remember I'm a bloody Seppo, myself."

"Mroww, mroww," TC interjected loudly, while glaring at Jake with brilliant blue-green eyes.

"If looks could kill," Lacey mused, *"Jake would be a goner."*

Lacey stroked TC's silky soft fur, while cooing to him. "Pay him no mind, TC. He's an Aussie. No further explanation needed." She smiled at Alex.

"Uncle Max is right. You do have spunk, Seppo. Just don't get all up yourself. It's not very lady-like."

His tone may have been arrogant, but his smile seemed to betray his true feelings. "I'm so sorry, Alex and Jake. I didn't mean to be so rude. But Steve is not easily put off. I told him I'd call him back later. I'm really enjoying our visit. If you'd like me to go now, I'll come back another time, if that's ok with you."

"You'll do no such thing, Lacey," Alex demanded. "Sit yourself back down. Have some more hot chocolate and another lamington. Or would you prefer a nice glass of wine?"

As if he could sense a party coming on, TC danced around the living room, strutting from one person to the other. He wasn't going to be left out. *"Purr, purr."*

Lacey sat back down. "Thank you, Alex. No wine or lamingtons for me. They were scrumptious, even though they were made by an Aussie." Lacey ventured a look in Jake's direction. Arching a brow, she prepared for a volley of insults.

He didn't disappoint. Fixing his intensely beautiful eyes on her, Jake let loose some Australian slang which one didn't have to be an Aussie to interpret.

Lacey didn't flinch outwardly, but she did feel her cheeks becoming flushed. "*Once I've dealt with Steve, I'll deal with Mr. Australia. He could use a few lessons in manners.*"

"Jake!" Alex interjected. "What you just said was rude, even for you."

"Don't worry about it," Lacey replied. "I'm sure Jake will apologize. If he doesn't, then no worries. In the meantime, I really must be going. I have another prickly pear waiting for my phone call."

"And, you can't handle either one," Jake muttered as he turned his back and walked out of the room. She did manage to catch part of his diatribe. "You give a bad name to the Blueys of the world."

Alex explained, "A Bluey is what they call redheads in Oz. Don't try to figure it out. Remember, he's an Australian." He was kidding, she knew, but the wistful look in his eyes told yet another story.

They walked down the hallway to the front door where Lacey retrieved her jacket from the hall tree. Alex helped her into it.

Turning to face Alex, Lacey remarked, "They certainly have some strange expressions, don't they? You seem to understand them."

Alex encircled Lacey's arms with an avuncular hug. TC came toddling into the hallway, purring, with his tail held high. He stopped in front of Lacey, stood on his hind legs, and pawed Lacey's legs with soft, furry paws.

"When you're around him long enough, you learn a lot. I know he has a rough exterior Lacey, but it hides a world of pain." I hope you'll give him a chance. Get to know the real Jake. You might even find that you like him. His bark truly is worse than his bite."

"Purr, purr."

Lacey picked up her favorite little guy, and then kissed him on his big head, his boof head. "Well, that's one heck of a bark, Alex. I would certainly hope his bite isn't worse. I don't know about getting to know him though. I'm quite sure he doesn't like me. If he does, he has some colorful ways of showing it."

"I'll give you that. He uses very colorful language, and he can be a bit of a larrikin. But, once you get to know him, and I hope you will, you'll find there's a big heart beating beneath that gruff exterior. He can be a bit of a yobbo at times, I know."

Lacey was surprised by the new term Alex had just used. Alex admitted that Aussie terms rolled off his tongue without his even thinking. Since his nephew had come to live with him, it had become second nature to him.

Alex explained to Lacey that he actually tripped over Jingles, while walking through his darkened bedroom to the bathroom. He was unaware that

Jingles was lying on the floor near the bed. "I'd broken my right hip, and yelled out to Jake for help. What was supposed to be a short visit, turned into eight weeks. As time went by, Jake decided to stay with me.

"It became obvious that we needed each other. I needed Jake for physical support, and Jake needed me for emotional support. A yobbo is an uncouth person—a lout. But I'm sure you've already figured that out," Alex remarked." But he's fair dinkum."

Lacey patted Alex on the arm, looking at him tenderly. "Not to worry about that one. I think I can sense what it means. And, if you say he's a genuine person, then he must be. But for now I'll just have to take your word for it."

A gruff voice coming down the hall interrupted Lacey's goodbye. "You sure do take a long time to say goodnight. I could have gone walkabout three times in the time you're taking to walk out the door. Strewth!"

Lacey and Alex exchanged knowing glances; she commented to Alex in a stage whisper, "I've figured that one out too, Alex."

"You're really up yourself, aren't you?" Jake said, with a sarcastic edge to his voice. He turned to walk away. "Oh, Uncle Alex, I'm going to crack a tinny. Care for one? None for you Lacey, because you *are* leaving, right?"

"And, not soon enough apparently," Lacey said,

aiming a trace of sarcasm at Jake. "TC, Jingles, or Boofhead, I'll be on my way. I'm sure it's a lot less cold outside."

"I do believe I'll have a beer, Jake," Alex said. "You're certainly welcome to stay and have one with us, Lacey. Don't let the boofhead, oops, I mean, Jake, run you off." Alex grinned at Lacey. She smiled warmly in return. "May I call you tomorrow, Alex? Maybe we can arrange to have lunch on Friday. I have a wonderful kitchen, and I know I'll be feeling better by then. I'd love to take advantage of it. Plus, I'm not a bad cook either."

"Meow, purr purr."

Alex and Lacey looked at Jingles, and laughed. "I'd be delighted to come to your place for lunch. Apparently, I'm not the only one. Would you mind if His Highness joins us?"

"Meow, purr purr," TC uttered loudly.

"My goodness, TC. Of course, you're welcome. Was there ever any doubt? I'll set an extra place, but don't get too excited; it'll be on the floor."

Hearing no complaint from TC, Lacey assumed the arrangement met with his approval. It was a good thing too, because she'd let him join them at the table, if he insisted.

Alex inclined his head toward Jake's back, silently questioning if Jake would be welcome.

Lacey wasn't sure if she wanted Jake to come

along, but she didn't want to hurt Alex's feelings. After all Jake was his nephew, even if he was a yobbo, Aussie, larrikin. And, a darn good looking one. She'd been led astray by good looks before, and she wouldn't fall into that trap again. Besides, he'd made it abundantly clear that he found her annoying. "Talk to you tomorrow, Alex. We'll set a time that's suitable for all of us. And yes, that means you too, TC."

CHAPTER TWELVE

Lacey walked out into the crisp air. The delicious smell of burning wood from many fireplaces wafted up her nostrils as she walked along the well-lit street. She would be home in no time, which was a two-edged sword. On the one hand, she'd be warm and comfy, in her own place. On the other, she'd have to call Steve. After all, she'd promised him.

After taking off her jacket, she poured herself a glass of wine, then her cell rang. Steve had taken the decision out of her hands, as to when to call him. Left up to her, she'd have postponed the call indefinitely.

Lacey sucked in her breath, forced a smile, and answered the phone. "Hello, Steve." So much for the forced smile. She could hear the biting edge to her voice and hoped Steve wouldn't notice.

"Well, hello to you too. Gee, don't sound so happy to hear from me. I wondered how long I'd have to wait for you to call."

"I just walked in the door. Sorry." Lacy shrugged. *"So much for disguising my displeasure."* She sat on the sofa and tucked her feet under her.

"At least I don't hear that damn cat howling. Got rid of him, I hope. Now you can get serious about coming home. I can't stress enough how much I need you here."

"Steve. You can rant and rave as much as you'd like, but wait until *after* you hear what I have to say, okay?"

There was silence on the other end of the phone. Apparently, Steve was listening.

Lacey walked into the kitchen and poured a glass of iced tea, then she re-entered the great room. She took a large gulp, and then as if preparing for battle, she placed the glass on the table rather forcefully. If she thought Jake was difficult, he was a pussycat compared to Steve when he had his hackles up.

"Very well, then. I don't want to hurt you, Steve. I'm grateful for all you've done, but I'm not coming back to South Carolina. I belong here, in Ascot Vale, Vermont. This is my home. I'll have Summer pack up the rest of my belongings. You can have everything you've bought me." There was more silence. She knew Steve was seething. In recent times, she'd seen this side of him; it portended an ugly explosion. "Steve? Please say something."

"Oh, I'll say something." He said in a calm voice, belying the volcano she knew was brewing beneath the surface. "If you don't come home, and like it or not, this *is* your home, *sweetheart*, you'll be sorry. Very sorry."

Lacey took several deep breaths before speaking. She decided she'd need all her wits about her, to deal with the mean, nasty side of Steve. "If I didn't know better, I'd say you were threatening me, Steve."

"Oh, it's not a threat, Lacey. It's not a threat at all."

Again, that calm voice. Lacey knew him well.

Most likely his lips were stretched tightly across his face like a taut archer's bow; exposing perfect white menacing teeth. His dark brown eyes would be flashing, and his fists were probably clenching and unclenching. She knew he wanted to scream at her—insult her. Steve was used to getting his own way, and he wasn't about to let a woman disrespect him. She would come home. He'd see to it.

"I'm glad it isn't, Steve. I don't want our relationship to turn adversarial."

"What relationship? There *is* no relationship!" Steve's voice had gone from a barely audible sarcastic level, to a high-pitched decibel, threatening to boil into a full-blown rage.

"Okay, Steve. I don't want to upset you any more than you already are. I think we should say good-bye for now, and talk again another time."

"Oh, we'll talk again. This isn't the end of it. You'll be costing me a lot of money, and I mean a *lot* of money if you don't come back home. If I have to reschedule this dinner, you'll be here for it. I can promise you that."

"Good-bye, Steve."

Lacey ended the call with trembling hands. Steve's temper had been getting worse of late. With all the pressure he was under from the law firm, things were turning ugly, and scary.

Lacey sighed and headed for bed. There would be

time to worry about all this tomorrow, not tonight, or else she wouldn't get any sleep. Now, she could turn her attention to a more immediate concern, one Jake Anderson.

"His manners are atrocious – he's rude, and condescending. He's not really an animal lover, and he's only minimally nice to TC. But he is Alex's nephew, and he did stay on and take care of him, and he is gorgeous. Oh my, is he gorgeous." Lacey thought of him as a diamond in the rough, but feared that after polishing the rough spots there would be very little left.

Sleep came in fits and starts for Lacey. It seemed she spent half the night worrying about Steve's unpredictable behavior, and the other half wondering what it would be like to kiss Jake on his beautiful full lips. She chided herself for thinking such a thing. Then again, she was in a half awake, half twilight state and couldn't be held responsible for her thoughts.

CHAPTER THIRTEEN

Lacey awoke to broad beams of sunlight streaming through her bedroom window. Glancing off the large mirror over the vanity, it bathed the room in a brilliant glow. A gnawing in her stomach was a good sign. She hadn't eaten much since she'd been sick; with the exception of Jake's lamingtons, and Aunt Lois's famous breakfast patty. Now, she was hungry.

After showering, Lacey let her hair dry. The length of time it took always annoyed her, but she wasn't about to cut it. Her mother always said that your hair is your crowning glory. She felt like walking to Aunt Lois's for a nice breakfast, and inquire about Jake. Hopefully, Aunt Lois would have the skinny on him, and give her the unvarnished truth.

Donning her faux-fur-lined jacket, she wrapped a soft Midnight Lavender scarf around her neck, put on her good boots, a pair of gloves, and then set out for Aunt Lois's Hearth and Home café.

A feeling of guilt swept over Lacey for wearing the clothes that Steve had paid for. But, she had given him her love. Wasn't that worth something? She gave him her devotion; she gave him everything she had. If she'd had millions, she'd have given him that, too. But she wasn't rich, although she lived in a level of comfort compared to most people. Most of her discretionary spending was for pet charities. Had Steve treated her with kindness, she would have given him whatever he wanted.

The inheritance from her parents would keep her out of the poor house. Making her living as a freelance writer helped, but only a dreamer would count on that for security.

Now, she had the inheritance from Nana's estate, and didn't need to accept Steve's charity. She thought he'd bought gifts out of love and devotion. Unfortunately, that wasn't the case. He was merely adorning his prize, gilding the lily; using her as bait for his gain.

So wrapped in her thoughts, Lacy hadn't realized she had arrived at Aunt Lois's. When she walked in, once again, her senses were caressed by the wonderful aroma of the patchouli incense, and all the scented sachets. Instantly, her mood was lifted. What really pleased her was the warm reception she received from the locals, calling out her name and waving friendly hellos.

"Welcome back, Lacey," came the cheerful greeting from behind the counter. Aunt Lois wiped her hands on her apron and walked over to Lacey with her arms held wide. She hugged her, then led the way to the same table where she'd sat before.

"So, I understand you returned Jingles to Alex. I'm glad you did. I know how tempting it is to keep him, but he and Alex are devoted to each other, as I'm sure you found out."

Marianne came over to the table carrying a pot of steaming hot coffee. After pouring a cup for Lacey and Aunt Lois, she offered Lacey a menu.

"Oh, I don't need a menu, Marianne. My mouth is watering for Aunt Lois's delicious maple flavored breakfast patty. Thank you."

"Coming right up," Marianne said, as she picked up the menu and headed toward the kitchen. "Oh," turning back around, Marianne smiled and inquired, "Seen any Greek gods lately?"

"What Greek gods?" Aunt Lois blurted. Putting her cup down, she then looked expectantly at Marianne, then Lacey. "I can't believe a Greek god got by me."

"Oh he didn't, Aunt Lois. We're talking about Jake."

"Ahh, yes, he's a Greek god indeed; an ill-mannered god for sure. But then, he has his reasons. So, you were impressed by his looks? Everybody is. Too bad, he doesn't have the personality to match. But that's a story for another day.

"He looks so devilishly handsome when he's wearing his Akubra hat. If I were younger..." Aunt Lois murmured.

"Can you tell me about Jake? I have lots of questions. I met him at Alex's house. I got the distinct impression that he really didn't like me. I'd like to know why."

Aunt Lois finished her coffee, and then stood up, holding the cup. "Join the club, Lacey. Everyone thinks Jake doesn't like them. The truth is, the only person Jake doesn't like, is Jake."

"I'm sorry to hear that. It's not healthy to dislike oneself. I'm asking because I'm undecided as to whether or not I should invite him to dinner at my place."

"Well, sure, but..."

"Oh, don't get the wrong idea, Aunt Lois. Alex is coming to dinner on Friday, and he wants to bring Jake along. I'd really like to know something about him beforehand. He delights in having the upper hand and teasing me. I'd like to have some ammo against him. I know that sounds awful."

"I understand. Nevertheless, if you're the kind person I think you are, what I tell you—you won't use against him, right? I'm sure you take after your Nana, and she was the kindest person I'd ever met."

"She was, wasn't she? I'd like to think I'm like her, too. I promise I won't use anything you tell me against him."

"I know you won't. Why don't you come around after closing tonight? We can talk then."

Marianne brought Lacey's breakfast, and the aroma was tantalizing. "Thank you, Marianne. It looks wonderful."

Aunt Lois beamed. It was obvious she loved compliments about her café and food.

"I have a better idea, Aunt Lois. Why don't you

come to my place? Get out of your work place and relax at my home. Is that okay?"

"Fine and dandy with me, hon. Since I'm the boss, I can leave early. What time should I stop by?"

Lacey rested her fork in mid-air. "How about 5 o'clock?" She resumed her breakfast.

"I'll be there at 5:00, and please don't worry about preparing any food. That's my job! Just put on some coffee, and I'll bring something from here." Aunt Lois was called to another table. "See you in a little while, sweetie."

Lacey's cell vibrated at that moment. It was rude to hear ringing cell phones, and people yammering loudly when out in public. Noting it was Summer calling, Lacey didn't answer. She elected to send a text instead, and would call her within the hour.

Several of the patrons seemed like one big happy family. They'd stop by her table to say hello, and to welcome her return to Ascot Vale. Most knew she'd spent a considerable amount of her childhood here, and they also knew her Nana and Gramps.

When Lacey had finished her breakfast, she waved good-bye to everyone, enjoying the shouts of friendly good-byes in return.

"Yes, this is home–where I belong. Home is definitely, where the heart is, and my heart is firmly entrenched in Ascot Vale."

CHAPTER FOURTEEN

Lacey walked along the street reveling in the fresh air; taking in the beauty of Vermont. She noticed everything from the magnificent trees lining the street, to the songs of the birds and the pleasant sights of the saltbox homes. Everything was decorated for the holiday season.

When she arrived home, she checked the mailbox. Not that she was expecting any mail; she did it out of habit. She'd have to get into the holiday spirit. A big bow around the mailbox and a few pumpkins would be nice by the double front doors. This is how the holiday season should be, cold and snowy, not warm and muggy like it is in Charleston.

Lacey entered her home, and headed for the kitchen. She made herself a cup of coffee with a teaspoon of cinnamon, then added a dollop of whipped cream. After a couple of sips, she took out her cell phone and called Summer.

"Hi, Lace," Summer's sweet voice answered. "I'm glad you called me back. I've got my plane tickets and I'll be in your neck of the woods on Saturday. I'll text you the particulars, okay?"

"That's more than okay. I'm so excited, and really looking forward to seeing you. Wait until you see this place-*my place,* I mean. It's huge, but so warm and oddly cozy, you know what I mean?"

"I do. You can make anyplace comfy, no matter how large it may be. You could make Buckingham

Palace seem cozy." Summer laughed. "I can't wait to get there."

Lacey took another sip of her coffee, and then told Summer all about Aunt Lois and her charming café. "Well, I'd better get going now. I have one more call to make, and I'm curious to see what the outcome will be. Don't ask, I'll explain all on Saturday."

She finished her coffee, set the cup down on the coffee table, and punched Alex's number on her cell phone. Too late, she realized that it might not be Alex who answered. It might be *him,* that frustrating, gorgeous Aussie, Jake.

"Hello," Jake answered in his sexy voice. Yes, she hadn't realized how sexy his voice sounded before, probably because he was always insulting her.

"G'day, Jake. It's Lacey," she said, trying for an authentic Aussie accent.

"Who bloody else would it be? You haven't got Buckley's chance of sounding like an Aussie. Studying up on your '*Strine*' are you?"

"Oh, brother, here we go again!"

Lacey stuck out her tongue imagining Jake seeing her do it. Whenever she wanted to say something that she shouldn't, she always surreptitiously stuck out her tongue. It was satisfying to her without being overtly mean to the other person.

"First, I'd have to know what 'Strine' is. If it's Australian, then it's probably something I don't want to study. And, I think my accent was pretty good, by the way."

"What do you care if it's good or not? You just said you don't want to study anything Australian. Anyway, you didn't call to talk to me." She heard him shuffle, and then there was silence. "Nobody does," carried through the phone.

"Yes. I called to speak to Alex. I'm calling to set up a time for dinner at my place. You and Jingles are invited too."

"Bloody nice! I'm on the same social plane as Boofhead, now. Thanks, but no thanks."

Lacey tried to stifle a laugh, but it sneaked out as if she were a little girl in kindergarten. The only thing she didn't do was clasp her hand over her mouth. "Sorry, Jake. I wasn't laughing *at* you. I just thought what you said was funny."

"Yeah, right. You're just enjoying taking the Mickey out of me. Bloody seppo."

Her moment of levity was just that. He had managed to get her hackles up once again. She resisted the temptation to stick out her tongue, once again.

"Actually Jake, you are not on the same social plane as Boof—as Jingles. You can only aspire to be on the same level as that wonderful cat, and me included."

"Ha! You're pretty good at big noting yourself, I

see. But you wouldn't know what that means. I'll go get Uncle Alex, while you stew about it. "I reckon that's one Sheila who can give, as good as she gets," Jake muttered quietly to himself. "Should be interesting to see if she's up for it."

He was off the phone before Lacey could get another word in. Good thing too, because she couldn't think of any more biting comments. If she could surprise him by taking a crash course in Aussie lingo, that might take him down a peg or two. As much as he upset her though, she couldn't bring herself to be mean to him. There was a sad little boy beneath that rough exterior; someone who had been hurt badly. It was her nature to be a caregiver.

"Lacey. Hello, love," Alex intoned, interrupting her musings about this handsome man-boy, this Greek god, this maddening and infuriating hunk of a man with the kissable lips. At least the kissable *looking* lips. She hoped she'd have the opportunity to find out for sure.

"Hello, Alex. How are you?"

"I'm feeling great. It's good to hear a friendly, non-combative voice, if you know what I mean." He chuckled. "How are you? I heard the tail-end of the convo. That's Aussie speak for conversation, but I suppose you figured that out anyway. I heard Jake giving you a hard time."

"Nothing I can't handle. Just between you and me, I'm going to learn as much Aussie as I can. You seem to know a lot of the lingo; perhaps you wouldn't mind helping me?"

"No worries, Lacey. I'll have you speaking 'Strine' in no time."

"So, that's what 'Strine' is," Lacey interrupted." Aussie slang. Jake mentioned that word. Can we keep this between us, Alex?"

"Of course, love. I suspect he'll be pleased too, although he wouldn't let that on. Just quietly, Lacey, this is a bad month for Jake."

"Meow, Meow, came," an insistent voice accompanied by some very loud purrs.

"Now, now, Jingles. It's Lacey and you can say hello in a minute. I swear he knows it's you I'm talking to. You know what magical powers he seems to have."

Lacey was pleased that TC, Jingles, seemed to remember her." Alex, would you let the little prince know that he's invited to dinner on Friday, along with you and Jake? Not that Jake will come, but he *is* invited. "Is 6:00 p. m. a good time?"

"Any time you say, Lacey. We'll be there. Well, at least two of us will be there, not sure about the third invitee. I'll see what I can do. Would it put you out too much to cook for three, and have only two show up? I've got a pretty good appetite so don't worry about that third portion, okay?"

"It's all perfectly okay, Alex. I'm looking forward to it, and also to my private 'Strine' lessons. I'll see you Friday. And, don't bother bringing anything other than your appetite, okay?"

"Okay. It's a date, Lacey."

"Meow, meow, purr, purr."

Lacey beamed. She really liked Alex and she just loved that big bear of a cat. Learning a little 'Strine' beforehand would make the dinner convo lively. Lacey chuckled to herself.

CHAPTER FIFTEEN

The doorbell rang at precisely 5:00 p. m.. Lacey answered the door, dressed in a comfortable pair of jeans, and a favorite tee-shirt. Her long hair was pulled up into a stylish ponytail. She was surprised to see that Aunt Lois was dressed casually too. Beneath her jacket, she wore a pair of casual black denims. A white cotton blouse was perfect for the occasion. Lacey was surprised by how cool, yet elegant Aunt Lois looked in casual attire.

Beaming, Lacey welcomed Aunt Lois into her home, and then took the package of food from her arms. Whatever was inside, the package smelled delicious; a combination of sweet and savory.

Lacey led Aunt Lois in to the spacious great room where they each sat on the comfortable furniture. She poured them each a glass of iced tea from the tray she'd carried in with her.

After exchanging pleasantries and getting comfortable with each other, Lacey asked the question that had been burning in her mind. Especially since Alex had mentioned that this is a bad month for Jake.

"Aunt Lois, what can you tell me about, Jake? Why doesn't he seem to talk to people, or smile? Why is he so rude and gruff?"

"This'll be a long story, Lacey."

Lacy smiled. "So, let's eat while we dish, okay? We can eat in here, unless you'd prefer to eat at the kitchen table."

"Oh, let's sit here. I'll try not to spill anything." Aunt Lois's eyes twinkled as she spoke. "May I help you with the food? It's nothing fancy."

Lacey got up from the sofa, assuring Aunt Lois that crumbs or spills were not a problem. "It makes the home lived in," she assured. "My friend, Rita, and I have a rule. You don't do dishes or help with the food at my house, and I don't do it at your house. Sound good?"

With a broad smile, Aunt Lois remarked, "Sounds more than good to me, Lacey. I'll have to remember that rule!"

Lacey went to the kitchen to get napkins, plates and forks. Then she returned to the Great room with a tray. Aunt Lois had specially prepared roast beef and cheddar sandwiches with her special homemade sauce. Her homemade potato chips and hot cherry cobbler were absolutely divine.

"So tell me, what is the big mystery concerning Jake? He's quite abrupt, cynical, and quite frankly, a bit rude. But I suspect there's a good bit of sadness there."

Lacey took a bite of her sandwich, sat back, and waited for Aunt Lois to fill her in on the enigma known as Jake Anderson.

"Well, you're right about the sadness, Lacey. But first I should give you a little background on Jake."

Aunt Lois started with Jake's teen years. "Jake's mother was an Australian—a lovely, soft-spoken woman. His father was an American and a very successful, wealthy businessman.

"Jake was born in Tasmania, the island state of Australia and the family lived there for most of Jake's life, until coming here when he was sixteen.

Jake's grandfather lived here in Vermont and when he became ill, the family wanted to be here for him. Well, Jake was a natural caretaker. He developed an instant bond with his grandfather, and was devastated when he passed away after a lingering illness."

Lacey listened intently as the story of Jake unfolded with the patient, kind storytelling by Aunt Lois. It was obvious she cared for Jake very much.

"So, you knew Jake back then?" Lacey poured some iced tea for both of them and waited to hear more about the maddening but intriguing Jake Anderson.

Aunt Lois took a small sip of the beverage, then placed the glass on the coffee table, and pulled her legs beneath her.

"Yes," Aunt Lois began again. "I was good friends with Roy. That was Jake's grandfather. I had the pleasure of being in Jake's company quite often, along with his parents, Charles and Rebecca. They were lovely, kind people. Jake was well-mannered, smart, and possessed a maturity way beyond his years. He was a happy-go-lucky young man whom everyone loved.

"The family eventually returned to Australia after settling Roy's affairs. I was sorry to see them go, but Jake promised me he'd be back. I knew he would. And, he did. But when he returned, he was no longer the carefree, happy young lad he was fifteen years before."

Lacey sat up straight. "Why? What happened?"

Aunt Lois's eyes misted over as she thought about what had happened. "Life happened, Lacey. As John Lennon said, *Life is what happens while you're busy making other plans.* Jake grew up, became a master carpenter, and had a very successful furniture shop where he sold his custom furniture. He was very well off, and he also developed quite a talent for photography. A couple of the pictures in my café were taken by him, and they're the best ones in there.

"One day, a beautiful woman came into his shop, purchased a very expensive piece of furniture, and in the process, stole Jake's heart."

"Then broke it, I suppose. That would explain his attitude toward women."

"No, dear. They were devoted to each other until her death."

A gasp sneaked from Lacey's throat and her voice caught. A few seconds passed before she could formulate any words. "Oh, Aunt Lois. I'm so sorry to hear that. I truly am. How sad for him. I know how awful it is to lose someone you love. Eventually, you learn to live again, although you never get over the loss. Never. But I don't understand the anger."

Lacey's cell rang. She looked at the Caller ID, and then let it go into her voice mail. She certainly didn't feel like talking to Steve now or ever.

"Go ahead and answer it, Lacey. I don't mind."

"Well, I *do* mind." Lacey smiled, then asked Aunt Lois to continue.

"I understand his anger Lacey, and you will too. Jake's wife, Shanna, was killed by a driver who was drunk and high on drugs."

Lacey's mouth dropped. An overwhelming sadness overcame her, accompanied by a large measure of guilt.

"I've done him such an injustice. I've been mean, and teased him. I hate to admit it, but I just haven't been nice to Jake. I pride myself on being a nice person, but I guess I'm not as nice as I think I am. I feel awful."

Aunt Lois reached over and patted Lacey's hand. "Don't be so hard on yourself, dear. You had no way of knowing his story. *He* certainly wouldn't tell you. He keeps it stuffed inside."

Sitting silently for several seconds, Lacey tried to absorb what Aunt Lois had just told her. She'd lost her parents, and many pets. But, losing a life-mate had to be one of the worst experiences, second only, to losing a child.

"Lacey," Aunt Lois said softly, "don't beat yourself up over this. The only way to make amends for past, real, or imagined slights, is to start fresh. Just be the nice person you know you are."

Lacey wondered if it was too late to get Jake to see her as a nice, kind person. Or, would he take her new treatment of him as pity once he discovered that she knew about his past life? But, she knew she had to do something. He was hurting, and she didn't want to hurt him further.

"How did you find out about this? Apparently, Jake didn't tell you himself."

"No, dear, he wouldn't." She smiled wistfully." Alex told me. We've been friends for years. Alex's sister, Rebecca, is Jake's mother. For many years, we were as close as sisters. Rebecca was born in Australia, but Alex was born here, a few years after Rebecca.

"Rebecca's fondest wish was that Alex and I would develop our friendship into something stronger. I was young then, and driven with ambition. Didn't think I had time for a man in my life. It seemed all I was interested in was food. Oh, not to eat necessarily," Aunt Lois laughed. "I wanted to become one of the all-time great female chefs. So, I went to school. I actually attended a Culinary Institute, and knew that cooking would be my great love.

"I opened several successful restaurants, one in New York City, one in Chicago, and one in New Orleans. I was what some old-fashioned people might call a flibbertigibbet. I didn't have feet like normal people—I had wings and nobody was going to clip them. I traveled the country and the world, and never regretted it. My life was full beyond words.

"Then, one day you look at your life and wonder if you should have made wiser choices. No matter how great and successful my restaurants were; no matter how many places I'd visited, nor how many accolades I received, none of that will keep you warm at night, or take care of you when you're sick."

Lacey smiled." Alex would have."

"Yes, he probably would have." Aunt Lois agreed. "But I don't think I could compete with Jingles, or Tuffy as I call him, or any of the other names he ignores." She laughed. "Alex is bonkers over that cat, but then again, just about everybody in this town is. He'd be a hard act to follow."

"Aunt Lois. I just had one of those Eureka moments. Alex will be coming to dinner with TC, and maybe Jake too."

"Oh, no. Don't waste your time on this old broad," Aunt Lois shook her head. "Maybe you should concentrate on trying to tame that reluctant stallion. He isn't wild anymore, but he *is* beautiful isn't he? You might be just what the doctor ordered to mend his broken heart."

Lacey considered what Aunt Lois had said before responding, "No. He really doesn't like me. It isn't just that I've been mean to him. He hasn't exactly been a gentleman toward me either. It seems that he doesn't like women at all."

Aunt Lois shifted in her seat, and stretched her legs. "Lacey, I need to leave in a few minutes. But, before I go, I want to assuage any thoughts you have about Jake not liking you. Marianne mentioned that he smiled at you, well sort of smiled, when you saw him in the restaurant. He doesn't honor many people with a smile. It seems his smile muscles withered when Shanna died."

"Oh, he can smile alright, when he's making some sort of dig about my being a Seppo, or a Sheila. He seems to take delight in that."

Lacey and Aunt Lois laughed simultaneously over that remark, with Aunt Lois commenting that Jake meant no disrespect. "I expect you'll discover that on your own, the more you get to know him. He has, *had*, a dark side to him, but maybe Alex should tell you about that part of his life. Maybe one day, Jake will tell you. Anyway, it's in the past and I hope it stays there. But it's left its mark."

They stood and hugged. Lacey knew she'd met her first good friend here in Ascot Vale. She hoped she'd take advantage of the dinner invitation. Then, she would have an ally when dealing with Jake—*if* he came. But even if he didn't, she'd be happy because she'd get to see TC, and be entertained by his antics.

As Aunt Lois was leaving, she turned to Lacey and gave her a broad smile. "You know what Lacey? Life is short—too short for regrets; too short to pass up opportunities to socialize with good friends. I'll be here for dinner, but that's all."

"Aunt Lois that is fabulous. I'll make a phone call."

Aunt Lois held up her hand. "Don't think I'm agreeing to any set up. I don't want to ruin the friendship that Alex and I have. So, what can I bring? You must let me bring something, and don't say 'just bring yourself."

"Okay, okay. Bring whatever you'd like. I know anything you prepare will be terrific. Maybe a small appetizer would be good. I'll think of something for dessert, something Australian. Besides, Jake might not come. But I'll make sure I have some good tuna for TC. I know he'll be here for certain."

After Aunt Lois left, Lacey felt her mood deflate. She'd been avoiding thinking about Steve. Remembering that he'd called, he'd be expecting her to call him back. No, she'd rather be poked in the eye with a sharp stick! And, the sharp stick was waiting for her call. Lacey took a deep breath, and pressed #2 on her cell. Why hadn't she deleted his number, or at least changed it to another position. Before she could ponder it further, Steve answered. Whereas, once she was thrilled to hear his voice, now the sound filled her with dread.

CHAPTER SIXTEEN

"Hi, Lacey. Thank you for returning my call. I wasn't sure if you would. I hope this means you'll be coming back home. I rescheduled the dinner with those high powered clients I told you about."

"Steve!" Lacey practically screamed his name into the phone. Her voice welled with anger. "I'm sorry Steve, I really and truly am. I hadn't wanted to have this discussion before, and there's no way I want to have it again."

By the low, controlled measure of his response, Lacey could tell Steve's anger was rising. "There *is* another way, and it's the only way. You owe me. And, you *will* come home. Once you're safely back in Charleston, you'll see that I'm right. I'm always right, Lace."

She'd learned Steve was at his most volatile when agitated. Now, she was glad they weren't in physical proximity of each other. It was true he'd never used physical force, but lately she'd been in fear of that very thing. Her inner voice was telling her to beware. Just as certain animals can feel the trembling of an earthquake before it erupts—she had been feeling Steve's tremors for quite some time.

"Steve, I'd like you to listen to me—I mean really listen. Can you give me just five minutes? That's all I'm asking is for you to listen. Just five minutes. Please?" Immediately, Lacey noticed complete silence.

Although it would be fruitless, Lacey had to make Steve understand. She had to give it her best shot. "Steve?"

"I'm l i s t e n i n g," Steve said very slowly. "Isn't that what you wanted, for me to listen? Or do you even know what you want?"

Lacey chose her words carefully. She didn't want to be the match to his gasoline. "I want us both to be happy, Steve. I really do. You've been extraordinarily kind to me. You helped me so much after the death of my parents, that I will always be grateful. Always. But I don't think *I* can make you happy anymore. *I've* changed, Steve. Not you. I want to live here in Vermont—run around in jeans and shirts. I want to live a quiet life, not be on display and paraded around town for all to see. I want to be loved for what I am on the inside, and not for my outer appearance. I can't be your arm candy anymore, Steve. It's not *who* I am. You deserve what you want. I'm so sorry, Steve."

This time, the silence was ominous, Steve had hung up. No goodbye, no argument, nothing. Just silence.

Lacey placed the phone on the table and decided to take a walk in the garden, which was blanketed with beautiful white snow. Traces of footprints made tracks to and from the feeders that she kept filled. She needed some fresh air. She made a cup of coffee, put on her jacket, then went outside to sit on one of the iron benches. After wiping snow off the seat, Lacey settled in, positioning herself for the best bird's eye view. Watching the freeloading birds delighted her; she needed that respite. She needed to de-stress and take time to smell the roses or in this case, the fresh air filled with the scent of pine and spruce trees. There was a feeling that was foreign to her, but she wasn't sure what it was. Tossing some adjectives around in her head searching for the perfect descriptor, it finally hit her. It was contentment! Something she hadn't felt in such a long time. If she could be totally free of Steve she would be *completely* content and hoped it would be so. It had to be.

Lacey stood up, surveying the peaceful scene before her. Without a doubt she knew she'd made the right decision to stay here in this little hamlet. Though it was bigger than a hamlet, it felt like one. How she loved the intimacy of this wonderful little village, and its people. Home is where the heart is, and Lacey's heart was definitely here in Ascot Vale.

After a while, Lacey walked back inside the house. The warmth of the kitchen made her realize how chilly the outside had been. Before, she was too happy to notice. She was in the right frame of mind now to finish the article she'd been hired to write. But first things first, she'd call Alex and ask if he had managed to convince Jake to come to dinner.

"G'day," resonated the voice on the other end of the phone. Upon hearing Jake's voice, Lacey was surprised by the quickening of her pulse. Her stomach seemed to lurch into her chest much to her annoyance.

"Hello, Jake. It's…"

"Ya don't have to tell me who it is, it's the bloody seppo. How're you doing, Bluey? I reckon you're looking for Alex."

"Yes, but actually I'd like to speak to…"

"The bastard's gone walkabout," Jake interrupted. "I'll tell him to ring you when he gets home. He and that boofhead of a cat left here about fifteen minutes ago. I think they've gone to the bush. Hope they haven't come a gutser."

Lacey audibly sighed. "Do you deliberately try to antagonize me, Jake. Or, are you just a yobbo?"

"Well, look who's skiting about her Strine knowledge. Giving the old fingers a workout on the computer are you? Google, eh?"

"Never mind, Jake. I was calling to talk to *you* actually. But first, please tell me why you would call such a sweet man a bastard. He's your uncle for goodness' sake."

Lacey thought she detected a slight chuckle in Jake's voice when he answered her. "I see you're not such a bloody know-all after all. One bloke calling another bloke, a bastard, is not a bad thing. Quite the opposite, in fact. But don't worry your girly head about it. As the old bastard likes to say, *'I'm Australian. No further explanation needed.'* Now, why would *you* want to speak to *me?*"

Lacey reminded herself that Jake was hurting; a

hurt unlike any she'd experienced in her life. But, sometimes he made it so hard to be nice by testing her. And, to make matters worse, she was sure he enjoyed it.

"I'm inviting you to dinner tomorrow night, at my place. Alex and TC—Boofhead, as you call him, are coming. So is Aunt Lois. I'd like you to join us, Jake."

Jake let out a whistle." Are you trying to crack onto me, Lacey?"

Was he implying that she was hitting on him? Her inner voice told her there was an innate goodness underneath that steely exterior. One could hope. Nevertheless, it would be wonderful for his inside to be just as gorgeous as his outside, and boy, was he gorgeous with a capital G!

"Don't flatter yourself. I'm just being neighborly, and I know Alex would like you to come too."

"Feeling a bit clucky toward my Uncle Alex are you?"

"I think I actually get that, Jake. I suppose you could say that. He's a dear man and even though he's older than I am, I do feel a bit maternal toward him. It's my nature to take care of people."

"Even if they don't need you. Typical! Uncle Alex gets by quite well with just my help."

"I'm sorry Jake. I'm not trying to usurp your position. Aunt Lois told me how kind you are to Alex, and how well you take care of him."

"Did she now? Is there anything that woman doesn't know, or talk about?"

Lacey found herself laughing. "Well, it *is* a small town, Jake. I've found that out since I've been here. Anyway, can I count on you for dinner tomorrow night?"

"That would be nice but I'll have to say, no. Thank you for asking. I'm a bit of a piker, I know. Oh, here comes the bas…Here comes Uncle Alex now, and his fleabag sidekick. I'll pass the phone to him. "Here you go, Uncle. It's for you."

"Hello, sweetheart," Alex said with a smile in his voice. "You're not calling to cancel dinner are you? Jingles and I would be very disappointed if you were."

"Oh, no. I'm looking forward to tomorrow night. I can't wait to see you and Boof—oh no, Jake has me calling Jingles, Boofhead now. Don't tell him that though." Lacey laughed.

"Don't tell who? Jingles or Jake?"

Lacey laughed once again, "Neither of them."

Alex commented that Jake had left the room. He asked Lacey if he'd accepted her dinner invitation. "He isn't coming, Alex. I don't know why. His only explanation was that he's a piker. I suppose that has a different meaning for Aussies."

"You're spot on with that Lacey. A piker in Australia isn't a cheapskate, but someone who doesn't want to fit in socially. If he does come to a party he's apt to leave almost as soon as he arrives."

"I'm sorry about that, Alex. I think he'd enjoy himself."

Alex spoke quietly, Lacey knew, in case Jake walked back into the room. "He never used to be this way. In fact, he was too much of a partier according to his mother. Rebecca, was my sister; she was devastated when Jake turned to alcohol and other drugs. Wherever Jake was, there was a party, but it wasn't all fun and games. He was pretty hardcore."

Lacey gave an audible sigh. "I had no idea." She was shocked and didn't know what to say. No, she didn't have any experience with drugs, or with anyone who did them. As far as she knew, no one in her family had the addiction gene.

"The ironic part of the whole thing, is that it took Shanna's death by a drunk and high driver to get him sober. We thought he'd go on a drinking and drugging binge, until he died. But he didn't. He isn't really an addict; doesn't have that gene. But, he was a drunk and he did do drugs; not sure what type, maybe cocaine. All I know is that when Shanna was killed, he never touched drugs again. Occasionally, has a beer or two, or a glass of wine. If he had even a sip, he'd never think of getting behind the wheel of a car. I'm proud of that young man, but my heart aches for him."

Lacey had a hard time digesting all of this information. She wanted to reach out, hug Jake, and be there for him. However, he wouldn't allow it. Now, she realized his gruff manner was a method of keeping people at bay; keeping him from getting hurt again. How could she comprehend his pain?

"Thank you for sharing with me, Alex. I don't know what to say. I'm shocked, but I think I'm more saddened than anything."

"And, you want to help him. I know. We all do. The hard truth is, only Jake can help Jake. Nothing will stop us from trying though. But, I have hope. He was actually angrier when he first arrived here. We've had some long talks, but only when Jake has initiated the conversation. I've been able to draw him out, and he isn't quite as angry as he was. Lacey, the sadness is always there. Though, he's really a kind, gentle man, he tries to disguise it by being flippant and arrogant. I hope you get to see that kind side of him."

"Me too. See if you can prevail upon him to come tomorrow night, okay? I think it would do him a world of good."

"I'll try Lacey, but he's stubborn. Well, that's not fair I guess. He's just hurting. Give him time. We all grieve in different ways and there's no deadline."

"I know, Alex. Hopefully, he'll grow stronger each day. We'll try to help him. Oh, and Alex, it won't be just you, Jingles and me at dinner tomorrow night."

"Yes, maybe Jake will join us."

"Maybe. But I was talking about someone a whole lot less gruff. Well, she's not gruff at all. She's lovely, as you know. I've invited Aunt Lois."

"Lois? Good! She is indeed a lovely woman. I've always enjoyed her company. We've been good friends for years. And, I do believe I'm the only person in Ascot Vale who doesn't address her by her first name, '*Aunt*'!" Alex chuckled. "Can you imagine me, at my age, calling her 'Aunt' Lois? Well, I'll let you go dear. Your special little guy and I will be at your place at 6 o'clock tomorrow. See you then. Oh, wait! I believe someone wants to say hello to you."

"Meowwwww, purr purr."

"Hello to you, big guy. Helloooo, TC. I can't wait to see you tomorrow. Thank you, Alex. Bye."

"Meow."

Lacey hung up the phone with a smile on her face and in her heart. That cat made her feel so good. He was a super special cat, among cats.

She had so much to do in the next couple of days. This would be her first dinner party in her new home. The arrival of Summer, and the article she was committed to write, all made life worthwhile.

First things first. On the chance that Jake did show up, she was going to make an Australian dessert. She needed to do an online search. She found recipes for Pavlova, a popular Australian/New

Zealand dessert named after the Russian ballerina, Anna Pavlova, after her visit to Australia.

A check of the pantry revealed she had the necessary ingredients to bake a Pavlova, with the exception of the fresh fruit. That, she would pick up tomorrow. Passion fruit would be best if she could find any; raspberries might have to do. That decision made, Lacey settled in on the sofa. She channeled her efforts into finishing the article she'd been hired to write.

A few hours later, after several revisions, Lacey was satisfied with what she'd written. She emailed it to the editor, and put it out of her mind.

Even if Jake didn't come, she knew the others would enjoy the dessert, and felt certain Alex would tell him about it. Maybe he'd come the next time. Yes, she wanted there to be a next time. Though he irritated her like sand irritates an oyster, she didn't want to admit she was attracted to him. Hopefully, the end result would be a beautiful pearl; she wondered if Jake could be her pearl.

Lacey strolled to the kitchen, humming a favorite tune. After making herself a cup of hot chocolate, she grabbed a shortbread cookie from Nana's beautiful vintage cat-shaped cookie jar. Lacey had replenished the jar shortly after her arrival. It was an orange cat; much like Nana's dear Taffy.

Returning to the great room, Lacey sat down on the sofa and wrapped the eiderdown around her. Happy to be in Ascot Vale, she let out a deep, contented sigh. The only fly in the ointment was the discomfort she felt when she allowed Steve to intrude on her thoughts. She hoped he would come around and accept that their relationship was over. It was sad, but life wasn't always a bed of roses. Sometimes there were thorns, and sometimes those thorns were poisonous.

CHAPTER SEVENTEEN

The next morning, Lacey was awakened by welcoming sunlight streaming through her bedroom window, once again. She awoke with that strange new feeling, that feeling of contentment. If only she could imbue the taciturn, arrogant Greek god with this feeling. If only everyone in the world could experience it.

After doing her morning ablutions, Lacey dressed, went into the kitchen, and put the coffee pot on. Sitting at the kitchen table, Lacey wrote a small list of everything she would need for tonight's dinner. Drinking her coffee, she thought of Jake; wondering if he would surprise her by showing up.

Lacey put her jacket on, stuffed the list into her handbag, and walked outside into the brisk air. She enjoyed the walk to the town square; admiring all the beautiful homes bedecked in their best holiday finery— nothing showy, just tasteful elegance.

It seemed everyone had their fireplaces going. They scented the air and filled her nostrils with aromas of burning pine and oak logs. Lost in her thoughts, Lacey remembered all the happy times she'd spent here with her Nana and Gramps.

It was a quiet little village with minimal vehicular traffic, which tended to move at a slower pace than what she was used to in Charleston. A red car drove past at a particularly slow speed. It was going in the opposite direction. As it rolled by, the driver looked at her.

"Steve?"

No, it couldn't be. That much she knew. But even though the driver went by unhurriedly, she couldn't discern his features; plus he was wearing sunglasses. Steve never wore sunglasses. He was also wearing a baseball cap with the bill in the back; another style that Steve would not adopt. Still, it spooked her. Why was this man driving by her so slowly? Could he be an abductor? *"Silly girl."* She chided herself for watching too many true crime shows on TV.

Lacy stared at the car to let him know she saw him, and wouldn't be intimidated. He didn't have to know that she couldn't really see his features, and that she'd never be able to identify him.

Quickly, she continued down the street, and came to the corner of Hawthorn and Maple. Alex and Jake lived on the corner with the front of their home facing on Maple. She found herself wondering if Jake was inside and if he was, should she stop in and ask him to dinner again.

Lacey thought better after checking the time on her cell. She didn't wear a watch anymore and couldn't remember the last time she had. Steve had given her an exquisite diamond encrusted watch, which she kept in her jewelry box. Unbeknownst to Steve, she had finally sold it and donated the money to the local pet shelter. She didn't need the money; Steve most definitely didn't, however the shelter did. It was a win-win situation in her opinion. Steve never noticed she stopped wearing the watch after the first night. He thought he had dazzled her with the gift, then he put it out of his mind. Mission accomplished.

Soon, Lacey arrived home eager to begin preparations for tonight's dinner. Some of her favorite people would be here, not to mention her favorite cat. She found herself humming as she assembled the ingredients for the Pavlova. The main course would be a large Salad Nicoise, with a simple side dish of pasta, chicken with shitake mushrooms. She'd accompany it with a loaf of homemade parmesan bread. It was an unusual upside down combination of foods and presentation, but one for which she'd always received rave reviews. The Pavlova would be an interesting addition.

There was a knock on the door. "Hello, dear," Aunt Lois said as Lacey opened the door. "I thought I'd stop by to see if you need any help tonight. If you do, I'll stay. I hope you don't mind."

"Mind? Do I mind a dear friend giving me help? Of course not. I haven't lost my mind yet," Lacey laughed. "Come on in and make yourself at home. A cup of coffee?"

"Actually, I'd like a glass of grape juice if you have any," Aunt Lois added with a sly look.

"Hmmm, I'm all out of grape juice. The closest I can come to that is this lovely Lincoln Peak rose' wine," Lacey said, as she retrieved the bottle from the wine rack. "I understand this is a very good Vermont wine."

"Indeed it is," Aunt Lois agreed as she lifted the

bottle from Lacey's outstretched hand and then took a glass from the cabinet "Should I take out a glass for you too, Lacey?"

Lacey demurred. "Not now, thanks, Aunt Lois. I think I'll have a cold glass of tea while I prepare the dish."

Aunt Lois prepared all the vegetables for the salad, including boiling some eggs and potatoes. Lacey started on the Pavlova. While they were fussing with the dinner preparations they chatted like long lost friends.

"So, Alex is looking forward to dinner tonight, Aunt Lois. Are you?"

"Well, yes I am sweetheart. Very much. But just because Alex and I are dear friends. Nothing more. I was very good friends with his wife. Elizabeth."

Lacey was about to take a sip of her tea but paused mid-air; her eyes wide in surprise. "I don't know why I'm so amazed. It never occurred to me that Alex had been married. He hasn't mentioned a wife. Then again I don't know him all that well, and we haven't really had a good in-depth conversation, other than our talks about Jake."

"No, he's a bit like Jake in that regard. Although, he's not rude or gruff like Jake can be at times. He just keeps it in. Elizabeth died from a brain aneurysm."

"I'm so sorry to hear that. Life isn't fair is it?"

Aunt Lois placed the saucepan on the burner in

preparation for the pasta noodles. "No honey, life is not fair. As some wag from a play based on Hamlet or something said, *'Life is a gamble, at terrible odds – if it was a bet you wouldn't take it.'"*

"Well, whoever that somebody is, he knows what he's talking about for sure." They laughed then picked up their beverages and saluted each other.

Holding the glass to her chest, Aunt Lois turned serious for a moment. "Look, Lacey. Alex and I have teetered on the edge of taking our relationship beyond good friends, but I think we're both afraid of sabotaging a noble thing. I'd hate to lose a decent friend. And, I know he would too."

Lacey turned the oven on. The Pavlova was ready to be baked. She was quite pleased with her efforts and hoped Jake would appreciate it *if* he even deigned to show up. She got butterflies in her stomach at the thought. As much as she wanted him to come, the thought of sparring with him made her nervous. Now that she knew his back-story, she didn't want to say, or do anything to hurt him. It would be hard to bite her tongue if he started in on her.

"Well, then it will be good friends, enjoying a good dinner. No pressure. That works for me."

"Works for me too. And, I've been meaning to mention something."

"Uh oh, sounds ominous," Lacey replied hesitantly.

"No, not at all. Quite the opposite, in fact. You know, not everybody calls me Aunt Lois. Yes, just about everybody does, and I enjoy it, but Alex calls me Lois. And, I'd like you to call me just plain Lois."

"Okay, just plain Lois." Lacey laughed. "But you're anything but plain! You're a very elegant woman yet down to earth. That's a wonderful combination. You're my friend, and I hope you feel that I'm your friend, too. I don't have any family now, and I enjoyed calling you Aunt Lois. Would you mind if I continued to do so?"

Aunt Lois put her glass on the counter and wrapping her arms around Lacey, said "No. Not at all. We may not be blood, but we're definitely family. Some bonds form almost instantly like super glue. I've felt that connection since we met. I'm glad you did too."

"Good. That settles that. I really couldn't see myself calling you Just Plain Lois," Lacey chuckled and Aunt Lois laughed along with her.

The doorbell rang at 6:00 p. m. Lacey took a deep breath and opened the door hoping she'd hear a gruff Australian accent. No Jake. Alex was standing there with a big potted poinsettia in one hand, and a leash in the other.

"Meow, meooowwww, purr, purr."

The leash was immediately pulled from Alex's hand by the wriggling and squirming Jingles. Whoosh! He was down in an instant, twining himself around Lacey's legs and almost knocking her to the floor. Lacey removed Jingles' leash before he could trip someone. He danced, stood on hind legs; then pawing at Lacey he danced some more.

"Happiness, thy name is cat."

"He's not coming tonight," Alex said apologetically, as Lacey looked over his shoulder searching for Jake.

"I don't know what to say. Jake didn't give me an excuse for declining the invitation."

"Don't worry. I'm sure he has his reasons. Some people take a long time to grieve. We need to let them mourn in their own time, not ours. Well, come on in for goodness's sake. We're not heating all of Ascot Vale, you know."

Alex let out a booming laugh obviously remembering how Jake had uttered those very words to Lacey. "You've got a great sense of humor, sweetheart, and it's a good thing too. You'll need it when dealing with that nephew of mine. Bloody oath you will!"

"I recognize that laugh," sounded a sweet voice from down the hall. Aunt Lois walked up to Alex, gave him a big hug, and a slightly lingering kiss.

"Well, hello Tuffy. You're looking quite well, I must say." Aunt Lois bent down and lifted the cat. "You've gained a pound or two since our last visit. She nuzzled his face and gave him little kisses which brought on even louder purring.

"Meoooowww, purr, purr." This was accompanied by another little dance with an added touch. The little prince was now drooling.

"I wonder," Lacey said, eyeing Jingles's unabashed delight in all attention lavished upon him, "is there anyone Jingles doesn't love? Or, anyone who doesn't love him?"

"Not in this village. I swear if we put his name on the ballot for mayor, he'd win hands down...or paws down."

"We could do worse," Lacey replied.

"And, we have," Alex and Aunt Lois laughed together.

Well, come in and sit down. Let me take the poinsettia, Alex. Thank you so much, it's beautiful. I have the perfect spot for it." Lacey turned and removed a large candy dish from the entrance hall table, then positioned the plant in its place. "There now, that's much lovelier than a candy dish."

"And, much less fattening," Alex chimed in. Picking Jingles up, and pointing to the plant, he admonished. "Do not eat the Poinsettia. It won't kill you if you eat a leaf or two, but best to stay away from it. Besides I've read where they're not very tasty." Jingles must have agreed; his only interest in the plant was to give it a couple of healthy swats before turning up his nose and jumping to the floor.

They gathered in the great room for cocktails before dinner. Jingles provided the entertainment. Lacey swore he'd get dizzy and collapse, while running from one person to another. He was not the stereotypical image of a cat that non-cat people have—aloof and sneaky. No, he was anything but. He was super friendly, not just wanting attention, but demanding it, in his sweet way, of course. He was in your face with his wants and needs, and didn't have to be sneaky. People were too willing to acquiesce to his needs. After all, he had been instrumental in helping many of them heal, or at least feel better. The residents of Ascot Vale tended to view him as the male, feline equivalent, of Florence Nightingale. Nobody could explain the cat's healing properties, but they all agreed that he had helped them tremendously.

The conversation around the dinner table was lively with Jingles putting in his two cents worth. Oh yes, Jingles had a seat at the table. Not only was he sitting at the table with the humans, but he had decided exactly where he'd sit. Laughter reverberated around the room as he beat them to the head of the table.

"Who's going to tell him he's just a cat and as such, his place is on the floor? I certainly won't tell him," Aunt Lois snickered.

"Nor me," Alex proffered. "Well, I don't mind if you two ladies don't mind."

"Not only do I not mind," Lacey agreed, "but I'll

get some tuna and kibble for him. Of course, being a cat he'll probably sniff it, then jump down on the floor, and demand to be fed there."

"Meooww, purr, purr."

Jingles had no such intentions. While Lacey, Alex, and Aunt Lois were eating their Salad Nicoise and pasta, TC was munching his tuna and cat chow at the head of the table. His table manners left a lot to be desired, but his humans showed good manners and made no comment.

"Lacey, do you have a camera?" Alex asked. "This should really be documented."

"You're right. Nobody would believe us. I'll do better than a camera. I'll get my Flip video camera. Who knows, we might win some money from some TV show, or at the least we could post it on YouTube and make him even more famous."

Lacey was afraid that TC would jump down from the table by the time she retrieved the camera. Ha! She should have known better. The little ham wasn't going anywhere. He was sitting at his rightful place at the table; she was sure he thought that. Lacey recorded him eating, and surprising no one, he actually looked into the camera cocking his head to the side; showing his best side she supposed.

After dinner, they adjourned to the great room for coffee and some of Lacey's homemade Pavlova. Everyone agreed it was delicious, including TC. Of course, he pigged-out mainly on the whipped cream part of the dessert.

The conversation continued to flow effortlessly. Alex and Aunt Lois were regaling Lacey with tales of the little town's more eccentric residents, including the Tambors' notorious fights. They both laughed as Alex recounted the time when Jim Tambor, the owner of the local hardware store, was seen running out of the house in his underwear. He was shielding his head, while being chased by his wife, Cathy, who wielded a large frying pan. She was shouting threats of bodily harm. What made the story particularly funny to the townspeople was the disparity in their heights. Jim was well over 6′ and Cathy barely reached 5′. Everyone wondered why he would shield his head, when the obvious place of damage, if she managed to catch him, would have been his backside. Alex slapped his knee and hooted loudly. "It doesn't matter how many times I tell this story, it never fails to amuse me." Then the conversation turned serious as Alex mentioned Jake. Alex offered an apology in Jake's defense but it was clear that even he was bewildered as to why Jake didn't show up for dinner.

"No worries, Alex," Lacey remarked. "If he wasn't feeling up to it, I wouldn't want him to feel any pressure. Perhaps he'll come next time. And, there will be a next time, I hope."

Alex seemed to give careful consideration to her words before he spoke. "I think you remind him of his wife, and that's why he finds it so difficult to be civil to you. His anger stems not just from the death of his wife, and the tragic circumstances surrounding it, but he's angry because you remind him of her, and he can't have her back."

Aunt Lois offered her opinion too. "Yes, hon, you do resemble her—long red hair and your beautiful complexion. I don't know that from personal experience of course, having never met her, but I've seen photos of her. You do resemble her, quite a bit actually."

Lacey smiled. "Hmm, perhaps I should dye my hair black and pencil some freckles on my face, then."

"Lacey, that would give Jake more ammunition to hurl at you," Alex snorted.

"Well, I'm not about to dye my hair, that's for sure. But maybe if he gets to know me, he'll realize I'm not Shanna. Maybe he'll appreciate me for who I am, and accept me as a friend. I feel so bad for him."

"We all do. But he's a strong man, and given time, he'll come round. He has to forgive himself first, before he can move on."

Lacey stroked TC, who had left Alex's lap and jumped onto hers by way of a pit stop on Aunt Lois's lap. He always covered all his bases. There were no flies on this cat.

"Purr, Purr."

"You're making the rounds tonight aren't you, big guy?"

"Meowwwww, purrrrr."

"But why does he need to forgive himself? He didn't have anything to do with Shanna's death, right?"

"Oh no, of course he didn't. I think he feels guilty for his past, for drugging and drinking. He realizes that he could have been responsible for someone's death just like the guy who killed Shanna. It weighs on his shoulders as heavily as Ayers Rock, you might say. Oops, I mean Uluru as it's called now. Jake would have my head if he heard me call that rock by the wrong name. He's hard on me too, but he doesn't intend to be mean."

"So then, we'll just kill him with kindness. I know there's a nice person hiding beneath that hard exterior. Well, I think so anyway. I don't really know him that well."

"It took me quite a while to get to know him again, and understand him," Alex said wistfully. "But he's gotten better and I'll tell you what, this big guy here, has had a lot to do with it." Alex inclined his head toward his precious Jingles.

"I'm not surprised by that at all, Alex. TC, Jingles, I mean, has a wonderful effect on everyone, and I suppose that would even include Jake, although I notice he doesn't like to show it."

"You're right about that. My nephew is a good man. He's always on the side of the underdog, or, should I say undercat, in this instance," Alex chortled. "Why don't you stop by for lunch one day? You can come over to visit Jingles. At least, that will be partly true," Alex stated with a kind smile.

"It's a date," Lacey acquiesced.

Before they knew it, two hours had gone by. "Let me help you with the cleanup," Aunt Lois offered, pushing her chair from the table. "Oh sorry, never mind. I forgot about that wonderful rule of yours."

"What rule?" Alex asked.

"Walk me home," Aunt Lois said as she left the table, "and I'll tell you all about it."

Lacey walked her guests to the front door, giving them each a big hug and a kiss.

"Meow, purr purr."

"And, a special hug and kiss for you, big guy. I'll see you soon," Lacey said as she stroked his head.

As she was shutting the door, something caught her eye; it was a car. The same car, she was sure, had passed her slowly when she was walking to the town square. Only this time the car wasn't moving. It was parked across the street from her house and about two houses down.

CHAPTER EIGHTEEN

"Chill, Lacey. He's probably a neighbor, that's all." She made a mental note to check it out tomorrow. Still, she hadn't noticed that car before, but then, she wasn't looking for it either.

Her cell rang taking her mind off the car. It was Summer. *"It's about time. I need to know when she'll arrive."*

"Hello, my BFF. About time you called me with your flight details. I can't wait to see you."

A raspy voice cut her off. "Lacey Belle. I'm sick. I've never felt so bad in my life. I'm afraid I won't be able to visit. I guess I have what you had."

"Summer," Lacey interrupted. "Please don't say another word. If anyone understands how sick you are, it's me. I just wish you could be here to let TC nurse you back to health. He really could; he's done wonders for me, and a lot of the people in this town."

"I wish I could be there too, Lace. I honestly do. I'd accept help from the devil himself if he could make me better."

"Well, TC is no devil. He's a darling angel; a big fat angel actually. I'm sorry you can't be here now. You'll be here as soon as you're better. Now, take plenty of liquids and get plenty of rest. Is Bradley there to take care of you?"

"I'm here," Bradley's strong voice came over the speakerphone. "And, I'm taking good care of her,

Lacey. Don't you worry about it. She'll be up and about, if I have anything to do with it. Maybe not tomorrow. If you could see what she looks like you'd think she wouldn't be better any time this century." Bradley laughed. "I'm not leaving her. She's in excellent hands."

"I know she is, Bradley. You're a good man. You're both lucky to have each other."

"Thank you, Lace. I know we are. Speaking of men, I hope you don't mind if I say something about Steve—I feel I need to."

Lacey's stomach did a flip. She surmised that Bradley wouldn't have anything good to say about Steve. Steve and Bradley had been friends since college, but she'd noticed that lately Bradley had been distancing himself from Steve. It wasn't anything she could put her finger on, so she never mentioned it to either Steve, Summer, or Bradley.

"No, of course I don't mind, Bradley. Please, speak your mind."

Bradley dove right in apparently wanting to get it over with. "Lacey, I saw Steve the other day, and well, he almost scared me with his attitude. By this, I mean his attitude toward you. He told me you were talking about staying up there in Vermont, then his face turned really ugly. I mean, it was full of hate. Steve said, she'll stay there over my dead body, or hers."

Lacey was shocked. She knew Steve's temper was

growing worse but surely, it couldn't be that bad. "Bradley, do you think he really meant that?

Bradley hesitated before answering, and Lacey wondered what was going through his mind. Was he afraid to tell her the truth? Would his answer frighten her? She respected Bradley and decided he wouldn't sugar coat it. She trusted him to lay it out for her, knowing she would see right through him otherwise. "I'd stake my own life on it. He had a strange look in his eyes like nothing I've ever seen before. He tried to play it off, but I wasn't buying it. I'll never forget that look. I hesitated to say anything to you because you're miles away, and safe from him. I don't know, maybe I *am* making too much of it. Summer thinks I am, but then again she didn't see that face."

Lacey swallowed. It took her a few seconds to put what Bradley had just told her together with the worry about the car. "Bradley, I'm not so sure that I *am* safe from him. Tell me—have you seen Steve since then?"

Bradley thought for a few moments and then responded, "No, why do you ask?"

"Because, I could swear I saw him. Here in Vermont. On my street, as a matter of fact."

Bradley made a whistling sound." Are you sure?"

"No, I'm not sure, but I wouldn't bet against it either." Lacey told Bradley about the two incidents, and what she planned to do. Then she asked his opinion.

"Well, it's a good idea to get to the bottom of this Lacey. Please be careful. There are a lot of red cars, and a lot of men who could resemble Steve. It might be nothing at all. But see if you can get a look at the license plate. If the car's a rental that would up the worry factor a bit."

"Yep, he could have flown up here, and then rented a car. Before I do anything, I'm going to call his office and see what they have to say. I don't know what I'll do if they say he's out of town."

"Do you have people there to help you, Lacey?"

Lacey pondered the question; she really only knew three people here, but what could they do? Jake could handle himself against Steve, she was certain. But what if Steve had a gun?

"I do, Bradley but I don't know what they could do. This is a small town. Aunt Lois knows everybody. I'll bet she's good friends with the police chief, or sheriff, or whoever runs this town. I'll ask her for her help."

"Great idea, Lacey. Summer and I will rest a little easier if you get the police involved. It's a crazy world out there. We can never be too careful. Let us know how it goes. Call us if you need us, no matter if it's day or night, okay?"

"Absolutely, Bradley. And, thanks for telling me about Steve. Nothing would surprise me about him. His temper has been escalating out of control for quite some time now. I had to get away."

"I understand. Oh, and by the way, who is your Aunt Lois? I thought your only relatives were your grandparents, and they're gone now."

"They are—were. Aunt Lois is a wonderful, beautiful woman, who runs a charming café here in town. Everyone calls her Aunt Lois. She practically insists on it. I'm telling you, this is the most wonderful place, even more wonderful than I remembered. I'm home, guys. Really home. And, I expect both of you to visit when Summer is well. You hear that Summer?"

After several sneezes and coughs, Summer managed a weak, "I can't wait to be over this bug. Thanks for understanding. I love you and hope to see you soon. And Lacey, be careful."

Lacey walked to the kitchen and made a cup of hot chocolate. After adding a healthy dollop of whipped cream, she then took it into the great room. She sipped it slowly while sitting on the comfy sofa; her thoughts dominated by Jake and those kissable-looking lips. Sadness descended on her. It was possible she'd never have the opportunity to kiss those lips. And oh, did she want to kiss them.

Her thoughts were interrupted by the intrusion of Steve's face. She didn't want to think about Steve, or other noxious things in the universe. Brains are strange. They allow wanted and even unwanted thoughts into our heads. Steve was definitely in the unwanted category. He was like a rash that would eventually go away, but in the meantime, would have to be dealt with. Hopefully, it wouldn't kill her before it disappeared.

She dismissed thoughts of Steve by thinking about her new friends, Alex, Aunt Lois, and of course, her special little friend, the amazing TC. Once again, she was experiencing that delicious feeling of contentment.

Of course, that contented feeling was too good to be true, and too good to last. Dread filled her with visions of that red car. She tried to replace the thought with dreams of her Greek god, but it didn't work. Nothing could banish her fear. It was irrational, she told herself; still the fear would not recede. In the morning, she would have to resolve the problem. There was no way she could live in fear.

CHAPTER NINETEEN

Lacey slept fitfully for the first time since she'd arrived in Ascot Vale. The old house creaked, a sound she never noticed before. Now, even little noises caused her to catch her breath. Shadows inside the room took on ominous shapes of menacing figures, all of them resembling Steve.

"Stop it! Just get a grip, Lacey. Steve is in South Carolina. There's more than one red car in this state. Think of Jake – Jake."

When Lacey awoke the next morning, she was exhausted both physically and emotionally. Now, she was even more determined to get to the bottom of this mystery. Was Steve really in Ascot Vale? And if so, why? Why wouldn't he have let her know he was coming? Maybe Bradley was wrong. Maybe, Steve is lonely without her, and really misses her. Perhaps, he's going out of his way to do the right thing—come to Vermont, get on bended knee, and beg her forgiveness. Either way, she would have to deal with this today, if she expected to have any peace of mind.

She went into the kitchen; her absolute favorite room in the house. As big as her home was it really couldn't be called a house. It was definitely a mansion; a homey mansion, if there was such a thing.

After turning on the coffeemaker, Lacey prepared some blueberry oatmeal, which she sprinkled with a healthy dose of cinnamon. She kept up with all the latest health news, and whatever was supposedly guaranteed to keep you up and running until the age of 100 or better. Cinnamon was the latest in a long list of, *must take every day* to lower blood sugar, or to lower blood pressure, or lower cholesterol. She was only thirty-four, but she knew if she wanted to reach one hundred four or perhaps more realistically, eighty-four, she had to eat to live and not live to eat. Exercise and meditation was also important.

Before Lacey could have her breakfast, she had to see if the red car was still parked on the street. She couldn't delay it any longer.

With much trepidation, she walked into the great room and over to the front door, after opening it slowly. Lacey peered outside scanning the street. What a relief! No red car.

What she did notice, was the glorious weather. The sun was shining; the temperature was chilly, but not bitingly cold. There was no wind, just brisk, crisp air. She decided to take advantage of it before the next snow set in. Lacey walked back inside the house, grabbed her jacket and embarked on a nice, leisurely stroll to Aunt Lois's café.

When she entered the café, she received a warm welcome from Aunt Lois. "Hi, Lacey, come on in and take a seat, hon. I'll be right with you."

Lacey sat in her usual place by the magnificent hearth, and enjoyed the coffee that Marianne had brought her. Soon, Aunt Lois joined her for a cup of coffee. "I just wanted to tell you what a delightful time I had at your place. Alex acted younger than he has in years. He really enjoyed himself. He adores you, Lacey."

Lacey sat her cup down and smiled. "I'm quite enamored of him too. He's a wonderful man. I think he'd make somebody a terrific husband, don't you agree?"

Aunt Lois blushed and returned Lacey's smile. "Don't make too much of this, but I'm inclined to agree with you. Alex and I had a lovely talk when he walked me home. We talked again this morning. We're just taking it one day at a time, and not rushing into anything. We're good friends and maybe that's all we'll ever be. If that's the case, then that's wonderful too. We'll see how or where it goes. Oh, and we also talked about Jake. And, you," Aunt Lois said slyly.

"Now, it's my turn to say, *don't make too much of this.* I'd like to get to know Jake better. But he isn't interested, and I really think he doesn't like me. Truthfully," Lacey said with a serious tone. "I'm not so sure I even like him."

Aunt Lois finished her coffee and stood up. "I have to get back to work, hon. But I'll leave you with this, Alex knows Jake better than he knows himself. Alex feels that Jake does like you. He thinks he might even be smitten with you."

"Smitten?" Lacey chuckled. "Now, there's a term you don't hear very often."

"Well, Alex and I both think he has more than a passing interest in you. He just doesn't know how to show it. We also think he might feel a sense of disloyalty to Shanna, if he takes an interest in another woman. That's irrational, I know, but I think it's pretty close to the truth."

"You may be right about the guilt part. I seriously doubt he has any interest in me. But as Alex says, he's an Australian."

"Don't pay any attention to Alex, hon. He loves Jake and loves to tease him. They're quite a pair, those two. Here's some advice if you don't mind. Stop in and visit them. Just because Jake didn't come to dinner well, if Mohammed won't come to the mountain, the mountain must come to Mohammed."

*****

Lacey walked home at a brisk pace. The chill in the air had picked up to a rather chilly temp. She looked forward to getting inside, kicking off her boots, and getting warm. Searching for signs of the red car, Lacey scanned the street. All was clear; she let out her breath, which until now, she hadn't realized she was holding.

No sooner had Lacey sat down, when her cell rang, startling her. "Hello," she answered nervously. *"Please, don't let it be Steve."*

"Hi, Lacey. This is Suzanne, your favorite editor. How are you doing up there, in New England?"

"Hi, Suzanne. It's good to hear from you. I'm doing just great, well, now I am. I had been sick but

I'm rarin' to go. Do you have anything for me? How are you doing?"

"I'd be doing a lot better if I could find a way to add 8 more hours to my day. But, that's neither here nor there. I have an assignment and I think you can do this better than anyone, since you're my crazy cat lady." She laughed and Lacey laughed with her.

"I know you love all animals, Lacey, as do I, but I know you fall into the category of a cat person."

Lacey laughed again. "Yes, you're right, Suzanne. I think cats beat dogs, but only by a cat's whisker."

"Fair enough. So, having said that, here is my proposal; I'd like an article on special cats. I don't mean purebreds. They can be alley cats just as long as they possess some special quality. Maybe you can find a cat that's a seeing eye cat, or a cat who alerts hearing-impaired people to a ringing phone. You know, qualities attributed to dogs or even monkeys. Maybe something like that."

"Oh, I already have the perfect cat!" Lacey added excitedly. "I can't believe you want me to do this story. Perfect timing!"

"That's great, Lacey. I knew I could count on you. Now, I'll need a good professional picture of the cat to accompany the article. Maybe two pictures—one with his or her owner, and one of the cat. And by the way, what does this kitty do that's so special?"

Lacey gave a quick thought to her answer and

then said, "Just trust me on this one, Suzanne? You've always trusted me before, and believe me, this will be worth waiting for. All I can say is, this is one very special cat. Instead of nine lives, he has nine names."

"You've got me hooked, Lacey. And yes, I trust you. You've never let me down. A cat with nine names. I'm intrigued. I can't wait to read what you've written. Have it to me by the end of next week, okay?"

After they ended their call, Lacey's thoughts immediately turned to Jake. Could she talk him into photographing TC? Could he put aside his obvious dislike of her and TC, to help her with this assignment? He certainly didn't owe her anything. Perhaps Alex could intercede on her behalf.

Before calling Alex, she wanted to have a head start on the article she would write about TC. Then again, she should ask his permission first since TC, or rather Jingles, belonged to Alex.

"Hello," Alex answered in his usual kindly voice.

"Hi, Alex, it's Lacey. How are you?"

"Well, I'm doing just fine now. It's always nice to hear your voice. What can I do for you, sweetie?"

"Thank you. It's always nice to talk to you too. I'd like to see you."

Alex chuckled. "Is it me you want to see, or a certain handsome someone?

"No, Alex," Lacey interrupted. "It's you I want to see, not Jake."

"I'm not so certain about that, since I never mentioned my nephew. I was referring to that other handsome resident of this house, namely, one Jingles."

"Oh, you're such a devil. That's too funny. So where is His Royal Highness? And, before you say anything, I was referring to Jake. Just kidding. How is my big guy?"

"That's what I love about you. You have a great sense of humor. Both *royal highnesses* are here; one's in the living room, and the other is running down the hall, as we speak."

"So, Jake's into running now, is he?" Lacey snickered.

"Meowww, meowww."

"I certainly heard *that*. Hello, TC, I miss you, my sweet friend. And, I'll see you soon I hope. Maybe sooner than you think, big guy. Would you put Alex back on the phone now? I really need to speak to him."

"Right here, Lacey. Somehow, Jingles knew it was you on the phone. If I live to be a thousand years old, I'll never understand how he knows what's going on. It's really uncanny. He's doing his little happy dance right now. I think you'd better come visit him. He misses you."

Looking out the window, Lacey's attention was caught by freshly falling snow resembling confectioner's sugar, dusting the ground. She knew it wouldn't be long before the fine powder accumulated turning the area into a winter wonderland, once again.

"Great, Alex. You've solved part of my problem. I was calling to ask if I could drop by right now. I have a favor to ask of you."

"Indeed you can, my dear. The sooner you get here, the better. The weatherman is calling for a heavy accumulation. Good thing we live within walking distance of each other, eh?"

"Amen to that. Okay, I'll put on my boots and jacket—be there in a jiff."

"But first, I'll do a quick search of some Aussie expressions just in case." A smug satisfaction crept into Lacey's head followed by a feeling of guilt. She knew she was innately a kind person, and didn't want to hurt Jake. But, sometimes he goaded her into childlike behavior. Whether or not she teased him would depend on his treatment of her. She was really keen to speak Strine, if for no other reason than to see the look on his face when she did.

CHAPTER TWENTY

The snowflakes danced about Lacey as she strolled down the street. As she lifted her face toward the late afternoon sky, flakes landed on her cheeks. Though the air was chilled, the presence of snowflakes swirling around her, with the anticipation of seeing Alex, and TC, warmed her heart.

The door opened before Lacey could remove her hands from her pockets to knock. Alex greeted her effusively, and ushered her inside the house. "Come on in, we're not heating all of Ascot Vale," Alex uttered as he repeated the running joke between them.

"Meowww, meowww," uttered an insistent little voice at Alex's feet.

Lacey entered the hallway and removed her gloves and jacket. She exchanged a hug and a Continental kiss with Alex. This behavior seemed too much for TC, who pranced back and forth, demanding that attention be showered upon him.

"Hello, my sweetie pie," Lacey said, as she bent down to pick up TC. She nuzzled him against her chest. TC snuggled in, with a loud, continuous purr.

"Bring him into the living room. It doesn't look like he's going to walk in there on his own. He's a right spoiled little bugger."

"Listen to him, TC," Lacey said. "I think he's been hanging around Jake too much. He's speaking Strine."

Lacey sat on the chair nearest the fireplace still holding her favorite cat. His long white whiskers rubbed against her face and tickled her. She let out a small, contented giggle.

"So, my dear, how about a nice brandy to warm you up?"

Lacey positioned TC on her lap to make herself more comfortable. "I'd like that very much, thank you."

Alex poured them each a snifter of brandy. "I don't indulge in a lot of luxuries for myself, but I do enjoy this particular brandy. Oogy wawa," Alex said, as he clinked his glass against Lacey's, and then smiled at her expectantly.

"Umm, oogy wawa to you too, Alex, I guess. Another Aussie expression?"

"He's bloody well showing off again," announced the familiar gruff voice entering the room. "You'll have to excuse him. He's a Seppo, just like you." Jake actually punctuated his remark with a wry laugh. "Uncle Alex likes to dazzle people with his knowledge of unusual anythings. It's a Zulu toast which means the same thing as Cheers, or To Your Health. Now, aren't you impressed?" Jake crossed his arms and leaned against the wall, placing one foot across the other with a cocky look on his handsome face. His shirtsleeves were rolled up exposing his muscular, lightly hairy, forearms. Again, the gold watch was wrapped around his manly wrist.

"My god, can you be any more seductive? Any sexier?"

Alex's voice interrupted her thoughts. She was sure she was blushing like a virginal bride." Ah, Jake, it would take more than that to impress our Lacey here. Wouldn't it, Lacey?"

"Actually, Alex, I am impressed. I love to learn new things; especially new words. I make my living by writing. And speaking of writing, that's the reason I'm here."

"Ah. Should have known you didn't stop in for a social call." Jake ambled out of the room. "Typical Sheila, always wanting something."

"Wait, don't go, please. I'd really like to talk to you about a proposition I have."

"Aha! A proposition. I could see that one coming." Jake plopped down on his recliner as if waiting to hear what she had to say.

"Hold on, Jake," Alex admonished. "That's too much even for you. What was it you wanted to talk to me about, Lacey? It involves Jake, too. Right?"

Lacey hesitated, smiled at Alex and Jake, then began telling them about her assignment. "My editor wants me to do an article on special cats. Jingles, is the most special cat I know. I'd like to do the article on him."

Alex expressed his delight. "That's a bloody brilliant idea, Lacey. I'm sure Jingles will be thrilled in his own little cat way. After all, it's all about him."

"And this involves me, how?" Jake asked, with one eyebrow raised, a suspicious look on his face. He shifted his body on the recliner and gave his full attention to Lacey—his Paul Newman baby blues bored into her oddly colored eyes.

"Well," Lacey said slowly, "My editor wants a professional picture of TC. She'd like two pictures actually—one of him with his companion; that's you, of course, Alex. Then, she wants one picture just by himself. Maybe in a regal pose, reclining on pillows or something. But that's not set in stone. I think we should do a re-enactment of him sitting on someone's bed, curled up in their arms, or something like that."

"Again, this involves me, how?" Jake placed his thumb and forefinger on either side of his jaw, giving him a serious, contemplative look.

Lacey felt certain he was contemplating how he could needle her, not help her. She decided she'd just dive right in and ask, "Well, I was hoping I could entice you to take the photos of this big guy here." Lacey stroked the top of TC's head.

"Meow?"

"Yes, TC. We're talking about you, as if you didn't know it." He responded by arching his back, sticking his butt in the air, then doing a little circle dance. He then pranced over to Jake. After sitting in front of him, he cocked his head to the side, and placed a furry paw on Jake's knee. His pose was irresistible.

"Me? You want me to photograph this boofhead? I don't think I have a camera lens bloody big enough to photograph that wombat-sized head. And regal? I've seen rats that are more bloody regal than him. Are you daft, woman?"

"I must be, Jake—to even think an Aussie could capture TC's beauty and character. But I'm desperate. My friend, Summer, who's a *professional* photographer, was supposed to take his picture. Unfortunately, she came down with a really bad cold, and can't get up here. My editor is expecting this story, along with the pictures, by the end of next week. That doesn't give me enough time to find a *real* photographer."

"What is wrong with me? He'll never agree to do it now. Shut your big mouth and quit while you're not too far behind."

Jake stared at her, but didn't say anything. She squirmed, wishing a big hole would open up in front of her. Did she want to jump in the hole, or push Jake inside? At least, he could say something to her, anything.

"What a cheek, a bloody cheek!" This statement was followed by a booming laugh, which Lacey felt certain came from Jake's mouth. Surely it couldn't be. Jake rarely smiles, let alone laughs.

But, there it was again, another laugh. Only this time, it was accompanied by Alex's laugh. Lacey couldn't help herself. She joined in the laughter, not knowing exactly why *she* was laughing, but it felt good to see Jake's amusement. Judging by the grin on Alex's face, Lacey knew he felt good his cherished nephew was laughing.

"Mew, mew, purr, purr, meowww." The dulcet tones from Jingles's throat filled the room as he sat erect with all eyes upon him. His bearing was indeed regal; the only accoutrements missing were a crown, a scepter, and a purple robe.

"Look." Alex wiped a few tears from the corners of his eyes. "I could swear Jingles is laughing. Too bad you don't have your camera, Jake. That would make a great picture. He's certainly one photogenic cat, among other things."

"Yes," Jake added, "I could name a few other things he is, for sure. He's a bloody sponge—doesn't even catch mice, and he's a moggy—not a very good one at that."

"Well," Lacey twittered, "you've got me on that one, Mr. Know All or as you would say, Mr. Bloody Know All. What's a moggy?"

Jake gave her a long look before replying. "Bloody oath; must I always have to teach you something? A moggy is an old English word meaning *mouse*. Cats were known as, *Moggy Catchers*. Over time, it was shortened to simply moggy, and of course we Aussies shorten everything, so cats are called moggies in Oz, too. You'd have to be a boofhead not to understand that."

"You've got to be kidding! You expect me to know what cats are called in Oz? If so, then you must know about everything here in the US. Anyway, TC's a healer and you know it."

"What a bunch of rubbish. Cats can't heal. They *cause* illnesses, they don't cure them. Bloody oath! A bunyip could heal people more than Boofhead can, and they're not even real. What a bunch of drongos you Seppos are."

"I think you just make things up as you go. Everybody in this town knows that Jingles helps people. Especially people who were sick. He nurses them back to good health. I can vouch for that, just as well as anybody. And, it's been scientifically proved that cats purr because," Lacey paused for effect. "Never mind, you tell *me* why cats purr since you seem to know everything. Come on, Jake. What's the matter? Cat got your tongue?"

"Well. You're all up yourself now aren't you? Well, not only do I not know why cats purr, I also don't bloody well care. I reckon they do it just to be annoying, especially Boofhead here. He could wake the dead with his loud purring. Bloody annoying."

Lacey grinned. She was delighted to have something over Jake. The words practically jumped from her mouth. "Well, you—along with most people, Jake, probably think that cats purr because they're happy. That is true, but they also purr when distressed; which is probably why Boof-Jingles purrs so much when you're around. It's also been shown that purring improves their bone density, and promotes healing. So, if they can do that for themselves, it's no big leap to believe they can do that for others. In fact, research is showing this to be true." Lacey was so happy, she didn't know if she should purr, or do a happy dance. "H*a! Jake Anderson. Take that. Jake 1, Lacey 1.*"

"Well, if you ask me he's as cunning as a dunny rat. He's got you all fooled."

"That is so not true. All that notwithstanding, you still haven't answered me. Can I please count on you to take Jingles's, ok, Boofhead's, picture?"

"I don't know," Jake answered with a barely suppressed smile, "*can* you?"

"Okay. *May* I count on you? We're not speaking formally here, so it really doesn't matter, does it? I shouldn't have expected any other response from a flaming Taswegian."

Jake smirked. "Of course I'll photograph him, Lacey. I'll go you one better though. I'll take lots of pictures of him, not just one or two. I'll even provide the props, would that be good?"

"Oh, Jake. I'm so sorry. I didn't mean to call you a name or talk down to you. I really didn't. I just thought it was funny. I'm so glad you're not angry with me."

"What a bloody dill you are," Jake answered. "But what can *I* expect from a Seppo? You must have kangaroos loose in the top paddock if you think I'll help you after that remark."

"Pay him no mind, Lacey. He's an Australian."

To Lacey's surprise, Jake's laughter intermingled with theirs. It was a genuine laugh; she could feel it.

"Come on, Jake. Don't be a ratbag. Do Lacey and me a favor, and...

"Meow, meow, purr, purr." TC was twirling around them, doing his little dance. As if making supplication to Jake, he pranced over to him. Yes, he knew how to work people. There were no flies on him!

"And Jingles too. He's practically begging you. You'd have to be a whacker to refuse. Wouldn't he, Jingles?"

"Purr, Purr." Jingles turned on the charm, placing both paws on Jake's knees. Then, the little con artist pulled off his coup de main, by resting his head on his paws, and looking as if butter wouldn't melt in his mouth.

Jake stared at Jingles as though he were seeing him for the first time. He scratched Jingles on the head and said in a low, almost imperceptible voice, "You're a beaut, Boofhead."

Lacey caught herself gazing at Jake with adoring eyes. She felt she was beginning to see the real Jake; the kind human underneath the prickly façade. For once, she didn't see any traces of sadness or belligerence. She knew she was in real trouble. It was too late to back out. Her heart had been taken hostage by this modern-day Valentino.

"Thank you for the delicious brandy, Alex. I really enjoyed it. Unless I want to spend the night here, I'd better be going. The snow is really accumulating, and I need to get home before it gets too bad. I have some phone calls to make. Time is most definitely of the essence. I've got to research some good photographers in Burlington. I've got my work cut out for me and a deadline to boot."

"Mrroww, mroww." Obviously, Jingles picked up the vibes that Lacey was leaving. He left Jake and headed toward her, but not before giving Jake a soul-penetrating glare, that only cats can give. To everyone's surprise, he accompanied the glare with a well-intentioned hiss, a sound that no one had ever heard emanating from the lovable cat's throat. *"Who needs you, anyway?"*

Lacey was sure Jingles had just dissed Jake. What a cat, she thought. No amount of human words could have conveyed that feeling as succinctly as TC.

Alex scratched his head. "Jingles and I would have no objection to your staying, Lacey. We've got plenty of room, and I make a mean bowl of cereal for breakfast."

Lacey contemplated various scenarios, all involving clandestine romantic interludes with Jake, while Alex slept. She was a writer with a vivid imagination. Previously, she had published an anthology of romantic stories. Each involved the prerequisite; tall, dashing stranger, who seduces the equally alluring fair maiden. How could her fictional hero come to life in a little village in Vermont? Her fictional heroes didn't have a tongue as sharp as a razor, and a wit to match. She smiled thinking of their verbal exchanges, and how he always bested her. She did manage to get that Taswegian zinger in, much to her and Alex's delight.

"Does that smile mean you're anticipating my delicious breakfast?"

"Oh, I'm sorry, Alex. Sometimes my mind takes little holidays. It goes walkabout, you might say." Lacey felt a pair of baby blues staring at her. She returned the stare in kind, only to be unnerved by a devilish smile. He certainly knew how to keep her off balance." As much as I'd love to partake of your wonderful breakfast, I'm afraid I'll have to decline. I really need to leave now. Thank you again for your gracious hospitality. I'll give you a call as soon as I locate a good photographer, then we can make arrangements to have his nibs's pictures taken. Nice to see you again, Jake," she said, trying not to sound acerbic. Turning to TC, she said, "And you, my little prince, come here and let me give you a big hug."

Alex walked Lacey down the hall to the front door with TC leading the way. "Are you sure you won't stay, Lacey? The wind has started to pick up and it's blowing the snow around and about."

"Meow, meow, purrrr," TC chimed in, as if beseeching Lacey to stay. She'd love to curl up, and

then lavish him with belly rubs and massages. Next to Alex, Lacey felt she was just about TC's favorite person in the world. Did he formulate words in his little cat brain? Nobody would know for sure, but his body language certainly indicated he'd enjoy her company. "I'm sorry, Your Lordship, but I really must leave. Be good and don't pay any heed to Jake. His bark is worse than his bite, if you'll pardon the canine metaphor."

"Mroww." TC turned and danced down the hall toward the kitchen. Lacey knew TC was waiting for Alex to feed him. He had Alex wrapped around his big paws.

Alex helped Lacey into her jacket and waited while she put on her gloves. "I'll see if I can talk him into photographing Jingles. Hold off on those phone calls until I call you tomorrow. I know he sounds as cross as a frog in a sock, but he'll come around. He's really aces. You'll see. He likes you, Lacey. If he were a bit younger, I swear he'd be dipping your pigtails in the old inkwell." Lacey felt that way when he'd smile at her. But then, he'd hit her with a zinger that knocked the props from under her. "You hurry on home, now. I know we live on the same street, but it *is* a long street. Call me when you get home, okay? Then, Jingles and I can get a good night's sleep knowing you're home, and safe."

"I'll call you as soon as I walk in the door. It gets dark early here in the winter. This'll take some getting used to again. Goodnight."

Lacey pulled the collar of her jacket around her neck. Her hands were shoved firmly inside her pockets. Even with gloves on, and her hands in her pockets, she was still cold. She couldn't wait to get into the warmth and comfort of her home.

Approaching her block, which was four blocks from where Alex and Jake lived, she found herself staring at a familiar car. It couldn't be the red car. She hadn't seen it lately and hoped it had gone away. However, it was becoming increasingly covered with snow, so she couldn't tell the make or even the color from this distance. Lacey hurried her steps, taking care not to fall, but anxious to get closer to the car. Now, she was eager to get home, run inside, and then lock the door. Spooked, she wouldn't rest until she got to the bottom of this.

Lacey's gloved fingers were as clumsy as sausages. With some difficulty, she managed to retrieve her phone from her pocket. She'd need to dial 911 if it was indeed Steve. After looking around her, Lacy darted furtive glances at the car, and the house where the car was parked. Her heart skipped a beat when she discovered it was indeed a red car, and looked exactly like the car that had passed her earlier.

CHAPTER TWENTY-ONE

Lacey thought she heard footsteps behind her, but was almost too afraid to look. Summoning her courage, she turned quickly, wrenching her neck in the process. Her movement elicited a painful yelp. She was relieved that no one was following her. No bogeyman. No Steve!

Holding the right side of her neck, she increased the pace of her stride. Now, she was anxious to get home, and anxious to apply a heating pad to her neck.

Lacey unlocked her door carefully, moving slowly due to the pain in her neck. After entering her home, she locked the door. Since moving to Ascot Vale she'd felt safe. This mystery of the red car, however, had her on edge. She imagined all kinds of bad happenstances.

After gingerly removing her gloves and jacket, Lacey attempted to remove her boots. The movement aggravated her neck and she sighed. It would take several minutes to completely remove her boots.

With only a few winces of pain, each boot was finally removed. There would be a hunt for a heating pad, but first a few aspirins were necessary.

As Lacey rummaged through the bathroom cabinet, or fossicking as she'd learned the Australians called it, she heard her cell ringing in the great room. Earlier, she'd left it on the end table. As soon as she was finished fossicking, she'd return the call. The word entered her mind with a smile. She was certainly getting an education in the Australian slang known as Strine. The strange words and expressions came easily to her now. The thought crossed her mind that she'd love to visit Australia one day. A romantic honeymoon with someone would be great. Who was she kidding? She wasn't thinking of a *someone,* but of Jake; that annoying, but vulnerable Jake.

She found the aspirin, poured a glass of water, swallowed the aspirin, and then walked back into the great room. The heating pad would have to wait until she found out who had called her. It occurred to her that it was probably Alex whom she'd promised to call. A red car, and the wrenched neck, had distracted her.

Lacey checked her cell, and sure enough, Alex had called. Knowing it might have caused him some distress, distressed her too. That wasn't a problem with Steve. Steve only thought about his image, what others thought about him, and how he could impress everyone. How could she have been so blind to his faults? She was in a very vulnerable place when she met him, and he poured on the charm—at least what little of it he possessed. It was all aimed at her, and she fell for it in her desperate need to be loved once again. The death of both parents in such a short time had devastated her. It took a while, but slowly she discovered that Steve was the proverbial wolf in sheep's clothing. Enough thinking of Steve, she berated herself. He was out of her life for good, or so she hoped.

After Lacey called Alex, she was touched by how

relieved he was to hear from her. He was a fair dinkum friend. If only Steve had been as concerned for her. But, no use wishing for something that she'd never have, and truthfully never did have. She apologized to Alex for not calling him sooner, and explained everything to him.

"That's okay, Lacey. I'm just happy to know you made it home safely. Looks like it's going to be one heck of a snowfall. Welcome back to Vermont, my girl! I am concerned about that red car. We'll have to get to the bottom of this; find out who it belongs to. It might be a relative visiting one of your neighbors. Have you met any of them yet?"

"I did meet Maggie O'Conlon. She lives two doors down from where the red car is parked. I was walking to the town square the other day, and she was checking her mail. We chatted for a bit. Seems like a lovely person; invited me to stop in anytime. I think I'll do just that as soon as this snow stops. By the way, have you had a chance to talk to Jake about photographing TC? I'm sorry, I know his name is Jingles, but he'll always be TC to me."

"I told you sweetheart, it doesn't matter what you call him. I certainly don't mind. As you know, he goes by many different names. And, you know what? He recognizes all of his names, and he responds to them; at least when he feels like it. He's a cat. Hey, maybe he's an Australian cat."

Alex and Lacey had a good chuckle over that one. "But to answer your question, I'm waiting for the right time to speak to Jake about the photo shoot. After you left this afternoon, he's been very preoccupied. I think he's considering it. But then, as I was bringing up the subject, he said he was going walkabout. He left the house a couple of minutes after you did. I thought perhaps he was going to try to catch up with you, but I take it, he didn't."

"No, he didn't." Lacey remembered thinking she'd heard someone's footsteps behind her. It had to be her imagination because she hadn't seen anyone. And surely, if Jake had been following her, he'd have done so openly. There was no subterfuge about Jake. He'd look you square in the eye, and say whatever was on his mind, no matter the consequences. The truth was, he usually enjoyed the results. She wondered if he was always so forthright before his beloved Shanna was killed. Somehow, she thought he was. "Does he go walkabout a lot, Alex? Doesn't the snow bother him, being from a sun-burnt country, as I've heard it called?"

"He comes from tough stock, my girl. I've learned it's best to let him do his own thing. He takes a lot of solitary walks. I think it's his way of trying to clear his head—to come to terms with Shanna's death. He's coming 'round though. I've been noticing a slow but subtle improvement in his sad moods. I think he finds it easier to be angry, than it is to be sad. But these are all stages of grief. I have no doubt he'll be apples eventually."

"That's funny, Alex. That's one Strine expression that's new to me. He'll be apples, huh? Let me guess, he'll be alright. Is that right?"

"We'll make an Aussie out of you yet, girl. Listen to me sounding as if I'm an Aussie myself. But living with Jake, you can't help picking up his words and so forth, and using them. They have a wonderful way about them. And yes, you're right about what *he'll be apples* means. There was a book written long ago called, *They're A Weird Mob,* and they weren't talking about a mob of kangaroos either. Yes, they're definitely weird, but I mean that in the nicest way. *Different,* would be a better word I suppose, but then I didn't write the book."

"Meow, meow, purr, purr," sounded in her ear. "Well, hello my big guy. Were you earwigging on our conversation, you little devil?"

"I don't know what it is, but he always seems to know when I'm speaking to you, Lacey. His talents never cease to amaze me. And you too, are you sure you aren't an Aussie? Earwigging? You're something else, you are. I'm glad to know you're studying Strine. Even though Jake might make fun of you for trying to speak it, I know him and I know he appreciates it."

Lacey ran her hand through her hair, finger combing it as she often did when anxious. The problem was, she didn't know exactly why she was anxious. Was it the mysterious red car, or was it discovering Jake left his house right after she did? Where did he go? Why would he go out in such inclement weather, and more importantly, why wasn't he home yet? Her instincts told her something was wrong. Then again, she'd thought someone was following her home. She was apparently wrong about that, and all it did was give her a sprained neck. "I hope you're right. Listen, I'm a bit of a worrier. Okay, I'm more than a bit. I'm the queen of worry, and I admit it. Do you think there's any way you could call me when Jake gets back home, without him knowing it, of course?"

"Sure thing, Lacey. I don't like to admit it, but I worry when he takes off on these solitary sojourns, too. He never tells me where he's been, or what he's done. He doesn't say anything at all, in fact. But, he always seems to be a bit calmer when he returns, like he came to terms with his demons. Will you be up for a while in case he's gone longer than usual, this time?"

"I'll be up for quite a while. Once I start writing, I don't want to stop, especially when I'm writing about such a magnificent subject. Would you give him a big hug and a kiss from me?"

"Absolutely, and I'll also give Jingles a hug and kiss too. But I guess that's who you were talking about weren't you?" Alex and Lacey giggled like children when talking about Jake. Lacey loved the little private jokes she shared with Alex. She could tell he loved them too, no matter how often they were said. "If I do happen to nod off, which is highly unlikely, please leave me a message?" Alex assured her he would.

CHAPTER TWENTY-TWO

Alex hung up the phone and went to the kitchen where he brewed himself a nice cup of tea. It was a habit he'd picked up and a taste he enjoyed since Jake had come to live with him. He and Jake had spent many a peaceful evening reminiscing about Alex's sister, who was Jake's mother. The only time Jake spoke about Shanna was on her birthday, and during the holidays. Christmas was especially hard on him, and he usually busied himself by making furniture. One year he'd made Alex a beautiful cabinet for his collection of fine wines. Another year, he'd made him a fancy curio cabinet.

"Well, Jingles. It's just you and me tonight, until Jake gets home. I don't know what it is, but I have a niggling feeling that something isn't quite right."

"Mrroww, mrroww," Jingles responded. His tail was not held high as it usually was. It was as if Jingles thought something was amiss too. He was many things, including a very observant cat. He sauntered over to Alex, jumped on his lap, placed both front paws on his shoulders, and began kneading them. It always amazed him that Jingles didn't dig in his claws like most cats. For such a big cat, he was very gentle. A gentle giant was an appropriate nickname for him.

"Would you like a treat, Jingles?" The words had barely escaped Alex's lips when Jingles bolted off his lap. He dashed to the kitchen stopping at the exact cabinet where Alex kept his special treats. "Ok big boy, give me a minute to get in there. I'm not as spry as I used to be. In my heyday, I still couldn't run as fast as you."

"Mrowww purrrr," Jingles' purr sounded irritated. He wanted his treats, and apparently, his servant was not moving fast enough. Poking his head around the kitchen corner, he stamped his feet in an impatient manner. It was obvious that Jingles was not particularly happy, and he was making darn sure Alex knew it. "M*rrowwwww.*"

"I'm coming, Your Lordship. You might want to trade in some of your curiosity for patience, or run the risk of losing one of those nine lives."

"Hissssss," Jingles responded with his mouth wide open, eyes narrowed, and a slight swish of his tail. Alex knew that Jingles would never attack him, but he sure was doing his best to intimidate him.

"Jingles, you know I was just teasing you, you silly bugger. Here are your treats. You're getting like Jake, can't take a joke, eh?"

"Purr, purr," came Jingles' trilling reply. He was eating and purring at the same time. He was one happy and quite spoiled cat, for the moment. If Alex knew what was good for him, he'd better not make him wait for his treats again. Jingles ruled the house. *"Purr, Purr."*

Alex strode back into the living room, sat down on the couch, and waited. He knew the inevitable hurricane would barrel into the room momentarily and jump onto his lap. He'd no sooner had the thought when Jingles flew into the room, leapt into his lap, and crashed with a resounding thud. Then the water works let loose. Jingles drooled, a lot. Copious amounts of drool, in fact. There were times when Alex would cover his shoulder with a hand towel, much as a mother would protect herself from her baby's gurgling drools. Jingles would purr, drool, and knead his chest simultaneously. His eyes would be at half-mast, and he appeared to be in kitty heaven. Alex always kept a hand towel or tissue box within reach.

CHAPTER TWENTY-THREE

Lacey looked out the big casement windows in the great room; surprised by the large amounts of snow that had fallen since she'd left Alex's house. She changed into comfy, long flannel jammies, and a tee shirt she'd designed that said, *Neuter and Spay, It's the Humane Way*. Without a pet of her own, meeting TC had made her even more aware of the emptiness in her life. Now that she'd settled in her home, and didn't have Steve discouraging her from adopting a pet, she decided to visit the local shelter. At least, she could give a dog and one cat, a forever home. Hopefully, she could stop at just two. If she could, she'd adopt every homeless animal in the world.

With her cell in hand, Lacey settled on the comfortable sofa and marveled at how lucky she was. She'd had many rough spots in her life, but she had her health and good friends. Looking forward to a long conversation with her BFF, Lacey dialed Summer's number.

Bradley, Summer's fiancé, answered her phone. He explained that Summer was still sleeping after being up the night before with coughing spasms. "I'll be taking her to the doctor in the morning. I promise. I'll let you know what he says. I don't think it's anything more than a lingering bad cold. Maybe, it's the flu. Either way, I won't rest until she's cleared by a doctor." Lacey thanked him for always being there for her friend. He was a good man, and she was happy for both of them.

It was early, and Lacey was too wound up to go

to bed. She opened her laptop and started typing what would no doubt, be the first of many drafts. "TC, *The Amazing Wonder Cat.*" She hoped the animals she'd adopt would be as wonderful. Even if they were only half as wonderful as TC, they'd still be amazing. One thing was for certain, she wanted to adopt older animals who had lost their homes. If the owner died, or the owner couldn't take care of them anymore, Lacey was always saddened when she'd hear about abandoned pets. It wasn't possible to save them all, but she'd do anything, to help as many as she could.

Several hours passed before Lacey noticed how late it was getting. Surely Jake would be home by now. Perhaps it was Alex who'd nodded off and forgotten to call her. She wasn't sure if she should call, not wanting to awaken him if he had fallen asleep. Still, she was going into full-blown worrying mode. If she did call and wake Alex, he'd understand. He'd confessed that he was a worrier too. She punched the number three on her phone, which was speed dial for Alex's home phone. Aunt Lois was number four. While she waited for Alex to answer, she made a mental note to call Aunt Lois tomorrow. Even better, she'd pay her a visit at her café, if the sidewalks weren't too icy.

After about ten rings, Lacey hung up, more concerned now than ever. If both Alex and Jake were sleeping, she didn't want to be a nuisance. Instead, she occupied her mind with thoughts of what make and model car she should purchase. Aware of how quickly cars lost their value, a new car was not an option.

Perhaps Alex, or Jake, would drive her to a car lot that was owned by a person with an honest reputation. A big car was not needed, just one big enough to haul a few animals to the vet. Maybe she'd need a bigger car for the lanky Jake, and their kids. *"Well, Lacey. Mom always said if you're going to dream, dream big. And that's one really big dream."*

Lacey tried to resume writing her article, but her brain wouldn't cooperate. It took twists and turns like some bizarre maze. Her thoughts ran from Jake to Alex, and then back to Jake. There was no escaping it; she was seriously concerned, now. Her neck was still hurting although the pain had lessened. Luckily, the snow had stopped coming down as heavily as it had been. The anticipated blizzard never materialized. She'd trudge to Alex's house, hoping he wouldn't mind if she came over so late. Hopefully, she wouldn't hear any bogeyman following her.

With little effort, Lacey pulled on her boots. The aspirin had helped her sprained neck. Giving it some thought, she realized it was probably a strained neck muscle, and not a sprain. Heading for the front door, she felt her cell vibrating. She'd forgotten to set the ringer. Maybe Alex had called and she'd missed it. A feeling of relief washed over her. Alex had promised he'd call even though several hours had gone by.

Without looking at the Caller ID, Lacey quickly picked up the phone." Alex. I'm so glad to hear from you. I'm sorry. I had my cell on vibrate and must have missed your call. How's Jake? Is he home?"

A chill traveled up her spine, and she gasped at

the intrusion of the voice in her ear. "So, which goon is yours?" Steve grumbled." Alex or Jake? Or is it both, Lace?"

Stunned, Lacey fell to the sofa. She removed the gloves from her sweaty hands, grabbed a tissue, and wiped the beads of sweat off her neck. Her throat went dry and constricted. *"What did he say? Goons? What could he possibly mean by that?"* Now, she felt light-headed. Was she having a stroke? "Why are you calling me, Steve? And, what on earth are you talking about?"

"Playing dumb doesn't suit you, my dear. I came to talk you into coming back where you belong. You wouldn't talk on the phone, so I decided to fly up here. I rented a car, and I'm staying at The Old Oak Inn, which as you must know, is close by. I've been watching you, and trying to understand why you won't come home to me." As if he were in pain, Steve drew in a breath.

Lacey's heartbeat slowed, and her feeling of panic calmed. "Why didn't you come by, Steve? Instead, you seemed to be stalking me. That's really frightening."

"Yeah, well that's too bad. We can't always have what we want in life, can we? You know. I thought about coming up here, and dragging you home. I'll bet Bradley told you I made threatening remarks, didn't he? Don't bother answering. I know he did, whether you want to admit it or not. I may have had one drink too many and shot off my mouth about you, but I wouldn't hurt you, Lacey. I've never laid a hand on you, have I?"

"No, Steve, you haven't. But, you've frightened me on more than one occasion. I've noticed that your temper has increased with time; especially when you're drinking. I really think you need help, before you do hurt someone, or yourself. I hope you'll realize that before it's too late."

"So, if I get help and sober up, does that mean you'll reconsider and come back home to me? I can change, Lacey."

"No, Steve. I'm sorry. I just can't. This is my home, now. I'm no expert, but I know you have to change for yourself, and not for anyone else. It has to come from inside you. I wish you all the luck in the world, but I know it'll take more than good luck. It'll take a lot of hard work and dedication."

"So, that's it? I should have known I couldn't count on you. Well, don't worry, I'm leaving here tomorrow. This is the last you'll hear from me. I've finally realized that you're not worth it. I'm sure your goons will be happy to know I'm leaving. Goodbye Lacey. Have a great life, if you can."

"Don't hang up." It was too late, the phone was dead. What did he mean by that? She wasn't going to worry about it tonight. However, she was exhausted, too exhausted to walk to Alex's house. After checking her phone she saw that there were two messages from Alex. She was happy to hear Alex's voice explaining that Jake was home, and that Alex would call her tomorrow. Now, she would be able to get a good night's sleep. Boy did she need it.

CHAPTER TWENTY-FOUR

Lacey awoke to the familiar ring tone that meant Summer was calling. Maybe it was Bradley. Either way, she was anxious to hear about Summer's visit to the doctor.

"Hello."

"Hi Lace. It's Bradley. Just calling to let you know Summer was admitted to the hospital last night. Now, before you panic, she's fine. She has a mild case of left lobar pneumonia. At least, that's what the doctor called it. They're treating her, and expecting a full recovery. She'll be discharged in a few days. Dr. Bartsch said it was good that we got her in and didn't wait."

Lacey expelled a huge breath while listening to Bradley recount the night's events. "Good, but you know that I'll worry. I wouldn't be me if I didn't worry about something. If I don't have something to worry about, I'll invent something."

Bradley laughed. He agreed that Lacey would always find something to worry about. "Lacey, try not to worry, okay? You're always looking out for your friends; like you took care of your parents when they were dying. I know you want to be here, but I'm taking good care of our girl. I've got to give the doctors and nurses some credit. We both know it's my tender touch that'll heal her." Bradley's laughter elicited her laughter. "I promise we'll both come to see you, soon."

"That is a promise I'll hold you to. Give Summer a big hug and a kiss from me. I won't have to talk you into that!"

"You know it. Hey, before I forget, have you heard from Steve, or seen that red car again?"

Lacey made a quick decision. This New England living had been good for her. Now, she was actually making decisions, and not agonizing over them. She decided not to tell the couple about the strange call she'd received from Steve last night, or that he was actually in Ascot Vale. Neither of them needed to worry about her, especially with Summer in the hospital. She'd explain everything later, but she hated to lie. Her parents had drummed it into her, it was always better to tell the truth unless the truth would hurt someone. "I did hear from him, Bradley, but no worries. I'll tell you all about it another time. Right now, I have to call my good friend, Alex."

"Alex, is it? I can't wait to hear all about him and of course you know Summer, she'll have a hundred questions."

"Chill, Bradley, Alex is just a wonderful friend. Also he's a good thirty years my senior. I really do have to make a phone call. Talk to you later. Love to you, and Summer."

"Oh, you'll pay for that. Leaving us hanging; wondering who Alex is. Summer will squeeze it out of you. Whoever he is, I hope you find happiness. Love to you too, Lacey."

"Spoiler alert, Bradley. You can stop wondering about Alex and start wondering about Jake. That should keep you two busy for a while." Lacey said mysteriously.

"Maybe, I shouldn't tell Summer. You know her. This bit of non-information will drive her up the wall. Whoever it is, I wish you all the best."

"So do I, Bradley. So do I. But first I have to make him like me. First things first."

Lacey pressed #3 on her phone. While waiting for Alex to answer, she day dreamed about Jake. She was feeling like a teen, thinking about the hottest boy in school who chose to show his feelings by teasing her. How she hoped that was the case with Jake—that he liked her, but didn't know how to handle her. Alex finally answered the phone, interrupting Lacey's musings.

Lacey told Alex she was glad that Jake had finally arrived home. But, had Alex had a chance to talk to Jake about photographing Jingles? Alex seemed to evade the question, but told Lacey he'd like to talk to her later when he visited her. Aunt Lois's Hearth and Home was on her mind, so she asked Alex to accompany her. When Alex answered yes, Lacey said she'd be at his house within a few minutes.

CHAPTER TWENTY-FIVE

When Lacey arrived at Alex's house, she was surprised to see him waiting outside by the mailbox. Even more curious, Jingles was not with him. She felt certain Alex would bring Jingles to Aunt Lois's café to socialize with his old buddies, and former patients. Anyone who knew TC knew he loved adulation, as evident by the pools of drool he'd deposit on everyone's clothing.

Alex and Lacey chatted amiably as they walked along the beautiful tree-lined street. There was something a bit stilted about their conversation, but Lacey knew if she had patience, Alex would tell her what was on his mind.

They arrived at Aunt Lois's café. Alex, being the consummate gentleman, opened the door for her and stood aside as she entered. They were greeted effusively by all the regulars with one wag asking where Alex's better half was. Yes, where is Jingles, Lacey wondered silently? Aunt Lois walked over to Alex, and Lacey and gave them each a loving hug before ushering them to the table closest to the fireplace. Everyone recognized this as Lacey's table. She hadn't been in Ascot Vale very long, and already she was considered a regular with her own table in the café. For a long time, happiness had eluded her. Now, her happiness was momentarily shadowed by thoughts of her parents, and Nana and Gramps not being here. She always viewed the cup as half-full and lived in the present. Tomorrow was not guaranteed and the past was gone. All that remained were wonderful, loving memories of the people in her life. She would honor them by living here and making the most of her life.

Aunt Lois' unlined face conveyed kindness and sincerity. "So, to what do I owe the honor of having my two favorite people here today? However, Jake, with his quirky ways, is still one of my favorites. And speaking of Jake, why isn't he with you? I thought perhaps the situation had improved?" Aunt Lois' voice held a touch of whimsy. Lacey knew there was a fascinating history behind those clear, bright eyes. She looked forward to getting to know her. The thought suddenly struck her—her next article should be about Aunt Lois and her Hearth and Home café. There would be a lot of interesting material to write about. She'd submit her query to one of the magazines aimed at seniors, although Aunt Lois hardly looked like the typical senior citizen. Perhaps she was; people were living longer today and leading more active lifestyles.

Lacey realized she was smiling and staring. Aunt Lois returned her smile with a quizzical look. "I'm sorry, I didn't mean to stare. I was marveling at how young you look, what a beautiful woman you are. I didn't mean to be rude."

Alex spoke up while giving Lois a loving look. "She is a beautiful woman. Bet you didn't know she's a former beauty queen. As you can see, she's still a beauty."

"Hello. I'm sitting at the same table, and I can

hear you. You're not very good at stage whispering are you? "She chuckled. "Enough about me, you're making me blush. Tell me about Jake, how is he doing?"

Alex took a long sip of the coffee Marianne had just served. He patted Lacey on the hand, then began explaining why Jake was so late getting home last night. "Jake was worried about Lacey walking home in what looked like the beginning of a blizzard. And, he was concerned about the mysterious red car that seemed to materialize wherever Lacey was. Of course, Jake was not about to let her know he was concerned for her safety. So, he waited a couple of minutes, and then followed her from a distance. Keeping his sights on the weather and the red car, Jake watched Lacey until she got home. When she turned in his direction, he'd ducked behind a van parked on the street. He didn't think he made a noise. Perhaps she was just being cautious."

Lacey smiled broadly and her tummy did a little somersault. "Alex, I'm gobsmacked. To think, Jake actually cares enough about me to follow me home. I knew someone was following me; I'm glad it wasn't my imagination."

"Wait on, Lacey. I haven't told you the worst of it." Alex continued informing her of the events of the previous night. "Jake is okay, nothing too serious. I wanted to get that out of the way before I tell you what happened. It seems that after you were safely in your house, Jake walked over to the red car, and found a man sitting inside it. He was hunkered down on the front seat, apparently not wanting to be seen. Jake leaned down and knocked on the car's window just as the door flew open. It smashed into him nearly knocking him to the ground. Obviously, that ticked him off. He was so angry he didn't even notice the pain at the time. I won't repeat the exact language of course, but Jake asked him who he was and why he was following you. The man told Jake it was none of his business and Jake…well, you know," Alex said cautiously. Lacy didn't laugh. She was too anxious to hear the rest of the story. "One thing led to another and they really got into it. I'm surprised you didn't hear the commotion. Now, my nephew stands about 6'2 or so, and has muscles that most men would give their eye teeth for. I'm sorry to tell you this Lacey, but all the muscles and strength in the world are no match for a knife."

"A knife?" Both Aunt Lois and Lacey asked in unison.

Alex gave them both a reassuring smile and continued. "The man in the car swung at Jake, taking him by surprise. He managed to blacken his eye. Jake grabbed him, threw him on the ground, and pummeled his face. Jake, as big and strong as he is, is not a fighter. He detests violence. However, he threatened this guy with more bodily harm if he didn't leave Ascot Vale, immediately. He said he'd file assault charges against him if he ever saw him again, even though the guy got the worst of it. Jake helped him up by his arm–that's our Jake for you. The man suddenly produced a knife from his back pocket. He plunged it into Jake's arm–twice!"

"No!" Lacey cried holding her hand over her mouth. Although her hands were shaking, she quickly regained her composure while fighting back tears." Alex, are you sure he's okay? Did you take him to the hospital? How bad is it?"

Alex stood up and gave her a reassuring hug. "Yes. No. And not too bad. His wounds could have been much worse, but his chest is one big, purple bruise. The ratbag was aiming for Jake's belly, but Jake deflected the knife before it could do serious damage. The two wounds are in his left forearm. He bled like a stuck pig, I'll tell you. I'm sure there was a trail of blood in the 700 block of Hawthorn. Most likely, the snow has covered most of it up. Jake was as mad as a cut snake when he was stabbed, and even angrier that he had helped his attacker up from the ground. He said his left arm was immobile, but there was nothing wrong with his right arm or his legs so he punched him in his face, and then kicked him in the bollocks. I think he got the message. He crawled into his car and sped away. We hope that's the end of that story."

"It was Steve," Lacy admitted tearfully. "I know it was."

"You think so?" Alex asked, holding his cup mid-air.

"Beyond a doubt, Alex. It's got Steve written all over it."

Aunt Lois patted Lacey's hand to comfort her." But how did you treat Jake's wounds? How do you know there won't be an infection? Shouldn't he be seen by a physician, and given antibiotics or something? I'm not questioning your medical expertise, Alex. But it has been a while since you were a paramedic."

"You were a paramedic?" Lacey asked incredulously. "How fortunate for Jake. I had no idea. There's so much I want to learn about both of you. And Jake too, of course. When can I see him?"

Marianne brought more coffee and asked if they were ready to order. Lacey looked hesitantly at Alex, her eyes pleading. "Sorry, Marianne. We just stopped in to see Lois, and have a cup of coffee. We have to go," Alex said as he stood up.

"Okay," Marianne said, "by the way, where is Jingles?"

"Yes, where is Jingles?"

"His Lordship is home, thank you, Marianne. In fact, that's where we're headed now. I'll tell him you were asking after him." Alex chuckled. Then, turning to Lois, he gave her a hug. "I'll call you a little later, and let you know how Jake is."

"I'd like that very much. Please give Jake my love, and that rascal, Jingles, too. I'll talk to you later, Lacey, okay? How about giving Jake a hug and a kiss from me, huh?" Aunt Lois had a mischievous look on her face.

They waved goodbye to everyone and Alex

opened the door for Lacey. How she liked this old-fashioned chivalrous practice. She considered herself a very modern woman, equal to, but not above anyone. Certainly she didn't feel like a delicate flower, who couldn't open a door for herself. Contrariwise, she saw nothing wrong with a woman opening a door for a man. Whoever arrived at the door first should open the door for the other person. That's just good manners.

On the walk to his house, Alex told Lacey about his years as a paramedic, and how his knowledge of anatomy and physiology had been helpful in treating minor wounds. New Englanders were a practical bunch, he explained, and couldn't see the need to go to a doctor if it wasn't absolutely necessary. He was a little concerned about Jake's wounds though, and was keeping a close eye on him. At the first sign of infection he was taking him to the hospital, Jake's protestations notwithstanding.

"And if he has to go to the hospital, there will be questions by the physicians. Perhaps there will be a police investigation." One thing Lacey didn't want was an investigation of Steve. She didn't want anything to set him off. For him to travel to Vermont, then get into an altercation with Jake, proved to Lacey how out of control he was. He needed help, of that she was certain. Maybe it would be better if he was investigated. Someone could get him the help he needed before he went off the deep end. She shuddered at the thought of how differently the situation could have been. According to Alex, he was fine. Now, she'd have to trust his professional opinion.

"Yes, those things are possible, Lacey but let's not put the cart before the horse. I think he'll be fine provided there's no infection. And another thing, we should keep him calm so let's not make too much fuss about his nurse."

"He has a visiting nurse? I didn't think it was bad enough to warrant hiring a nurse. Why shouldn't I comment on his nurse? Is she young and pretty?"

Alex's booming laugh took her by surprise. "Well, handsome would be the correct adjective. We didn't hire a nurse. The nurse hired himself. He hasn't left Jake's side all night and this morning either."

"Oh, Alex, you've got to be kidding me." Lacey sighed with relief. "Jake is allowing Jingles to take care of him? According to Jake, Jingles is not a healer. In fact, cats cause diseases, yada, yada, yada."

They were both laughing by the time they reached the house. "Now remember, don't make too much of it, or else Jake will shoo him away. That would greatly upset Nurse Jingles. I'm telling you, he's been with Jake the entire time, licking his arm around the area where the stab wounds are. I've got them medicated and covered with bandages, but he's licking the skin in the surrounding area. You've got to see this; he's been sleeping on Jake's upper chest and right underneath his chin. Jingles is purring to beat the band while Jake rests his arm on him. When he thinks I'm not looking, he strokes Jingles' head, and practically coos to him. He likes to pretend that he merely tolerates Jingles, but he's quite fond of him, actually."

Alex opened the door and they were greeted by Jingles, who immediately launched into his happy dance. He was winding around both of them, purring and making some unusual sound that only Jingles knew what it meant. It sounded something like a cross between a purr and a meow. He darted in front of them, ran down the hall, and into the living room next to Jake. He gingerly climbed on the sofa and toward Jake's neck being careful not to step on his chest and arm. He took a couple of delicate steps toward Jake's head, then began licking his face. He gave a long, loud purr as if he were alerting Jake that Alex and Lacey were there.

Jake reached out to Jingles, stroked his head, and then made a noise that sounded suspiciously like baby talk. Lacey beamed. That cat had a way of breaking through barriers and melting the coldest of hearts.

"Oh, bloody oath. I didn't know you were here, Lacey. Put Boofhead on me, did you?"

She merely smiled at Jake, surprised to be greeted by his smile. He beamed as if he were glad his secret was out. He actually liked Boofhead.

"How are you feeling, Jake? Are you in any pain?"

"Bloody hell, woman. Is a koala a marsupial? Of course, I'm in pain. Nothing I can't handle though.

You should see the other guy." Lacey nearly fainted by what Jake did next. He winked at her which she found to be uber sexy. The desire to grab him and squeeze him with big, loving hugs overwhelmed her. Her feelings toward him were more than a bit clucky as he might say. These were not maternal feelings she had for him; these were romantic feelings, sexy, loving, romantic feelings.

"Here, let me have a look at those wounds, Jake. We need to keep a close eye on them; make sure they don't become infected. I'm sorry there's not much we can do for the ribs and sore chest. Time will heal that though. Do you need more aspirin now?"

"Nah, I'll be apples, Uncle. You know I don't like to take any kind of pills unless absolutely necessary, and right now it isn't absolutely necessary." Jake attempted to sit up, bringing forth a loud moan from him. Jingles didn't like that one bit, and swatted Jake on the cheek, staring at him in a most authoritative way. Was he defying him to get up? Jake obeyed Jingles' command and laughed at the pushy cat. He stole a look at Lacey, smiled, and winked again.

"I must be dreaming. From insults to winks and smiles in such a short period of time. Could he really be flirting with me? If he is, it must be the magical powers of Jingles." It doesn't matter why he's being flirtatious, if indeed he is. He was smiling at her. Lacey felt the color rush to her cheeks, but had no desire to hide it. She wanted him to know the effect he had on her. If Jake could take a step forward by smiling, then she could let her emotions show. If anything was to come of this, it had

to start somewhere.

Alex ignored Jake's protests and got him a couple of aspirin and a glass of water, which he accepted. Alex excused himself, but before leaving the room, he asked Jingles if he'd like to take a nap with him. He patted his legs attempting to entice Jingles into joining him. Jingles wanted none of it and expressed his desire to stay with his patient in a most vocal way.

"Mrroww mrroww," came Jingles' reply as he snuggled in between Jake's neck and shoulder. He gave Alex a *'Don't even think about trying to move me'* look. He began purring and licking Jake's face in a move that was both defiant and loving. He was going to take care of his patient and darned be anybody who would try to interfere. At least that's how Lacey interpreted his demeanor and she was pretty sure she was right. No matter what Jake thought, she knew Jingles was a healer. Jake was about to find this out if he hadn't already.

"Your ex is a real ratbag, Lacey. I reckon Alex already filled you in on most everything. He took me totally by surprise when he pulled that knife on me. I may be the one with two knife wounds and bruised ribs, but I gave him a hell of a lot worse than he gave me, I'll tell you. The dirty rat bastard can't fight like a man. I told him I'd better not ever see him again or I'd file charges against him and that would be the least of his worries."

She took a tentative step toward him, smiling hesitantly. She asked if there was anything she could do for him. His reply of *"You're not a bad sort, I reckon,"* surprised her. Perhaps she really could make him like her. *Dream big, Lacey, just like mom said.*

"You're not such a bad sort yourself, even if you are a bit of dill sometimes."

"Ha! I'll make an Aussie out of you yet, Lacey. I'll have to give you some lessons once I'm feeling better. Right now, if you don't mind, I'd just like to sleep. It was one hell of a night but I'll tell you all about it later if you'd like. Now if only Boofhead will let me sleep. He's determined to lick all the skin off my arm, the bloody drongo."

"It sounds like he's purring you a lullaby. He really is doing his best to comfort you. I know you don't believe that but trust me, you'll be feeling much better before you know it. Alex cautioned me about saying anything about Jingles' healing powers but I can't help it; I want you to come to know what a special cat he is."

"I'm a wake-up to you. You're just hoping I'll like him enough to do the photo shoot for you. I might be a Taswegian as you like to call me, but I'm not bloody stupid. Now, if you'll both let me sleep I'll think on it. No promises."

He drifted off with Jingles curled up by his head purring and licking his face. It was clear to Lacey that Jingles was determined to make Jake better. It was important to her for Jake to know it was Jingles who was responsible for his recovery.

Lacey knew she was anthropomorphizing but so what. Maybe Jingles could have those thoughts. What do we know what goes on in cats' minds? It was good enough for her to know the cat was a healer. Hopefully, Jake would know it too. Standing by the sofa she watched one of the most angelic sights she had ever seen. There was her gorgeous Greek god sleeping peacefully. Snuggled next to him was his very special feline male nurse now sleeping peacefully himself. Her heart felt like it would burst. She couldn't wait until Jake was feeling well enough to come home with her so she could cook for him.

Reflecting on her career choice, she wondered if she would have been a good nurse too as she really did enjoy taking care of people. And, she really wanted to take care of Jake. She envisioned him sitting on her couch, both of them sipping a good Australian wine, talking, getting to know each other and then Jake taking her in his arms.

"Meow, meow, purr purr," Jingles interrupted her wishful thinking. He was staring at her with a loving, sleepy look, extending his paws but no nails. He was kneading Jake's upper chest, carefully avoiding his rib area just like any other good nurse would do. But Jingles wasn't just any nurse, he was super nurse and the rascal seemed to know it.

Jake made a slight sound of contentment but didn't wake. Lacey knew her special TC was working his magic. Soon, Jake's picture would be on the wall at Aunt Lois's Hearth and Home café holding Jingles in his arms. She smiled, thinking his picture, however, would be inscribed, *'Jake and Boofhead'*.

"I'm too wound up to rest," Alex said, as he poked his head around the corner. He raised his eyebrows and gave Lacey a questioning look. Lacey responded to Alex's unspoken question. "Yes, Jake's asleep."

Alex came into the room. "That's quite a sight isn't it, Lacey? Too bad it took a couple of stab wounds and a blow to the chest to give us such a picture."

"Do you really think he'll be alright? You don't think his wounds will become infected, do you?"

"Everything looks fine, Lacey. I've seen a lot worse in my Paramedic days. I clamped the wounds shut after tending to them and I have no doubt they'll knit back together very nicely. The bruised chest and ribs will heal; he's fortunate they weren't broken. Jake was absolutely insistent about not going to the hospital. But if anything untoward does happen I'll have him at the hospital before you can say Bob's your uncle. There will be no argy bargy about it. That's an Irish expression, by the way, and a good one, I think."

"Indeed it is." Lacey smiled and blew the sleeping Jake a kiss before petting TC on the head. He gave a soft purr, not wanting to disturb his patient. "Well, I'll be going now. I have to write this article about our favorite cat and—and I think that Jake will take the pictures. He said he'd give it some thought. I take that as a yes don't you?"

"I haven't doubted it for a minute. When he left the house to follow you, I knew that was a major breakthrough in his grief journey. He'll never forget Shanna and will never get over her death, but he'll get on with his life, knowing that's what Shanna would want for him. And, I really do believe you're playing a big part in his recovery process. He wants to get his life back, Lacey and I know if you'll allow him to keep a part of her in his life and allow him to talk freely about her, that'll be the best medicine for him."

"Meow, meow," Jingles interjected in a soft voice again.

"Sorry, Jingles, I meant to say you and Lacey will be the best medicine for him. Okay?" Alex and Lacey admired Jingles as he laid his head back down on Jake's shoulder again. He gave them a look that Lacey could only interpret as smug.

Jake would thrive under Jingles' undivided attention. Lacey hoped Jake would recognize it. He didn't have to admit it. It would be enough that he knew.

CHAPTER TWENTY-SIX

Lacey walked home with a light heart, remembering Jake's smile. It would be up to her to make the first move, mostly because she feared he wouldn't. Inside that gorgeous Greek god's body was a little boy. A little boy who needed someone to heal his broken heart. Her hopes were high that she could be that someone.

Work on the article about TC consumed her until she fell asleep on the sofa. It have slept several hours because it was dark when she awoke. And, she was hungry so she went to the kitchen and prepared a large salad. One could hardly call Lacey's salads *diet* food as full as they were with all kinds of veggies and lean turkey. Everything went in them but the kitchen sink as her mother had liked to describe them.

When she'd finished eating, she called Summer. It was a delightful surprise when Summer answered the phone. She took that as a good sign and Summer affirmed her supposition, stating that she was already feeling tons better.

Lacey filled her in on Jake, knowing that Summer's curiosity was at a level ten. They talked for a long time and each felt better when they said goodbye.

Lacey wanted to call Jake, but decided to wait until morning, to let him have more time to rest. If she were really being honest, it would be to give TC more time to work his special magic. The memory of the funny cat curling up against the Greek god brought forth a smile.

On opening the laptop she quickly resumed writing her article. The words flowed and she was surprised by the few rewrites that were required. Her most successful articles were always ones that she had such a passion for and this was one of those articles.

As she sat on the sofa, after having finished the article, she began thinking of something Jake had said to her. The comment had been residing quietly in her mind waiting for her full attention." A*lex has already filled you in on most everything."* What did Jake mean by *most* everything? Was there more, something worse that Jake and Alex were keeping from her? She'd have to ask Alex about that.

Lacey went back to the kitchen and made a cup of her favorite Acai berry green tea. The memory of the smile from Jake warmed her more than the tea. Tomorrow she would call Alex and inquire if Jake was up for a visit. And even if he wasn't, she still wanted to see her precious TC. The more she thought about it, the more she liked that name. Anything was better than Boofhead, although Jake seemed quite fond of it. Then again, he's an Australian, as Alex loved to joke.

Upon awakening the next morning she felt content and eagerly anticipating the day. Would Jake smile at her again? She'd never felt this giddy before, not with Steve or any other man she'd dated. Jake was special. He needed her. The only problem was he didn't know it yet.

After hurrying through her morning routine in record time, she picked up her cell, and called Alex. It was a relief to hear how Jake was doing. He was much better than he would have expected, Alex explained, given his wounds and the short amount of time since he was attacked.

"TC to the rescue," Lacey exclaimed.

"You're absolutely right as we both know. And..."

"And what?"

"And my pig-headed nephew knows it, too. He as much as admitted that Jingles was helping him feel better. He said he couldn't explain it, but his wounds and the aches and pains were lessened while Jingles was with him. Better than any pill, he said. I'd say he's ready for a visit from you, what do you think?"

Lacey agreed wholeheartedly and told Alex she'd be by shortly. A glass of orange juice, and several vitamin pills, satisfied her. A quick brushing of her hair would suffice and then she'd be off to Alex and Jake's house.

It was no time before she arrived at their house. A knock on the door brought forth Alex and TC. She followed Alex down the hall with TC bouncing along quite happily beside her.

"Well, come on in," a sexy voice shouted from the living room. "We're not heating all of Ascot Vale, you know." This was followed by a warm laugh that took Lacey by surprise. TC, not wanting to be left out of anything, did his usual happy dance in a more exuberant fashion than usual, trilling as he was twirling.

Lacey picked up His Lordship and cuddled him, then she turned her attention to Jake who was sitting on the sofa. "G'day, Jake, how are you feeling? You look better than you did yesterday and I'm glad to see you sitting up too. That's progress."

"Well, I'm not a bloody baby, of course I can sit. I'm feeling a lot better. I reckon I'm ready to go walkabout by tomorrow and before you say anything, I'm healing on my own and not due to any magical Boofhead powers."

Sensing he was being disparaged and not appreciated, TC let out a long and loud meow and glared at Jake; at least that's how Lacey viewed his actions. Raising an eyebrow, she looked at Jake and crossed her arms. "He knows you're not giving him any credit for all his help, Jake."

"Ah, don't be a Galah. I swear you Sheilas will buy into anything. It's merely coincidence that I'm feeling better, and he was by my side."

"How about all the other people who've had miraculous recoveries while TC was with them? What do you say to that?"

"Mass hysteria, that's what I say."

"Mrowww!" Jingles complained vociferously. "Mr*owww, mrowww.*"

Jake couldn't help himself; his face broke into a huge, heart-melting smile. His gorgeous Paul Newman baby blues bore into her. "He's having a lend of you, Lacey. He's as cunning as the rats under the porch."

Exasperated by Jake's refusal to admit TC had helped him, Lacey said she was leaving and turned to go. She never expected to hear "Okay, maybe he did help a little. Now don't get up yourself, I'm just saying *maybe* he helped a little bit. Does that make you happy?"

Lacey felt a smug expression forming but she quelled it. She knew she'd have her hands full with Jake but she was not a quitter." Actually, Jake it does make me happy. And you know what else would make me happy, as happy as Larry? If you'd accept my invitation to a nice dinner at my place tomorrow. Alex will be there, Aunt Lois, and of course, his nibs here. You can't refuse to show up twice. If you do, that would make you dill, a drongo, *and* a larrikin, a Taswegian larrikin!"

Jake's robust laughter reverberated through the room, surprising Lacey and delighting TC. He joined in the laughter with several loud purrs and his special little cat noises. Then he jumped onto Jake's lap. Jake was obviously moved and scratched TC's head affectionately. "If you can cook better than you can speak Strine, I'll be there. What time?"

Lacey was surprised, but managed to reply, "Come over about 7:00, then you can decide if I prepare a meal good enough for your delicate palate." Lacey reached over and petted TC on his head. Her hand briefly brushed against Jake's where it rested on the cat's head. He didn't pull his hand away, and shocks of electricity went through her. When she looked from TC to Jake, she was surprised to see him staring at her with a wistful smile on his face.

After Lacey bid Jake and her precious TC adieu, she prepared to leave the room. "Don't get up Jake. You still need your rest. I'll see myself out. Hooroo." Lacey left the room with a smirk on her face. She didn't have to look back; she knew Jake's eyes would be following her.

CHAPTER TWENTY-SEVEN

Lacey welcomed Aunt Lois who had stopped by early to lend a hand. They chatted like long lost friends while preparing the food and the table. Lois was impressed with the meal that Lacey prepared; a rack of lamb with all the trimmings and another Pavlova for dessert. "You'll knock his socks off with this meal, Lacey Belle. It might even bring some joy to his heart."

Unbelievably, promptly at 7:00 p. m., Jake rang the doorbell. Standing next to him was his Uncle Alex who was holding Jingles. Lacey couldn't suppress her glee. Her three favorite males, standing there in front of her.

TC led them into the great room which was now abuzz with joyful conversation. Within half-an-hour they adjourned to the kitchen. Much to everyone's surprise, TC did not take his place at the head of the table. Instead, he jumped on the seat next to Jake, and rubbed his head against him and purred.

"Yes, Uncle Alex" Jake remarked. "The cat is brilliant and the greatest healer the country has ever seen. Why, I'll bet he can even cure every disease known to man. He's bloody amazing, a miracle worker, I'll tell you," Jake said with more than a trace of good-natured sarcasm.

"I noticed you winced slightly when you got up from the sofa, Jake, and apparently Jingles noticed you're still feeling a bit crook, too. He's not going to leave your side until you're one hundred percent."

All of them gathered at the table laughed including Jake, who was laughing at himself. "Look, I've already admitted that he's probably helped me. Everybody happy now? Oh, and to make you even happier, Lacey, I'll do the photo shoot."

"That's my boy," Alex chimed in, "I do believe Jingles is posing for you already. Look at the little blighter, sitting there with his head held high. I reckon he fancies himself a prince."

TC swung his head in Alex's direction and narrowed his eyes. "Oh, sorry, Jingles, "Alex chuckled, "I meant to say a king." Alex patted Jingles on the head, which seemed to mollify his highness.

After the laughter settled down, Aunt Lois announced that she had something to share with them, now that they were all together. She explained that she was selling her café to her namesake, Lois, her only niece. Jake and Lacey bemoaned the fact that there would be no more Aunt Lois's Hearth and Home. Aunt Lois explained that it was a good thing and that the only name change would be the dropping of the *Aunt.* It would simply be known as Lois' Hearth and Home café. Mostly, everything would be the same, and Aunt Lois would stop in to see her favorite customers. She was absolutely delighted about it and so was Alex.

Alex had an announcement of his own. He and Aunt Lois were talking marriage which drew much enthusiasm from Lacey and Jake. Jake seemed truly happy for his uncle, and Lacey was absolutely delighted.

Aunt Lois commanded their attention once more by telling them that she was throwing a Christmas party at the café, where she and Alex would announce their engagement and let her dear customers know of the change in ownership. It would be worth the wait, she reasoned.

They sat around the kitchen table talking enthusiastically about the revelations of the evening. Later when Aunt Lois and Alex left, Jake hung back purportedly to arrange a time for him to do the photo shoot. Jake thanked Lacey for such a delicious meal. "I reckon you have every reason to skite about your cooking, Lacey Belle. It was bloody delicious. Even Boofhead enjoyed the scraps I fed him. Of course, that's not saying much is it, given his voracious appetite? Anyway, can you come by tomorrow in the afternoon? I'll have everything set up by then."

"You're not such a bad sort, Jake. Yes, I'll be there tomorrow about 2 o'clock if that's okay with you."

Jake gave Lacey a hug, a quick friendly hug. Certainly not a romantic hug but it was huge considering how standoffish Jake had been since she'd known him. *Progress!*

Lacey didn't sleep very well that night. Her mind was working overtime. So many decisions to be made and even though she had improved with her decision making dilemma she still dreaded making them; always fearful that she would choose the wrong path or her decisions would adversely affect others.

She busied herself in the morning, inspecting the three floors of her home and envisioning layouts for a perfectly wonderful B&B. This would be down the line of course but definitely something to begin preparing for. She had the money to do it and was really looking forward to being an innkeeper.

The sky outside the great room windows was sunny with brilliant, almost blinding rays of light glinting off the cars parked on the street. The presence of the sun belied the cold weather awaiting her as she opened the front door. She needn't have worried about adding any color to her delicately pale skin in the form of blush; by the time she'd arrive at Alex and Jake's home, she'd have the rosy complexion of a little English girl.

She walked briskly along Hawthorn holding her head down and pulling her scarf snugly around her neck. By the time she reached Alex and Jake's, she was chilled and could see her breath. She hoped the unseasonable frigid temperatures wouldn't last long but found herself thinking how cozy it would be to be snuggled in front of a blazing fire with Jake.

When she arrived at Alex and Jake's she was pleasantly surprised to find Jake waiting for her in front of the door ready to usher her in the house and out of the cold. "Oh, thank you Jake. Funny how a short walk can turn into a long walk when it's cold like it is today. That's very considerate of you."

"No worries. I'd do the same for any Sheila or *anybody* for that matter."

Before Lacey could think of a suitable comeback, Jake winked. Would she ever not go weak in the knees when he winked at her? It was doubtful as she was inexorably under his spell and…she liked it! This was not like her. Lacey was the very definition of a 'modern' woman, independent, self-assured, and impervious to insincere flattery. She was able to navigate the world on her own, not needing any man to take care of her. But Jake wasn't just *any man.*

"Meow? Purr, purr," TC came running to greet Lacey and surprised her by jumping up into her arms. He landed with a thud nearly causing her to drop him. "Goodness, somebody needs to go on a diet."

"Well, it isn't you, Lacey, my girl. You're looking as beautiful as ever," Alex said as he greeted Lacey, trying to give her a hug while Jingles was playfully swatting at him.

"Thank you Alex, you're looking well yourself."

"Ok, enough of the bloody love fest, let's get Boofhead posed for his pikkies while he's still in a good mood."

Lacey groaned and Alex shook his head. Jingles was always in a good mood. He was a happy cat and Jake knew it. He just loved to take the Mickey out of everybody.

Lacey was surprised to see the professional setup that Jake had put together. Summer couldn't have done it better. Jake had the recliner positioned at a right angle to the fireplace with the fire blazing, creating a perfect Christmas card scene. He had placed a plump royal blue pillow with gold tassels on the recliner on which he would sit TC. He had no doubt that Boofhead would cooperate being the world-class ham that he is. That fancy pillow would require some explaining later.

To no one's surprise, when TC entered the living room he immediately jumped on the recliner. Stepping gingerly onto the pillow, he turned around once and then sat up waiting. *All right, Mr. DeMille, I'm ready for my close-up.*

Jake nodded at the cat. "You're as silly as a two bob watch, Boofhead."

Lacey was delighted by the scene, although she would be hard pressed to say which delighted her more, the cat's imperious manner or Jake's smile and gracious demeanor. Who was she kidding; Jake wins every time hands down, with her precious TC a close second.

"You said you wanted a picture of him with one of his former patients, right, Lacey?"

"Yes, Jake, so we should ask one of them if they'd be willing to pose with him. Maybe Aunt Lois?"

"Maybe you?"

Again, surprising no one, TC jumped down from his regal perch and danced over to Lacey, winding around her legs and purring. "Well, I think that settles that. He wants to pose with you. Let's do that picture tonight. That way I can be done with all this falderal and you can submit your story with pictures to that silly cat magazine; what's it called? *Cats are Useless Bludgers,* something like that, eh?"

Were it not for the disarming smile he leveled at her, perhaps she and Jake would have gotten into a blue. The thought occurred to Lacey *"Australians are Drongos.* There's a good name for a magazine. Hmmm, actually that would be a good title for my next article. What do you think of that?"

Before Jake could respond, Alex chimed in with his idea for a better title for her next article. "I think, *'Never mind him, he's an Australian'* would be an even better title. Now, what do you think about that?"

"Bloody perfect." They laughed, both of them noticing Jake's attempt to remain stone-faced and failing miserably at it. When he smiled at Lacey and then laughed, she thought it was the sweetest sound she'd ever heard.

Jake picked Jingles up and deposited him on the pillow. Most cats, being quite contrary, as cats are wont to be, would jump down off the pillow just as quickly as they were placed there. Not Jingles; heaven forbid. The world was his stage and he seemed to know it. He sat patiently, posing, while Jake took several pictures. "That does it for this session, Boof. You can get down now."

"Wait. That's it? I'm not finished posing." Judging by his reluctance to get off the pillow, Lacey deduced that's what the little prince was thinking. Apparently,

Jake and Alex were thinking the same thing as they all looked at TC and then one another and laughed wholeheartedly.

"Okay, you silly buggers, I've got to lie down for a bit. The old ribs aren't one hundred percent yet. How about if I bring Boofhead to your place about 7:00 p. m.? Would that give you enough time to get all tarted up in your best bib and tucker?" Jake laughed so hard at his own comment that he winced in pain and wrapped an arm about his chest.

"Serves you right, Jake. And I'll have you know I'm not a tart and have never gotten tarted up for anyone and I never would, especially a Taswegian." Lacey said it with no rancor. She smiled, something she noticed she was doing a lot more of lately.

He laughed again. "Are you trying to make me crack a rib, woman? If you'd leave now, I could get some rest, thank you very much."

"See you and Boof—darn it Jake, I don't know what to call this poor cat now. He has so many names anyway. I'll see both of you around 7:00 tonight. Make sure you keep him warm. It's quite chilly outside and I wouldn't want him catching a cold."

Alex reminded Lacey once again that it didn't matter what she called Jingles. He would answer or not as he saw fit.

"I'll see you out, Lacey Belle. Don't get up Jake. Get some sleep. We'll have something to eat later."

Jake stared directly at Lacey but directed his comment to Alex. "Don't worry, Uncle Alex, I'm sure Lacey will be a gracious hostess and feed me."

"Indeed. I have plenty of cat kibble that you and TC can share."

TC purred loudly and then took his position on the sofa next to Jake's upper chest. He gave him a few gentle kneads with his big paws and then closed his eyes and settled in for a nap. *"What a perfect picture that would make. Two of my three favorite guys."* Lacey gave Alex a hug and then bundled up and walked out the door. The weather didn't seem quite as cold now or maybe she was just feeling the warm glow from her encounter with Jake.

CHAPTER TWENTY-EIGHT

Lacey changed into a flattering blue-green satin top with a modest but alluring V-neck that complemented her unusual eyes. She wore a pair of wedge peep toe shoes that would give her some height although she knew that readers of the magazine would be focused on TC, not her. Then again, she wasn't dressing exclusively for the cat magazine.

Lacey set the table for a casual dinner; no romantic candles or other frou-frou. She wasn't about to make it look like she went out of her way for Jake. Because he would surely have some smarty-pants remark being the little boy that he sometimes was. Now, she didn't want to be with the little boy Jake; she wanted to spend the evening with her Greek god, Jake. In keeping with the casual *I'm not out to impress you* theme, Lacey decided on spaghetti Bolognese, a simple salad and garlic bread. Nice, but not over the top.

The doorbell rang and Lacey's heart skipped a beat. Jake was on time, not early. She really disliked it when guests arrived early because she was always rushing around right up to the last minute. She opened the door and was overwhelmed again by the vision before her; a Greek god and a regal cat. Jake was wearing his sexy Akubra hat, which was sitting at a jaunty angle atop his shiny black hair, a dark blue dress shirt tucked into his perfectly fitting jeans and a pair of stylish boots. She invited them in but of course Jingles had already jumped out of Jake's arms and was sprinting into the great room. Lacey's and Jake's eyes met. Jake took a tentative step toward her and then stopped. Lacey felt a sudden rush of empathy for him. She knew what it was like to be shy and Jake, for all his sharp remarks and diffident attitude, was not as confident as one would expect of such a gorgeous hunk. "So, it looks like TC is ready for the photo shoot, but he'll have to wait. Dinner's ready." Lacey gestured at the hall table. "You can put your hat on the table here. I suppose I'll have to buy a nice hall tree like the one you and Alex have."

Lacey led Jake to the kitchen and he seated himself at the head of the table, casting a sly look in her direction. *Yes, Jake that's where you belong at the head of the table and you know it.* TC took his rightful place at the table too, not on the floor where an ordinary cat would sit, heaven forbid. "*Purr, purr.*"

Lacey opened a can of cat food and served it to TC in a crystal bowl, not because she was being deferential to him but because it was the first bowl she came across in the cupboard. She brought the salad bowl and chilled salad plates to the table along with the steaming hot spaghetti Bolognese and garlic bread. She asked Jake to pick out a nice wine from the wine rack. He chose a nice Merlot and poured a glass for each of them, although his glass contained a mere ounce or two of wine, the same as Lacey's.

"Ahh, spag bol. One of my favorites," Jake said, as he inhaled the spicy aroma.

Lacey sat down and gave Jake a quizzical look.

"Do you Aussies shorten every single word?"

"Ya."

"Funny, Jake. I hope you enjoy your dinner. I didn't know you liked this dish."

"Or you wouldn't have made it, right?"

This is going to be one interesting evening. "Or made it with an inch thick layer of hidden hot peppers."

Jake turned to TC who had nearly finished his dinner already and said "Pay no attention to her, Boofhead, she's a Seppo."

Another dazzling smile. Another weakening of her knees. Jake raised his glass and clinked it against hers. "Cheers, big ears. Before you do your block, Lacey, it's a friendly Aussie cheer to which you would reply, Same goes, big nose."

"You Aussies are a weird mob and I mean that in the nicest way, but sometimes you really are a dill." Lacey pushed a strand of hair behind her ear and gazed at Jake.

They ate their dinner with Jake commenting on what a good cook she was. She noticed that Jake took just a few sips of his wine and remembered what Alex had told her about Jake not drinking and driving. However, he wouldn't be driving, he'd be walking. Good for him though, she thought.

They talked for quite a while and actually had a civil conversation with only the occasional barb slipping from Jake's mouth. *More progress!* "I didn't make dessert, Jake. I hope you don't mind. Alex told me you Aussies have a sweet tooth, but I didn't have time to make anything."

"Aww, don't get your knickers in a knot, Lacey Belle. That was beaut tucker and I don't know if I could fit any more food in. Besides, I need to take the pikkies of His Highness. I'll want you sitting up in bed with Boofhead snuggled next to you. I don't think there'll be any problem getting him to cooperate, do you?"

Lacey straightened up from the table and told Jake she'd pick up the dishes later after the photo shoot. She headed to the great room with TC following alongside her. "No, Jake, that won't be a problem. He's the biggest ham I've ever met. Come on into the great room and we can get started."

"But the shoot should take place in your bedroom if we want it to be authentic. I'm sure you would have mentioned the locale in your article."

"Yep, I did. And, the locale is the great room. *Why didn't I say it took place in my bedroom? You idiot, Lacey, you bloody stupid drongo.* I was too sick to get off the sofa so TC and I stayed there. That's where the big guy snuggled with me and kept me company. He virtually didn't leave my side."

"Oh." Jake appeared a bit crestfallen but quickly recovered. "Okay, well you set it up like it was during that time."

Jake turned his back to Lacey to pick up his camera when he muttered something unintelligible. Lacey thought she heard one word, bedroom. But she couldn't be sure so she kept her thoughts to herself.

Lacey sat on the sofa with her back against the armrest and her legs stretched out on the sofa in front of her. She pulled the eiderdown over her and called for TC to join her. She was sure he had little springs on his feet as quickly as he had jumped up onto her lap.

Jake took many pictures while Lacey and TC sat quietly and patiently. "Perfect! I think you'll be happy with these, Lacey. I'll develop them in my dark room in the basement." Jake must have noticed the surprised look on Lacey's face because he commented, "Uncle Alex and I have all the mod cons. You can pick the ones you want."

Jake asked Lacey to let him help her with the dishes. Her first inclination was to be polite and refuse but in so doing Jake would leave soon and that wouldn't do. She wanted him to stay. She wanted to get to know him if he'd let her.

She gave TC a kiss on the top of his head and then moved him to the end of the sofa. "Sure, that'll be beaut, Jake. It'll be nice to have some help." Jake gave her a big grin as if he was pleased to hear Lacey using the Aussie expression. Lacey was rewarded for her attempt at Strine by a warm smile from Jake. They went into the kitchen to do the dishes. A black and white streak preceded them and jumped on his chair at the kitchen table.

"If you're waiting for dessert, TC, you'll be sadly disappointed."

"Meow?"

"Well, okay I do have some whipped cream. I know you like that."

"Purr, purr."

"You're welcome. Now, if you'll excuse us, Jake and I have to do the dishes. *How wonderfully domestic that sounds.* That quickly she caught herself envisioning a life with Jake.

"You've got a grin as big as the Great Australian Desert, Lacey. I only offered to help with the dishes. You Sheilas are something else."

"What? Oh, yeah we are. Wash or dry?" Lacey asked, pointing to the sink and then to the dish towel. "Whichever one you don't want to do. How's that?"

"Righto then, let's get to it. These dishes aren't going to clean themselves."

"Fair enough," Lacey said as she threw the dishtowel at Jake, laughing as she did so. With a deft hand, he caught it and gave it a snap.

With Jake's help, the cleanup went quickly, too quickly for her liking. She asked him if he'd like coffee and he replied, "A cuppa tea would hit the spot."

Lacey served Jake his tea and then coffee for herself. They sat at the table and talked into the night. TC had long toddled off into the great room to curl up on the sofa. "So, tell me, Jake, do you really dislike me, or do you treat all women in the same manner?"

"I think it's obvious Lacey. I don't dislike you. Sometimes. Well, most of the time, I say something and immediately I want to pull out my tongue." Jake went on to explain his situation.

"As you know, I was married back home in Australia. Her name was Shanna and she was the love of my life. I never thought I'd meet a woman like her, and if I did, I couldn't imagine such a woman having any interest in me. The day she walked into my shop, I knew I'd never be the same. I was immediately captivated by her beauty. Of course, that's what first attracted me to her. But it went so much deeper than that. Not only was she beautiful on the outside, she was even more beautiful on the inside. The joy she brought into my life was amazing. I'd never known that feeling before.

"I was a hell-raiser—drinking, drugging, and always getting into trouble. I gave my poor parents so much grief. I got in trouble with the law, and spent time in jail for petty theft. The life of an addict is not a pretty one. You're always chasing that first high, and the truth is, you can never recapture that feeling. But, that doesn't stop you from trying. Once you're hooked, you spend the rest of your days self-loathing. Your brain has been hijacked by the drugs. I call it the Addiction Monster. He has you in his grip, and only the lucky ones escape.

"I was still drinking and drugging when I met Shanna, but I managed to hide it from her, or so I thought. But, she saw something in me I can't explain. One time I asked her what she saw in me, and she said a little boy, a handsome little boy. A good person with a bad disease. She never gave up on me. Neither did my parents. I'll always be grateful for their love and support.

"Shanna and I were married within six months, and she was helping me become a better drug-free person. She never asked anything of me. All she wanted was for me to overcome the monster. She didn't care if we were penniless, or homeless, just as long as I was clean. We were making great progress; me, cutting back on the drugs and her encouraging me. We were happy. We were looking forward to the day when I could be totally free from the monster and we could start a family.

"I received *the call,* the one that everyone dreads. It was 3:30 in the afternoon. I was at the shop, finishing work on a beautiful custom cabinet made of the finest Australian Huon pine. I had to buy a special license to purchase my supply because most of the stands of Huon are protected, which is a good thing. Anyway, I reckon I'm avoiding talking about it, aren't I? It's still hard to even think about it, let alone talk about it.

"That was the last day I took any drugs. Alcohol was never really the problem for me. It was the bloody drugs. Shanna was killed by a driver who was drinking and drugging. How's that for irony?"

Lacey listened intently, hanging on to every word when she felt the little rivulets of tears sliding down her face. She wanted to reach out, hug him, and keep hugging him; this little boy that Shanna had seen inside the man's body. Lacey saw it too. At that moment, she knew she was falling in love with him. She also knew it was probably hopeless, a no-hoper as the Aussies would say.

Lacey wiped the tears with the back of her hand, and then looked into Jake's amazing baby blue eyes, wishing she could absorb his pain. "What can I say, Jake? There are no words for that kind of pain. It's unimaginable. I can only hope that time will ease the pain. I know it will never erase it."

Jake cleared his throat before he spoke. "I'm touched by your concern, Lacey. Time is helping. I never thought I'd be able to say that, but it is. It's like a scab on a wound that is slowly healing. You go along each day and then something happens to rip the scab off. It might be a scent that reminds me of her, or someone's voice that's similar, or seeing someone who resembles her. Then the scab has to form again, and each time the scab becomes a bit thicker. But a scar remains; the scar is always there and always will be. You just become stronger, but it doesn't happen overnight, so yes, time is helping. It also helps to have good support and Uncle Alex has been a great support to me."

"I know. He's a wonderful man. I know we don't know each other very well, Jake. We seem to rub each other the wrong way, but I want you to know that I do like you. I don't pity you, nobody wants to be pitied, but I do have a lot of empathy. After all, you're not a bad sort." Lacey reached across the table, grabbed Jake's hand and squeezed it.

Jake placed his other hand over Lacey's and smiled. It was still just a friendly smile. There was nothing romantic in it. Still waiting for him to zap her with one of his zingers, she was surprised by what he said next. "I actually do like you, too. You're not such a bad sort either, for a Seppo." Jake smiled sheepishly. "I have to explain why I've been giving you such a hard time since we met. You resemble her, Lacey, so much so that it's bloody uncanny. I wanted to avoid you. That's why I didn't show up for dinner that first night. It's been hard to look at you, and not see Shanna. I'm sorry for giving you such a hard time, but I am an Australian, you know." He laughed and she laughed along with him.

"Oh, pull your head in, Jake. Yes, I've been studying Strine." She then gently removed her hand from his, not that she wanted to. But Jake hadn't made any overt romantic moves.

"There's something I need to know, Jake. You said that Alex had told me 'most' everything. Is there more, Jake, something I should know? If there is, I really think you should tell me."

Jake shifted in his chair and leaned closer across

the table, looking Lacey squarely in the eyes. "You're right. I was trying to spare you, but you should know. The reason I didn't involve the police in this and don't want to go to the hospital because of the questions they'll ask, is...well, he threatened to come back and kill you if I called the police. Normally, I wouldn't pay much attention to something that was said in a fight, but he was serious, Lacey. You'd have to have seen his eyes. He had a crazed look, not just angry, but definitely crazed. He was away with the pixies, like he'd lost all touch with reality."

"That's what Summer's fiancé, Bradley, told me, too. He said Steve had a look in his eyes that frightened him. He's afraid that Steve will do something to me. He's never hurt me physically, so I haven't been afraid of him, but now that you're telling me the same thing, I *am* frightened of him. I really think we should go to the police about this, Jake."

"Let's think about it. Now that you know, you'll need time to absorb it. Let's not make any rash decisions, now. Oh, and he also threatened to kill 'that damn cat that she's so crazy about. ' Even *I* wouldn't want anything to happen to Boofhead, believe it or not." Jake said facetiously.

"Of course, you wouldn't. Whether you admit it or not, you like TC. And, I know you wouldn't want to see any animal harmed. But right now I have to think on this. I don't want to do anything to set Steve off. Then again, I know he needs help. His anger has been building. If I could be sure that the judicial system would put him into a mental facility, I'd feel so much better. He's not a bad person, at least he wasn't, but he's very sick. He does have some good qualities, but I think his mental illness is overshadowing them. He needs help. But, he'd better not ever lay a hand on TC. He can threaten me all he wants but not that innocent cat."

"Don't worry your pretty head about it. I'm a wake up to him now and if he's bloody stupid enough to show his mug around here again, he'll be one sorry bloke. I promise you that."

"Thank you, Jake. That does comfort me."

Jake stood, preparing to leave.

"I'll call you tomorrow and we can take a Captain Cook of the pikkies of Boofhead. I reckon about 3 in the arvo, is that good for you?"

Lacey wasn't about to let Jake get the better of her by admitting her ignorance of his latest salvos lobbed at her. Instead she simply replied "that'll be fine. Let's get His Lordship up so you can leave."

Upon walking into the great room they discovered TC flat out on the sofa snoring! "Come on, Boofhead; get off your fat date," Jake said. He nudged the cat's legs which were dangling over the sofa, with his left knee. "Time to go home."

Meow? TC lifted himself up and stretched to his full length, front paws extended in front of him, bum and tail high in the air and yawning. It was followed by what could only be called a glare directed at Jake. *How dare you wake me? I'm staying right here, if you don't mind, or even if you do.* TC laid right back down, curled his tail around his face and burrowed in.

"Well, I think that settles it, Jake. His nibs wants to stay here. Also, that must mean you're healed otherwise he wouldn't leave you. Uh uh, don't get into an argy bargy with me, Jake Anderson. If TC says you're healed, then you're healed." Lacey giggled which brought a smile to Jake's gorgeous face.

"Well, Boofhead's medical acumen notwithstanding, I am much better so he can stay here if he wants. Uncle Alex won't mind. Whatever Boofhead wants, he gets. He's spoiled worse than any ankle biter you've ever met. I'll call you tomorrow." He paused for just a second. Did he want to say more or perhaps ask if he could stay but thought better of it? "Have a good night."

Lacey closed the door behind him and leaned against it while wondering why he didn't hug her. Wondering if she'd ever be able to break through that hard shell. Her thoughts went to her friend, Summer who had suffered the death of her husband and who, in time, had learned how to go on. Though she would never be the same, when she met Bradley she allowed her heart to open again, to accept love. Now she was making a new life for herself. Lacey wanted that for Jake, even if it meant it couldn't be with her. Of course, she wanted to be the one who could make him happy, but the important thing was for him to find happiness again. Lacey was a born 'fixer' who always wanted to help people with their problems. And, she desperately wanted to fix Jake. Would he let her?

"Come on, TC; let's go to bed, in a real bed, not on the sofa. We have a big day tomorrow. We're going to look at the pikkies that Jake took of you." TC meowed in agreement and followed her to the bedroom, yawning as he walked. "Stop that, now you've got me yawning."

CHAPTER TWENTY-NINE

The sound of tuneful trilling in Lacey's ear woke her the next morning. Lifting her hand she reached out and stroked TC's face which brought on even louder purring. "Let's get some breakfast or brekkie as Jake would say, although I suspect you got up and ate during the night. Well, I didn't and I'm hungry so let's go."

After breakfast, Lacey went through her usual morning routine and then put on one of her prettiest cashmere sweaters. She added a splash of her two favorite perfumes; a combination of the old-fashioned Chanel #5 and Opium. An array of modern perfumes sat on her vanity, some of which she liked a lot, but none as much as she loved her own concoction. Others liked it too judging by the many compliments she received when wearing it. TC sneezed. Apparently, he was not a fan.

Picking up the phone, Lacey called Alex's number to let him know she and TC would be coming over soon. She thanked him for allowing TC to have a sleepover, which made him chuckle.

The two of them arrived at Alex's house after a delightful stroll down Hawthorn Street to where it intersected with Maple. TC had walked ahead with Lacey following about two steps behind which she was certain delighted him; after all, such a royal being could not allow anyone to precede him. Her vivid imagination amused her although sometimes she wasn't so sure that it *was* only her imagination. She knocked on the door and was surprised and delighted to be greeted by Jake.

"Well, G'day, Seppo, what's with the silly look on your mug? Damn, woman. You tend to bring out the worst in me. Bugger."

Lacey opened her mouth to respond with a wisecrack, but noticed that Jake was wearing a slight frown. She didn't have time to ponder that because he took her off guard in the next instant by giving her a warm smile. He was harder to figure out than a Rubik's Cube. Maybe seeing her reminded him of Shanna again, so she took the high road and merely said, "Well, G'day to you too, Jake. May we come in? Sorry, I guess I mean may *I* come in since TC is already in? He doesn't stand on ceremony, does he?"

Jake smiled and relaxed. He looked at Lacey as if seeing her through different eyes. "You don't need a royal invitation to come in, Lacey; after all, you're with him." Jake said as he raised his arm and crooked his thumb toward Boofhead who was busy cleaning himself in the hallway.

Jake hung Lacey's jacket up on the hall-tree and the three of them went into the living room, Boofhead leading the way, of course. "You'll like the shots I took, not because I'm such a great photographer, which I am, of course. But because you like anything that involves that wombat-headed cat. Here, take a look at them. Uncle Alex likes them. Bloody surprise, eh?"

"*Quelle surprise*, indeed," Lacey commented. "Oh, TC come here. What a little beauty you are. Jake has captured your unique beauty and personality."

"Purr, purr," TC responded, jumping up on the coffee table and staring at the photos and unabashedly admiring himself. Lacey could think of no other reasonable explanation for the cat's fascination with the pictures. Another normal cat would simply ignore the photos or promptly sit on them. But one thing that TC isn't is normal.

"This is simply beautiful, Jake," Lacey said as she stared at one of the photos she'd just maneuvered from under TC's firmly placed foot. "Just look at him posing on that pillow like Little Lord Fauntleroy, all sweetness and innocence. You did a great job, Jake. I even like the picture with me in it and I rarely like pictures of myself. You're quite the artiste!"

"Ta, I think they're bonzer, too. If the article you're writing is half as good as the pikkies, then it's London to a brick that it'll be read by heaps of people."

In her best exaggerated Southern drawl, Lacey replied, "You really think so, Jake? Ah cain't imagine li'l ole me writing anything that could be on par with your photos or even come within cooee of such excellence."

Jake laughed so hard he actually snorted. "You little ripper. Where's that bloody uncle of mine? I know he's been coaching you in Strine. Uncle Alex! Get your arse in here," Jake yelled while still laughing.

Lacey wasn't surprised to see Alex walking into the room with a big grin on his face, and holding a cup of hot chocolate which he proffered to Lacey. The kitchen was right off the living room so it was no problem to earwig. "Here you go, love. Have a cuppa. Sorry I didn't greet you at the door but I was busy making the hot chocolate. You're like family, Lacey so there's no need for formalities now, right?" Looking at Jake, Alex said "She's a good student isn't she, Jake? She'll be teaching *you* Strine before you know it that is if she's still speaking to you, as rude as you are at times."

Jake didn't seem to take offense. It appeared to Lacey that he was actually having fun and enjoying a good laugh. "You know I'm not rude, Uncle Alex, I'm Australian. Isn't that right, Seppo?"

"Oh, you're an Australian, but I don't think it's fair to lump all the other Aussies in with one rotten apple, and a Taswegian rotten apple to boot." Lacey's smile grew broader with each second that passed without a wisecrack from Jake. "Well, I wonder whose tongue the cat has now, Alex?" Lacey said, casting her eyes from Alex to Jake. Her comments were met with a lazy smile from Jake and a chuckle from Alex.

The three of them seemed to observe a silent and amicable truce and began reviewing the photos. Lacey chose several she thought were the best. It wasn't easy to narrow the selection because they all captured TC's personality. She knew this piece would be a popular one. In fact, the seeds for a full-length book about TC had begun to germinate. Of course, it would require many photographs of TC. Either he was one very photogenic cat, or Jake was one bonzer photographer. Most likely it was a combination of the two. The ease with which she was picking up Strine amazed her.

Lacey picked up TC and held him in the crook of her right arm while petting his head with her left hand. He returned the favor by inclining his head up and licking her cheek, and of course, purring. Then, looking up through his half sleepy eyes, he glanced Jake's way with a *She likes me best* expression on his smug little face. As he did so, Lacey felt a strange sensation of a pair of eyes on her and looked up to see Jake smiling longingly at her. Their eyes locked onto each other and neither spoke nor looked away until Alex announced he needed to take a nap.

"Do you mind if I take Jingles with me, Lacey?" Alex grinned. "He's taken to keeping me company lately when I nap. I sure hope I'm not coming down with something. I've been rather tired lately and you know our Jingles here, he knows things that we don't."

"You and Boofhead go on and take a nap. Are you sure you're okay?" Jake asked, turning his gaze on his uncle.

After having reassured them he was okay, just a little tired, Alex and Jingles headed off. Lacey thought it odd that TC didn't do his special little dance around her legs; he seemed more concerned with Alex.

"I'll see you out. It'll be quiet around here this arvo with those two napping instead of them making little goo-goo sounds to each other. Don't laugh. They really do. One's as bad as the other. Anyway, this'll give me a chance to work on the bedside table I've been making Uncle Alex for Chrissie. That's Christmas to you, Seppo. It's a surprise."

Lacey said "Don't worry, Jake, I won't spoil your surprise by telling Alex about the prezzie you're making him." Reacting to the pleased smile on Jake's face, Lacey commented, "If I hang around you and Alex long enough, you might have to start calling me a dinky-di Aussie and not a bloody Seppo."

"You're a beaut, real ridgy didge. But it'll take more than a minimally passing knowledge of Strine to be a dinky-di Aussie."

"I suppose you're right. It's just like having a minimally passing knowledge of manners doesn't make you a gentleman." *Touche'*.

As if reading her mind, Jake grinned and said "touché." He walked her down the hall with a tentatively placed hand on her shoulder. "I'll ring you tomorrow. I'd like to know which two pikkies you chose. Walk carefully."

CHAPTER THIRTY

Lacey had no sooner settled down on the sofa, when Aunt Lois called with a question for her. "Lacey dear, how would you like to help an old woman on Thanksgiving?"

"Well, I always like to help people, but who is the old woman you want me to help? Lacey asked. Before the older woman had a chance to reply, Lacey cheerily responded that she'd help her in any way she could.

Aunt Lois told her about her annual free Thanksgiving supper she gives for the residents of Ascot Vale. "We have a wonderful celebration. It's like one big happy family. Some of the people who attend don't have family at all so they come to my café. I like to think we nourish their souls as well as their bodies. It's my small way of giving back to the community which has supported me for so many years."

Lacey was honored to be included in the festivities and was thankful that she wouldn't be spending Thanksgiving alone. Aunt Lois informed her that Alex would be there of course, as he is every year, helping in the kitchen. And yes, before Lacey could ask, Jingles would be there delighting all the customers with his usual antics.

"Does Jake attend the Thanksgiving Supper?"

A few seconds elapsed before Aunt Lois responded thoughtfully with, "Well, he never has, but somehow I think this year could be different. I've told you I think he's sweet on you, but doesn't know how to show it." Maybe he'll surprise us this year. But, don't think that Jake doesn't help. Every year he comes to the café after closing and does all the dishes and cleaning up and I mean he does it all."

"That's so sad, Aunt Lois. It seems he has two sides to him. One is a cocky self-assured, brash, almost rude man and the other is a shy little boy who doesn't like to be outside of his comfort zone. I want to help him so badly. I just don't know what to do, I just don't know."

Aunt Lois reassured her that Jake just needed some time and understanding. Jake would be personally invited to come for dinner and not just clean up. "I'll tell him you'll be here to help and then we'll wait and see, okay?"

"It has to be okay, because there's really nothing we can do short of kidnapping him." They both laughed at the concept of two women trying to abduct a man who was at least 6'1"about 220 pounds and all muscle. They hung up and Lacey thought about how much she'd like to kidnap Jake. She was not what one would call a wanton woman, but her ruminations about kidnapping Jake and what would happen once she had him in her clutches, had her on fire. Eventually she fell asleep on the sofa and had wonderful dreams of Jake.

True to his word, Jake called Lacey the next day surprising her that he'd called so early; she wasn't expecting to hear from him until early evening. Her invitation to him for lunch was declined with Jake explaining that he didn't want to leave the house. He told her that Alex was feeling even more tired and was having chest pain. Alex was adamant that he would not go to the hospital, but Jake was doubly adamant that he would. He was calling to let Lacey know what was going on; he knew she'd want to know.

Lacey was bright and alert now with this news and very concerned about her precious Alex. In her mind, he was a father figure and she couldn't bear it if anything happened to him. She didn't have a car, but she wanted to go to the hospital. "I'm rushing out the door now, Jake. Can you please pick me up and let me go to the hospital with you? Please?"

"Stay where you are, Lacey. I'm not driving Uncle Alex to the hospital. I've already called 911; that's the sensible thing to do. I'll be in the ambo with him. Sorry, the ambulance. If you want to walk here, I'll leave the key to the car under the front seat. Yeah, I know, not very original, but this is a safe town. I could even leave the key in the ignition with a note that says *Take me,* but let's not take any bloody chances. I'll see you at the hospital. Oh, the ambo's here now so we've gotta go before Uncle Alex runs away. I'll talk to you when you get here. And Lacey, try not to prang the car." She heard the smile in his voice as he hung up. She didn't have the chance to ask him what *prang* meant but it didn't take a rocket scientist to figure out that bit of Strine.

CHAPTER THIRTY-ONE

Lacey power-walked to Alex's house. When she arrived, she went to the car, found the key and got in. Before starting the engine, she took her cell phone out of her purse and called Aunt Lois. She began by telling her about Alex. Aunt Lois interrupted, explaining that Jake had just called her. Lacey could ride with her to the hospital.

The three of them kept a vigil in the waiting room. Jake explained that Uncle Alex had been having intense pain in the ambulance and he was so distressed that he'd agreed to let Jake call 911.

When the Attending Physician walked into the waiting room after a long afternoon of waiting and teeth gnashing by the three of them, it was Jake who popped up from his seat first, asking urgently how Alex was. The physician, Dr. Dale Andrews smiled at them before speaking. It was as if, after many years of dealing with anxious family members, he'd learned that a smile, made it easier to communicate with them. "I'm Dr. Andrews," the doctor said as he offered his hand to Jake. He then shook hands with Aunt Lois and Lacey." Alex should be fine. We just want to keep him here for a day or two and run some standard tests to rule out anything serious such as a cardiac arrest. But from the tests we've done so far it looks like Alex's primary problem is hypertension. He's given me permission to speak to you about this so I have to let you know that his BP was alarmingly high. Without going into a lot of medical mumbo jumbo right now, I'll just tell you that we're getting it under control. He'll have to be on medication from now on. He should lose some weight of course, and take the usual dietary precautions."

"What about the severe pain he was having in the ambo, I mean the ambulance. He was in a lot of distress," Jake said, with a catch in his voice.

"We're checking everything but right now it appears that he was having a bad hypertensive episode and an anxiety attack. He's been stable with no pain since we gave him an IV and we had a good talk. But we'll know more tomorrow. He'll be moved to the cardiac unit tonight and we'll do more tests in the morning. If nothing untoward shows up, he'll be ready for discharge the day after that when all the test results are in."

Lacey noticed Jake's lip quiver and realized he was having difficulty controlling his emotions. *Jake has emotions, how about that? And, he's letting them out. Even more progress.* Lacey and Aunt Lois breathed a huge sigh of relief, both with tears in their eyes and obviously relieved.

"You can visit with him in about an hour," Dr. Andrews said. "Have a good night and I'll be talking to you tomorrow. Alex is a strong man who's in pretty good shape, but this has been a wakeup call for him. I think we should all realize that life is short and we should make the most of it. It looks like Alex has a lot of good years in front of him but it's always good to take stock of our lives. Well, I'll be going before I get on my soap box again, something which I'm always accused of doing." He smiled.

"Let's go to the cafeteria and have some coffee and maybe a bite to eat," Aunt Lois suggested to which Jake and Lacey readily agreed.

After grabbing a bite to eat they returned to Alex's room." Alex, you're looking so much better," Lois and Lacey said simultaneously.

"Too bloody right, mate. I reckoned you'd come a gutser by the looks of you in the ambo. But there's no keeping a bastard down."

Alex laughed and thanked Jake for having the good sense to take him to the hospital. He hadn't realized he had high blood pressure most likely because he never went to the doctor. "You go to the doctor and they always find something wrong with you; it's their job," Alex was fond of saying. "Now, all of you run along and let me catch some Z's or Zeds as you Aussies would say. Isn't there someone you have to take care of? Someone who won't be very happy right now being left out and not told what's going on? Run along now. I'll see you tomorrow."

Jake and Lacey left the room. Aunt Lois hung back for a second and gave Alex a kiss goodnight. "We'll talk later; get your rest now."

"That's my girl. I'll call you at our usual time," was the last thing Alex said before he drifted into a peaceful sleep.

CHAPTER THIRTY-TWO

The ride back to Lacey's house was spent in companionable silence with all of them tired from their recent scare.

"Jake, do you still want to see the pictures I chose for the article? I can give them to you and let you take them back home and look at them."

"Better yet, Lacey, why don't you get them, then we can go back to the house and look at them together? That would be after we've attended to His Majesty's needs, of course. He's got his dry kibble to eat, but by now he'll want his wet food, followed by a bit of whipped cream."

"Gee, he's not spoiled or anything is he?"

"You can blame Uncle Alex for that. You know I wouldn't bloody well give him any whipped cream or spoil him."

"Then don't give it to him, Jake. With Alex in the hospital, he'll never know you didn't give him his treat and TC certainly won't be able to tell. Then again he does have his ways of communicating."

"I couldn't do that. The cat expects his whipped cream. Uncle Alex has him into the habit, not me."

Lacey suppressed a grin. She was testing Jake and sure enough, as she had long suspected, Jake had a soft spot for the cat. She smiled inwardly thinking Jake was an even bigger pussycat than TC.

Aunt Lois brought the car to a halt in front of Lacey's home and waited. Lacey went into the house and fetched the photos. Ignoring their protestations that they would walk back to Jake's house, Aunt Lois drove them instead, and then bid them a good evening. They had barely walked in the door when TC came running down the hallway, stopping to look behind them and then scratching at the door. "No, Boofhead. Alex isn't here. He'll be home tomorrow and he's fine. No worries mate. Let's go in the kitchen and get your tucker."

Lacey was surprised at what Jake did next. He picked TC up and carried him to the kitchen. TC looked back at Lacey over Jake's shoulder. Nobody could convince her that he didn't have a self-satisfied look on his face. She was a wakeup to that cat.

Once they were all settled in the living room, they perused the photos. Jake agreed that Lacey had selected the most flattering ones, even commenting on how beautiful she looked.

Lacey felt her cheeks flush. This was promising. Jake was actually being nice, not only to TC but to her.

Jake went into the kitchen and came back out with a bottle of wine. After he poured them each a glass, he sat on the sofa. Lacey noticed that this time he sat much closer to her. He toasted her, then placed his glass on the table. He took Lacey's glass from her hand and placed it next to his.

He looked at her intently with those incredible

baby blue eyes, and then placed his index finger under her chin, and lifted it up. When she didn't object, he placed his arm around the back of her neck and kissed her with a soft, short kiss. He then gathered her in his arms and gave her a long, deep kiss. She wound her arms around his shoulders and kissed him back with a fervor that surprised even her.

There's nothing that can compare to that first kiss, that first blush of new love; that thrill, that excitement. There's nothing like that time-stopping moment when nothing else matters but *the kiss*. Lacey didn't want this kiss to ever end. This was that moment in time that she'd never forget and knew that it could never be recaptured. There would, she hoped, be many more kisses and more intimacy. That first kiss was the most magical, that moment when you realize that the object of your desire also desires you and you never want that moment to end. You fuse it onto your brain and keep reliving it, hoping that each memory will permanently seal it, not allowing even one magical second of it to be lost.

One must come up for air though, Lacey mused. She gazed at him and ran her hands through his hair while feathering kisses on his cheek and then kissing him full on, on his beautiful, warm, full lips.

His breath was hot on her face. Lacey could feel his passion, his need for her as he pulled her closer and tighter to him. "I'm sorry, Lacey. I really am."

Lacey's heart skipped a beat and she held her breath. Why was he sorry? How could he kiss her with such passion and then apologize? Was he sorry it happened? She could feel tears beginning to well in her eyes.

"I've treated you so badly, teasing you mercilessly, trying to deny that you intrigued me. It's been so long since I've experienced such passion. I've been wracked with guilt, feeling disloyal to Shanna because of the strong feelings I have for you. But I have to face the fact that Shanna is gone and life is for the living. She loved me enough to want me to find happiness after her death. We discussed this, and decided that when one of us died, the other should go on living and try to find happiness. Like most couples, of course, we never thought it would happen to us." Jake sighed, "and now..."

Lacey's voice cracked as she asked, "and now, what, Jake?" She was fearful of his answer and thought she was going to be sick.

Jake took a deep breath and hesitated long enough to make Lacey know for sure that she was not only going to be sick but would also pass out. "And now, and now I have to come right out and say it." He took Lacey's hands in his and kissed them and murmured in a low voice, "And now, I think I love you."

"You what? Did I hear you right, Jake? Or is this more teasing, taking the Mickey out of me? Please! Be serious. Don't do this to me. I couldn't take it."

"Not the reaction I expected, Lacey Belle. But there, I've said it. It's out in the open and there's no taking it back. I really do think I'm falling in love with you. I'm so sorry I've treated you so badly. I know you like me. I don't know if you could ever love me. I bloody well hope so but I'll be happy if you just like me for now."

"Jake Anderson, I could knock your block off. You just put me through ten seconds of pure hell. I don't like you."

Jake smiled a broad smile from ear to ear. "You do like me, Lacey. I know you do."

Lacey threw her arms around Jake and kissed him hard. "What I'm trying to say, Jake, is that I don't like you, I love you! And, I'm not kidding, sometimes I don't like you. Seriously. Well, maybe I don't like you sometimes just a little bit but Jake, I do love you. I love you with all my heart. You took my breath away the very first time I saw you."

"In Aunt Lois's café. I felt a connection the instant I looked at you. I couldn't bring myself to act on it. I knew I'd feel disloyal to Shanna if I ever became involved with another woman. That's how quickly the thoughts fly through your brain, you know?"

"Yes, Jake, I do know, in an instant. Some people say there's such a thing as love at first sight. Perhaps lust at first sight might be more appropriate. All I know is that when I saw you, my stomach did a flip-flop. But it was more than that, somehow. It was more than your Greek god looks."

"What's that? Greek god? That's what you

thought when you first saw me? That's too bloody funny. That's a ripper! I've been called many things in my life but never a Greek god."

"Well, probably not to your face, Jake. But I know for certain that thought has been echoed by other women and before you ask I'm not telling. You'll probably revert to your Aussie wise-cracking ways and then I won't like you again."

Jake shook his head in amazement. He had no clever retort. "I don't want to tease you or say those things to you anymore. Well, I'm sure I'll slip from time to time because it is a lot of fun, but I'd rather say nice things to you, and kiss you, and make love to you. I'd like to hear you tell me how much you love me."

"I do enjoy our repartee, Jake, and I have to admit it gives me great satisfaction to give it right back. But one thing you'll hear from me a lot is how much I love you. I will never get tired of telling you that."

As they sat on the couch, they shared stories, giving each other glimpses into their past in an effort to understand their present.

Jake put his arm around Lacey and stretched his legs on the coffee table. He kissed her intermittently on the cheek while telling her about his love affair with Shanna. "I think I owe it to you, Lacey, to explain how I felt about Shanna, why it's been so bloody hard for me to open my heart to anyone else. If you don't want to hear about it, I'll understand."

Lacey took Jake's hand, lifted it to her lips and kissed his fingers. "I want to hear all about you and your past life and about Shanna. She was such an important part of your life. I don't want you to feel you can't talk about her. Please tell me."

Lacey laid her legs over Jake's lap and snuggled her face into his neck while he spoke of his life and loves. "I thought I was in love before I met Shanna. I had the usual experiences with puppy love while growing up, but that all paled in comparison when I discovered true adult love. We were happy together. I didn't know I could be that happy. I didn't think I deserved it because I was a drunk and was abusing drugs. No addict thinks they deserve happiness, and even though I didn't fit the definition of an addict, I still felt like one. But she stood by me and helped me kick my alcohol dependence. When she was killed by that drunk driver it devastated me. The man was drunk and he was also high on drugs. But it was the fact that he was drunk that got to me. I did do drugs, but knowing she was killed by someone who was drunk, drove it home for me. I made up my mind that I didn't want to be that person. I didn't want to be responsible for taking someone's life and causing them such horrific grief."

Lacey interlaced her fingers with Jake's and urged him to continue. She felt it was important for him to get it off his chest. "Go on, Jake. Take your time, if you need to. I'm here for you."

Jake smiled and ran his hands down Lacey's legs. He looked into her eyes before continuing. "I was attracted to you immediately and I can tell you I bloody well hated that. Then when you showed up here, I was even more aggravated. I didn't want to get to know you because of the strong attraction to you. I wanted to keep my distance because I was so bloody afraid if we connected, I might lose you, and I couldn't bear that. So I pushed you away, and like a damn boomerang, you kept returning.

"And I'm so glad I did, Jake."

"Not as glad as I am," Jake murmured. "And I reckon I lied to you. I don't think I love you. I know I do. That's fair dinkum. I'll never give you a chance to dislike me again, Lacey. At least I hope not but, remember what I am."

"Yes, you're an Australian. How could I forget?" They both laughed and then at the same moment grabbed each other and kissed deeply and lovingly. He then lay back on the couch and gently pulled her down to lie alongside him where he could hold her and caress her. She draped her left arm across his chest and playfully twined her fingers around his longish locks. She propped herself up on her right elbow while he dropped little kisses on the top of her head and then her forehead. She lifted her face up to his and eagerly met his mouth with hers.

They both knew where this was heading until suddenly Lacey yelped." Bloody hell, what was that?" Jake cried out as his eyes flew open and he found he was staring at? At Boofhead? Boofhead standing on Lacey's bum and then walking up her back meowing mournfully. "Lacey, are you okay?"

Lacey rolled off Jake's chest and reached her arm around to pet TC.

"Mrroww, mrroww," TC cried.

"I'm fine, he didn't hurt me. I just didn't expect to feel a huge sack of bricks land on my bum. TC, what's wrong? Are you hurt?" Lacey noted that even Jake seemed concerned. He showed no evidence of his usual annoyance with the cat but showed compassion.

"What's up, Boof? Let me take a look at you. Did you hurt your leg or something? Ahh, Lacey, you and Uncle Alex have *me* talking to the cat now. Not only that, I'm asking him questions. I must be daft."

"No, you're not daft, Jake. Something is wrong. I know it. TC knows it. Maybe we should call the hospital and see how Alex is doing. Maybe something happened."

By now, both Jake and Lacey were sitting up staring at the cat, as if waiting for him to suddenly start talking.

"Well, I have this premonition, you see…"

"Okay, we're being really silly now. I think if something had happened to Uncle Alex, the hospital would have called us. I know neither of us will rest until we're satisfied Uncle Alex is okay."

As Jake got up from the sofa to fetch the phone,

TC zipped past him and ran down the hallway to the front door, meowing all the way.

Just as Jake was about to call the hospital his cell phone rang. It was Uncle Alex. Turning to Lacey, Jake smiled and said "Hello, Uncle Alex. Is everything ok? Are you alright?"

"Jake, slow down, will you? I'm fine, but it's Lois." Jake asked Uncle Alex what was wrong with Aunt Lois. He'd already put him on speaker so he wouldn't have to remember everything to pass along to Lacey. "That's just it, Jake. I don't know if anything is wrong, or I'm just being a silly old man, but I've been calling her for the past ten minutes and she isn't answering her phone." Jake tried to reason that ten minutes was nothing to worry about. But Alex explained that he and Lois always spoke to each other at this time. Even though he had dozed off as she had left the room and they had just seen each other an hour or so before, they still had their standing phone call that neither of them ever missed.

"I'm going to drive to her place now, Uncle Alex." Lacey was motioning to Jake that she was going too. "Lacey is going with me. I'll call you as soon as we find out what's going on, if anything. Oh, and Jingles sends his love."

Lacey was touched once again by Jake's thoughtful remark to Alex. He was full of surprises. She was falling even more in love with him if that were possible.

Jake suggested they give Aunt Lois a call before

they leave the house. Lacey called but no answer. Now she was becoming just as concerned as Alex.

They hurried down the hall and were preceded by TC who was not going to be relegated to sitting in the house like any ordinary cat. No, he would go where he was needed.

CHAPTER THIRTY-THREE

It didn't take long to reach Aunt Lois's house since they all lived in rather close proximity to each other. On any other day, they would have walked there, but this was not any other day. TC had alerted them in his own way that something was wrong. How else to explain his sudden leap onto Lacey and his mournful crying at the same time that Alex was trying to reach Aunt Lois? No, there was definitely something wrong.

They arrived at Aunt Lois's house and discovered that her car was in the driveway and the lights were on in the house. Jake got out of the car and of course, TC was way ahead of him. He ran up to the front door before Lacey even had the chance to catch up. TC was standing on his hind legs and scratching furiously at the front door.

Jake knocked on the door, and also rang the bell. Standing on the porch Lacey looked through the window. She was glad there was no body sprawled on the floor. Yes, she chastised herself; she watched too many true crime shows on TV.

Lacey yelled out Aunt Lois's name and waited anxiously for her response. When there was none, Jake thought of calling the police. It was either that or breaking down her front door. Contrary to what they show on TV and in movies, kicking in a door is not that easy. But Jake had the muscles and strength to do it if necessary.

"TC, be quiet, please. Shhh. I think I hear

something inside. Jake, listen. Do you hear that? It sounds like voices, or one voice. I can't be sure. Or maybe it's the TV or radio."

Jake listened and also heard what sounded like a human voice, not the TV. "Wait here, Lacey. I'm going around back. Maybe she's in the kitchen and doesn't hear us, although I don't know how anyone couldn't hear Boofhead's wailing."

Jake ran around back and in no time, Lacey heard a crashing sound coming from the back of the house. A minute or so later, she saw Jake through the window, walking quickly from the kitchen area into the living room.

He opened the door and TC streaked into the house. Jake smiled at Lacey. "She'll be apples. No worries, but she is in a fair bit of pain."

"What happened?" Lacey asked Jake as she pushed her way into the house.

"Put simply, she fell down and couldn't get up. And I'm not being a smart-aleck either, Lacey."

"Well, did you at least call 911?" Lacey asked as she rushed into the kitchen to comfort Aunt Lois. TC was already ahead of her, and before Jake had time to answer, she was already in the kitchen.

"Purr, purr." Lacey could hear TC's lovely musical purring as she neared the kitchen. Aunt Lois lay prone on the floor letting out little whimpers of pain. TC was sitting next to her, licking her face, purring

and offering her the best comfort that he could.

Jake dialed 911 and then came into the kitchen to offer support. He told Aunt Lois that help was on the way. He didn't want to lift her, in case she had broken anything." Alex. Did you call Alex, Jake? Lacey, did you call him? I know he's worried because my phone has been ringing off the hook. I missed our nightly call."

By now, Lacey was sitting on the floor next to Aunt Lois, stroking her head, and offering words of comfort. She and TC were doing their best to make her feel better and Jake was taking care of business.

"Uncle Alex," Jake said, as Alex answered the phone. "Lois is okay—not great, but she's okay. You may have to move over and make room for her in that bed. She had a fall, and couldn't get up. Don't laugh. I know you were thinking the same thing."

Alex apparently uttered his agreement, causing Jake to comment, "Well, it seems that you and I are the only ones with such a wicked sense of humor. Lacey was not amused when I said the same bloody thing. Anyway, the ambo is on the way. She looks okay but she's experiencing some pain. I don't know if she broke anything. I think she can move, but she's afraid of doing any damage."

Lacey called out to Jake. "Tell Alex that Aunt Lois looks fine and she sends her love to him. Now, make sure you use those exact words, Jake. She sends her love. And, say it in English, in Seppo speak, not in your bloody Oz talk. I want to make sure he gets the message."

"Uncle Alex. Lois is not going to cark it, and I think Lacey thinks she's cracking on to you, but don't spit the dummy, she'll be Aces."

Lacey could hear Alex's booming laugh through the phone, accompanied by Jake's equally loud laughter. She wanted to knock his block off, but found herself caught up in the amusement. Because she didn't want to offend Aunt Lois, she stifled a laugh

Alex stopped laughing long enough to take stock of the situation. He told Jake how concerned he was about Lois. Jake told him, she'd be okay. Relief had flooded through him. Now that he could think clearly he asked about Jingles. "Never mind, Jake, you don't have to tell me. Jingles is right there next to Lois, isn't he?"

Jake smiled. "You're spot on about that, Uncle Alex. He's sitting next to her, and being a good little nurse. I didn't want to mention this until I knew that Aunt Lois was okay. He knew before we did, that something was off. Lacey and I were sitting on the sofa, when out of nowhere Boofhead ran into the room and jumped on Lacey. He began meowing very loud. It was quite different from his usual meow so we knew something was up."

"He's really something, Jake. I don't know how he knows these things but he does. He's a real treasure."

"Yep. The bugger is a real beaut, Uncle Alex. Lacey and I were getting ready to call you to see if you're okay. Then you rang and we put two and two together.

"I'll talk to you later, Uncle Alex. The ambo just got here. Don't worry; we've got it all under control."

TC was not at all happy when the paramedics shooed him off the gurney where he had deposited himself. He fully intended to stay with Aunt Lois on the ride to the hospital.

Lacey picked up TC, cuddling him, but wincing each time she heard Aunt Lois emit a cry of pain. TC tried to jump out of Lacey's arms but she held onto him a little tighter.

Jake squeezed Aunt Lois's hand and told her how relieved Alex was to find out she's okay.

"Lacey, I think I should take Boofhead home with me and you ride in the ambo to the hospital. After I've dropped him off, I'll meet you there and we'll get the good oil from the doctors. Sound good?"

"Sounds good to me, but a certain someone is not going to be very happy about being left out. You might want to give him some treats when you get home. I'll see you soon." Lacey handed TC to Jake and kissed him on the cheek.

Aunt Lois was being wheeled out of the kitchen. "Oh come on, sweetie, kiss him on the lips. You know you want to. Make me happy before I die." She must have noticed the horrified look on Lacey's and Jake's face. She gave a weak smile. "I was just kidding."

*****

Lacey hopped into the back of the ambulance. Jake drove home with TC sitting on the seat next to him. "I reckon the Seppo and Uncle Alex might be right about you, Boof. And, okay, those other people who seemed to recover from their illnesses because you were with them. Maybe they're right and you are some kind of special moggy. But don't tell Lacey I said that, or she'll be grinning like a shot fox."

****

"Ok Boof. We're home. Let's go into the kitchen, and you can bog into your tucker. That'll bloody well keep you occupied until I get back home. I've gotta nick off now, so behave yourself. Uncle Alex will be home tomorrow."

Jake was whistling as he walked out the door. He had told Lacey earlier why he'd denied himself any chance at happiness. Now being happy was his gift from Shanna, he'd said.

CHAPTER THIRTY-FOUR

Once Jake arrived at the hospital, he went straight to his Uncle Alex's room, only to find it empty. "Excuse me," Jake said to the comely nurse's aide who entered the room, "could you tell me where Mr. Kelly is?"

"I really don't know, but I'll be glad to help you look for him."

Jake wouldn't have known she was flirting had she not been so obvious about it. A seductive smile accompanied by the saucy placement of her hand on her hip gave it away. Jake muttered under his breath, *"Maybe I am a Greek god. Bloody oath."*

Jake excused himself and headed out of the room. He had one of those moments when you *feel* someone's looking at you. He didn't bother to turn around, but simply walked to the nurses' station where he inquired about his Uncle Alex.

"Are you Mr. Anderson?" the male nurse asked. His name badge identified him as Scott, Charge Nurse.

"I'm Jake Anderson, Alex Kelly's nephew, and he's not in his room. I suspect I might know where he is though. Has Lois Lindsey been admitted?"

"She sure has. Your Uncle Alex told us to be on the lookout for you. He's visiting Mrs. Lindsey now. She has another visitor—Lacey, I believe she said her name was. They're laughing and having a good time. That's always a good sign." Scott grinned. "Mrs.

Lindsey, excuse me, Aunt Lois, as she insists we call her, took a hard fall, flat on her back, and she can't move without experiencing pain.

"They'll be taking her in for x-rays pretty soon to rule out any possible fracture, or fractures. But, in my opinion, I don't think Dr. Andrews will find any.

Anyway, we'll have to wait and see what the x-rays show. She's in Room 302. You can go in there now before they take her down for them."

Jake thanked Scott and walked quickly down the hall. It wasn't difficult to locate the room; he merely followed the boisterous laughter of his Uncle Alex.

"Jake!" three voices sang out in unison. Aunt Lois beckoned Jake to her side. She thanked him for helping her and gave him a big kiss. "Where's my nurse?" Aunt Lois said, with a mischievous grin on her face.

Thinking the pain pills were causing her a bit of brain fog, Jake explained that there was a nurse in her room. Lacey added, "She's referring to her own private nurse, Jingles.

Alex was sitting on the bed; holding Lois's hand. Once again, he broke out into raucous laughter. He was well known throughout Ascot Vale for his great sense of humor, and he never disappointed.

Within minutes, two orderlies came into the room to wheel Aunt Lois down to x-ray. "I'll see you soon, love," Alex whispered tenderly.

Alex sat on a chair, with his arms crossed over his chest, deep in thought.

"I smell wood burning, Uncle Alex." Jake chuckled. "I hope you're not worried about Aunt Lois. She'll be apples in no time."

"It's not that," Alex said, looking up at them. "We've got a wee problem, and I can't fix it without help from both of you. Lacey, I know you'll jump right on it, but Jake..."

Jake raised his arms wide in front of him. "What is it you want me to do? Just say it and I'll bloody well do it. You know it. Anything for Aunt Lois, and for you. As long as it doesn't involve me taking care of Boofhead for any length of time." Before Alex could protest, Jake laughed and said of course, he'd take care of the cat. He added unnecessarily, "Boofhead's not so bad, after all.

With a sly grin on his face, Jake turned his attention to Lacey. "I'll admit I did recover from my wounds much quicker than I expected. I'm not sure what he did but I do think now he might have done something. With him next to me I had much less pain. Okay, are you happy now? Don't get all up yourself, Lacey. I may be a bit stubborn but I'm not a drongo."

Lacey surprised Jake by putting her arms around him and kissing him. "There now, that wasn't so hard to say, was it?" Jake grinned that beautiful Greek god grin of his, then turned his attention to his Uncle Alex. He asked him what he wanted Jake to do.

With a thoughtful look, Alex asked them if they would be able to take over the annual Thanksgiving Dinner for Lois. He explained that all the arrangements had been made, and Lois would not be able to do any of the work. "As you know, Jake, this annual dinner is a big deal. A lot of people depend on us. Some have no family to share the holiday with. I'd hate to disappoint them."

Jake looked at Lacey and was gratified to see the eager look on her face. "No worries, Uncle Alex. It's a goer," he answered for both of them.

"Thank you both. I knew I could depend on you," Alex said with apparent heartfelt gratitude.

"We'll take care of everything and you take care of Aunt Lois," Jake said. "And don't forget to take Boofhead to her house, once she gets discharged from here."

Alex shook both their hands, hugged Lacey, and then Jake. He wiped a tear away with the back of his hand. "I'll tell Lois as soon as she gets back from the x-rays, and speaking of that, where is she? How long does it take to x-ray somebody's back? It's not like she's a giraffe or anything."

Jake and Lacey laughed, evoking a laugh from Alex too. "You know," Lacey said, "it's too bad we can't smuggle TC in here. That would speed up her healing for sure. I'm pleased to know that we can *all* vouch for that." Lacey looked pointedly at Jake, and he responded by hugging her affectionately.

Alex beamed. "It does my heart good to see the two of you hugging instead of slinging off at each other." Just then, Aunt Lois was wheeled back into the room; this time accompanied by Scott, the Charge Nurse, who was wearing a broad smile.

The staff must have learned that smile technique from Dr. Dale Andrews, Lacey mused. "So, how is the patient, Scott?"

"Hale and hearty, I'd say. Nothing broken. Though she'll be a pretty shade of purple tomorrow. The soreness has already started. I understand she tripped on a throw rug and took quite a nasty fall. It'd be good to get rid of it before she comes home. Dr. Andrews will be back to check on her and give her some prescriptions. The most important prescription for right now is rest, of course."

"Actually, Scott, I'm inclined to disagree," Lacey said demurely.

"What? You're disagreeing with me? The greatest Charge Nurse on the planet? In the whole universe, I'd say." Scott had a great sense of humor.

"I'm sure you are the very best, Scott. But we have an even better nurse *and* he makes house calls, "Lacey said with a wry look on her face.

"Well, he must be good. Very good." Scott grinned.

Come to think of it, she thought; Dr. Dale Andrews was quite a looker too. She just hoped their talents were as extraordinary as their looks.

"Actually, the nurse I'm referring to is—are you ready for this? A cat! And, he's not just any ordinary cat. He helps people heal, whether they've got a common cold, broken bones, or whatever. Okay, I know you think I'm crazy but this cat is seriously special." She looked to Jake for confirmation and he shook his head in the affirmative but without vocalizing his agreement with her. Apparently, he wasn't ready to admit that.

"No, I don't think you're crazy at all. I've heard about this cat. Really, I have. I'm new to this area, but my uncle is Dr. James. His wife, my Aunt Grace, had a stray cat visit them while she was recuperating from pneumonia. His name's Hippocrates, right?"

Lacey replied, "No, his name is Jingles."

A confused look came over Scott's face. "Surely there can't be two such cats in a small town like this. I thought for sure you were talking about Hippocrates."

It was Jake's turn to jump in the conversation. "That's exactly who we're talking about, mate."

Scott arched his brows in surprise.

"You've heard about cats having nine lives? Well, this cat has nine names. Everyone he's helped has given him a special name. His companion is Alex Kelly" Jake said pointing to his Uncle Alex, "and the cat's real name is Jingles. Lacey, here, calls him TC for

Tuxedo Cat, and others in town call him different names. I call him Boofhead."

"Aha!" Scott exclaimed." Aussie or Kiwi?"

"Aussie," Jake replied amiably. "From Tasmania. Most people guess Sydney or Melbourne, but there are other beautiful places in Oz and Tasmania is one of the very best."

Scott told them about his experience in Australia." After I finished my residency, I treated myself to a trip to Oz, New Zealand and the Fiji Islands. Did a lot of surfing had a great time, and met some of the most wonderful people in the world. That's also where I heard the term, *Boofhead*. From everything I've heard about this cat, he really can't be called a boofhead. He sounds bloody smart to me." Scott said as though pleased to be speaking to an Aussie again, and engaging in a bit of Aussie lingo. "Didn't get the chance to visit Tassie, as you call it, right?"

Jake responded, "Too bloody right, mate. The next time you go to Oz, be sure to visit Tassie. Be prepared for rugged beauty and lovely little towns and of course, some bloody wonderful people."

A floor nurse came up to Scott at that moment. Clipboard in hand, she told him she needed to talk to him about a patient. Scott reluctantly excused himself and wished them all well.

CHAPTER THIRTY-FIVE

Jake and Lacey left the hospital, and Jake headed back to his house. Lacey realized how exhausted she was. She stole a look at Jake and felt he looked a bit frazzled too.

"Would you mind if you took me home instead, Jake? I'm really beat. I need to be on top of my game to get everything ready for Thursday's Thanksgiving Dinner. We both have a lot to do."

Sighing, Jake said, "You're right, my love. I didn't want to be the one to say it, because if it were up to me I'd throw caution to the wind and deal with being tired tomorrow."

Jake pulled into Lacey's driveway, brought the car to a stop, then kissed her. Locked in his embrace, Lacey felt he wanted to change her mind. Life was short, carpe diem.

The next morning, Lacey awoke to find Jake's head propped on one hand, his eyes bored into hers, while his other hand roamed through her tousled hair. Caressing Lacey, he kissed her delicately on the neck. "Wakey, wakey, sweetheart," he said, and kissed her deeply. When he kissed her again, she responded enthusiastically. "Did you sleep well, love?" Jake asked with a sly smile on his face. "I know I bloody well did."

"I had a wonderful night, and I slept like a baby. You're a very persuasive man. I'm so happy about that. I love you, Jake Anderson."

"I'll settle for half as much as I love you. That would be more than enough, Lacey. You've brought such happiness into my life; something I never thought would happen to me again."

"I feel the same way, Jake. I've never met a man like you in my life. I love you."

"Umm, love you too, Lacey Belle," Jake murmured as he kissed her on the neck. "Hey, there's something I've wanted to ask you. How did you get the name Lacey Belle? I love it. It's so musical, just like your voice."

Lacey laughed, thinking Jake's words were like music to *her* ears. "Funny you should say that, Jake. My mother said that I didn't cry like most babies. My crying reminded her of a little tinkling bell. She and my dad had already decided to call me Lacey. When the time came to sign the papers, they added the name Belle, and Bob's your uncle." She was really cottoning on to these Australian expressions.

"And, your laugh is still musical, my little Seppo. My little Seppo Belle. Hey, I'm hungry."

"What?" Lacey said somewhat shocked.

"I'm sorry, Lacey. Sometimes, I just say whatever pops into my head. And, it just popped into my head that I'm hungry. So, do you have any Weetbix and Vegemite? Also I'd like a couple of googies. Think you can handle that, love?"

"Jake, what will I do with you? I've never heard

of Weetbix and don't have a clue what a googie is. But, I have heard of Vegemite and from everything I've heard, it's awful. So the answer to your question is a resounding no."

"I'll give you a hint, love. Googies come from chooks. Got it now?"

Lacey took a moment to think like an Aussie which was getting easier. She still couldn't completely understand them. "Okay. It's morning, so I'm assuming googies is a brekkie food. How am I doing?"

"Aces, so far. You called it brekkie and not breakfast. You're a quick learner, my little Seppo."

"Sooo, if it's a breakfast food, and chook sounds very close to chick, then I'm guessing a chook is a chicken. Therefore googies must be eggs, although I don't see any rhyme or reason for it, but it's Australian, what can I say?"

"My oath, you'll be an Aussie yet. Indeed, a chook is a chicken, and they lay googies. You can call them googie eggs if you'd like. You're an amazing woman, Lacey Belle Robertson. Did I tell you I love you?"

"No, tell me again. I can't hear it enough." Lacey kissed Jake and smiled at him. He was truly the most remarkable man she'd ever met and she couldn't believe he'd given his heart to her. Part of his heart, she knew, would always belong to Shanna and she accepted that with no reservation. It just showed what a good, loving and faithful man he was.

"Never mind. We'll get something at Aunt Lois's café, but first I have to get home and take care of Boofhead. He'll probably have gobbled up all his tucker by now and will be whinging for his wet food. He won't be one bit happy that I didn't come home last night. Tell you what, I'll go home and take care of His Royal Highness, get a shower, and then come back to get you. I'll call Marianne and ask her to open the place up and then we'll go there and do whatever it is that we have to do. The show must go on, right?" Jake kissed Lacey goodbye and headed to his car.

CHAPTER THIRTY-SIX

Jingles was not happy and he let Jake know so in no uncertain terms when he finally walked in the front door. There, Jake was met with loud, insistent, raucous noises. There would not be one purr forthcoming until Jake did his penance and took care of him. He might even sniff the food and then put his head up and airily walk away in disgust. This is an act sure to tick off even the most ardent cat lover and especially a non-cat lover.

"Look, Boof, eat it or not, I can't hang around. Lacey and I have business to take care of at Aunt Lois's."

At the mention of Aunt Lois's name, Jingles's ears perked up. He turned around and walked back to Jake, cocking his head to one side.

"You little beauty, you really do know what people are saying, don't you? Well, I'll be buggered. Okay, here's the ridgy-didge, Aunt Lois is fine, and Uncle Alex is fine. In fact, I'll be bringing him home today but right now I've gotta go, mate. There's your food so bog in and we'll be back later."

Jake hastened down the hall, opened the door and tripped over TC who had bolted ahead of him and out the door. Jake wasn't going anywhere without him.

"When would they learn?"

"Okay, let's not play silly buggers. You can come along. I know Lacey will be happy to see you."

"Purr, purr."

Jake and Boofhead arrived at Lacey's and found her waiting outside her front door. She was anxious to get to the café and was absolutely delighted to find TC sitting in the front seat. Lacey maneuvered her way onto the seat and once she was settled, TC jumped on her lap. The thought crossed her mind again: *Happiness, thy name is cat.*

Jake leaned across the seat and kissed Lacey softly while Boofhead pressed his head against Jake's chest. "G'day, love. His nibs here wasn't about to let me go anywhere without him and when I said I was picking you up, he insisted on coming along. And, by insisting I mean he ran down the hall and out the front door. The cat's bloody mad about you."

When they reached the café they were pleased to see that Marianne had it open and the coffee brewing. The kitchen staff was there and preparing the food for the day. Marianne was busy making a sign to be placed on the front door, reminding the customers that they would be closing at 5 p. m. They'd need the time in order to prepare for the annual Thanksgiving Day Dinner tomorrow.

As the customers began coming in, Jake and Lacey pitched in, taking orders, pouring coffee and helping the cooks with whatever was needed. Once the café was closed for the evening, they'd decorate the place and set out all the dinnerware and silverware and set up the buffet table.

Then when that was all taken care of they'd begin

prepping all the veggies, making the dressing and all the trimmings and baking the pies. By this time it would be about midnight. Aunt Lois always began serving the meal at 11:00 a. m., so they had plenty of time to get everything ready and then take a catnap before opening.

TC was not allowed in the kitchen of course, the reasons for which he most definitely did not understand. So he naturally serenaded them with his caterwauling. Finally, having exhausted himself, he fell asleep on the floor outside the kitchen door. He gave one last loud, *mrroww* though before giving in to the inevitable. *Happiness, thy name was most definitely not cat tonight!*

CHAPTER THIRTY-SEVEN

Jake and Lacey awoke early Thanksgiving morning after having spent several hours cat-napping on a cot. Aunt Lois kept the cot in the back of the kitchen for her staff that might need a small break during a long shift.

"I don't know how she does it. I'm exhausted already and I'm a lot younger than she is. But we'll get through it won't we?" Lacey mumbled.

"I think I can get through anything, if you're with me." Jake took her in his arms and held her tightly by the waist. Lacey wrapped her arms around Jake's neck and kissed him until she thought she'd lose her breath.

"I could stand here all day with you, Jake, but I guess it's time for you to pick up Alex. I know he won't want to leave Aunt Lois but he needs to get home and get some rest. TC will be glad to spend time with him because he's not a very happy cat right now."

"Well, he should be happy. I'm sure he got more sleep than we did last night," Jake said, beaming.

"Meow, meow, meow, purr, purr." TC was awake and was raring to go. Where he was going to didn't matter, he just wanted to be with his people. It seemed he'd forgiven them for banishing him to the dining room.

"Okay, Boof, pull your head in. I'm coming." Jake opened the kitchen door and TC zoomed into the kitchen. He made a dash for Lacey who promptly picked him up for a cuddle. "Let's go home. Then, I've got to pick up Uncle Alex and bring him back to the house. And then, it's back here again."

She never thought she'd see the day when Jake would be talking to TC and actually enjoying it. Now she wondered what other surprises were hidden beneath that Adonis-like exterior.

Lacey was busy boiling mounds of potatoes to make fresh mashed potatoes and sweet potatoes. The cranberry sauce was made, both jellied and with whole cranberries. Fresh loaves of handmade bread were ready to be taken out of the ovens along with the fruit pies. The salad ingredients were chilling in the refrigerator waiting to be set out on the buffet table. She knew Aunt Lois would be pleased.

Jake had showered, shaved, and changed into a very flattering teal shirt, which set his eyes off beautifully. He complemented the shirt with a nice pair of black denim form-fitting jeans. Around his neck, he wore a simple but nice silver chain. He was a vision to behold, understated and masculine. There was also a faint scent of musk cologne.

While Jake was taking care of things at the café it was Lacey's turn to go home and shower. She wanted him to appreciate her as much as she appreciated looking at him.

CHAPTER THIRTY-EIGHT

When Lacey was ready to leave the house her cell rang. She was happy to hear that it was Summer. They couldn't talk long because Lacey had to get back to the café. But in their typical fashion they managed to blurt out a month's worth of news in about five minutes. Summer and Bradley were coming up for a Christmas visit and they were getting married. Summer wanted Lacey to be her Maid of Honor. Lacey regaled Summer with her news about Jake. And so, it went.

An hour later, Lacey was back at the café, all tarted up as Jake commented when he looked at her. "Don't take offense, Lacey, my love." Lacey had worn her prettiest emerald green dress that was cut two to three inches above her knees and showed off her long, slim legs. She always felt desirable when she wore this dress. It was an oldie but goodie that had served her well through the years. The fact that Jake had never seen it was a plus.

"That dress is a beaut color, and I've gotta say it really shows off your ham and eggs."

"Lacey blurted, "It doesn't take an Aussie to know what that means, Jake, at least I think not. Thank you for the compliment, on my legs, right? You didn't mean something else, I hope?"

"Come here, gorgeous. Of course, I meant your legs but every part of you looks gorgeous. It's a shame to throw an apron over that package but we've gotta think of the customers. The men won't be able to eat if their mouths are hanging open looking at your Ginger Meggs."

"Oh, so ham and eggs are legs and now you're talking about something else entirely, aren't you? It's rude, isn't it?"

"Nope, still talking about your legs, Lacey." Jake smiled and grabbed her by the waist. "Give your Greek god a kiss. You're not an Aussie yet, but we'll work on that."

Lacey gave Jake a look of pure exasperation. No sooner did she think she had a handle on Strine, when Jake would confuse her again.

She reluctantly took off her heels and replaced them with a pair of sturdy sneaks. She didn't want to fall on any of her customers although some of them probably wouldn't mind. But wearing the heels, if only briefly, had garnered the desired effect from Jake.

Lacey heard shouts of "Hello, Alex and hello, Jingles," coming from the dining room. She was delighted and hurried out of the kitchen to greet them. She was too late to get Alex's undivided attention, though. All eyes seemed to be on Jingles. The little bugger was soaking up the attention, dancing around, rubbing his head against everyone. He was purring and even touching certain people's faces with his paws. They must have been his former patients, Lacey thought, judging by the special attention he was giving them. He knew how to work the room.

No one complained that he was standing on one of the tables. Wouldn't do them any good to complain anyway because Jingles was not going to allow anyone to steal him away from the spotlight - from his well-deserved spotlight he was surely thinking.

"Lacey was born to be a hostess," Jake muttered to no one in particular. She treats everyone as though they're family and pays special attention to those customers who came in alone. They didn't remain alone for long. Lacey made sure all tables were filled with friends and strangers together. She introduced herself and had a way of getting everyone to introduce themselves. Before long the room was filled with chatter and laughter. The customers made new friends and had a filling dinner and a fulfilling time.

After all the customers had left, Jake took Alex and Jingles home. He then hurried back to the café to get the cleanup started. He arrived in the kitchen to find Lacey stretched out on the cot and Marianne and the cooks busy cleaning up.

"Well, who's the bludger now?" Jake grinned as he walked over to Lacey. Marianne chimed in, "Aww, let her rest, Jake. She's worked hard all day and just needed a few minutes to relax. I insisted she lie down until you arrived back here."

Lacey began to sit up until Jake placed his hands on her shoulders and gently pushed her back down. "You just lie here and close your eyes and dream of your Greek god. That would be me."

Lacey smiled and didn't fight the veil of sleep that

was enveloping her conscious mind. She thought she thanked Jake but couldn't be certain if she'd said it or thought it.

"I never thought you'd be one to chuck a sickie," Lacey heard someone saying as she began to come to. When she opened her eyes and the brain fog had cleared, she realized it was Jake, her handsome Greek god.

"How long have I been asleep? And, what do you mean about chucking a sickie? I'm not sick."

"No, you're not sick," Jake interrupted. But you're pretending to be sick to get out of work, ergo chucking a sickie."

"Jake Anderson, you know that's not true! I don't know why I got so tired. All I wanted to do was sleep."

Jake kissed Lacey gently and softly on the lips and pulled her up off the cot. He held her close to him as she nuzzled against him. "Looks like all the work's been done. I feel awful about that."

"No worries. You worked harder than any three people last night and today. Let's close up and go back to my place; that is, if you're up to it. Uncle Alex will still be up and I know he'll want to see you. Boofhead will too. You don't have to stay long. I'll take you home, after I pack my toothbrush," Jake murmured with a sly expression.

CHAPTER THIRTY-NINE

Lacey had a nice visit with Alex, and Jingles too, of course.

Alex told her that Lois would be discharged from the hospital tomorrow. He'd already let her know that the Thanksgiving Dinner went off without a hitch. "She told me she never doubted it for a minute and she'll be eternally grateful to both of you. Oh, and Jingles, too, of course, for providing the entertainment. She'll give you a call tomorrow, she said, to thank you in person. And I can't thank you both enough, either."

"Purr, purr." TC rubbed against Lacey's legs and even against Jake's. Then he ran back down the hall to Alex, jumped on his lap and licked Alex's face before settling down for a good cat nap.

Jake and Lacey decided to walk back to her house instead of driving. It was a beautiful night, cold but not bone-chilling cold. It was the kind of cold that was meant for walking in and then snuggling up in front of a fire.

Lacey awoke to the smell of freshly brewed coffee on a serving tray. It was accompanied by a cup of fresh orange juice and a slice of toast with something unpleasant, actually smelly on it when she lifted it to her nose.

"Go on, have a go, Lacey. You'll like it, or not. Most likely not, but you can't be a real Aussie unless you've had some Vegemite."

"But, I don't have any Vegemite here."

"I put a jar in my coat pocket when we left the house. I make sure I have a supply of it. Uncle Alex won't eat it so I won't be offended if you won't eat it either. It's an acquired taste."

"Just like an Aussie is." Lacey giggled, took a gulp of the orange juice and then picked up the toast and brought it to her mouth. "Yuck! You actually eat this horrible stuff?" Lacey said as she tried to discreetly deposit the offending morsel in the paper napkin.

Jake took the rest of the toast from her hand, bit off a large chunk and sighed, "Ahh, you can't beat Vegemite. You Seppos don't know what you're missing."

"Well, I do now, Jake, and I'll be glad to be missing it for the rest of my life. It's so, so bitter. Even the worst tasting medicine doesn't taste that bad. You Aussies truly are weird. Don't you ever make any disparaging remarks about us Seppos again! We'd never eat anything so awful. Yuck and double yuck."

"Well, good, I'm glad you don't like it; that means there's more for me. You can stick to your Limburger cheese. Now, that's smelly and bloody awful tasting."

"That's not American, Jake. It's German, but *they* do eat a lot of it in America, I guess. I said *they,* because I sure wouldn't eat it. I think we've got a tie between Vegemite and Limburger."

"So, let's get you some real brekkie then, Lacey. We'll decide what to do for the rest of the day, after we help Uncle Alex bring Aunt Lois home from the hospital. Marianne said she'd run the café today. It's all taken care of. So we have this arvo to do whatever we want."

"We have right now to do whatever we want, Jake," Lacey murmured as she lay back on the bed, pulling Jake down with her. He grasped her head in his hands, and ran his fingers through her hair. He leaned over her, kissing her, pashing her, and loving her.

Lacy slowly floated down from her cloud. Seemingly, neither wanting their union to end. On their way to the hospital, they picked up Uncle Alex.

All were greeted enthusiastically by Jingles once they settled in the house. Aunt Lois sat down on the sofa and accepted the glass of mulled cider that Alex had poured for her.

Aunt Lois thanked them all profusely for coming to the rescue and saving Thanksgiving Dinner. TC jumped on her lap and did his little dance nearly causing her to spill her drink. "Yes, and you helped too, Jingles. I understand you were very entertaining. You're a great little ambassador for the café. But I've already told you this several times today. You can never get enough praise, can you, you little ham?"

TC trilled contentedly with his tail held high and his eyes shining. A large amount of drool suddenly puddled on Aunt Lois's lap. TC was most definitely happy.

Lacey and Jake excused themselves while Jingles was doing his happy dance on Aunt Lois's lap and purring. They'd almost made it out the door when Jingles raced down the hallway and came to a sudden halt in front of them. He stood on his hind legs and pawed Lacey's legs and then Jake's. He gave a happy meow. Then as soon as he'd appeared there, he'd disappeared, and was right back on Aunt Lois's lap. Good little nurse that he is he didn't want to leave her side for long. He knew where he was needed and never shirked his duties. As Jake might say, he's as cunning as a dunny rat.

"Well, the chariot's at your disposal, Lacey Belle; your wish is my command. Where would you like to go?"

CHAPTER FORTY

An hour later, Jake and Lacey were sitting in the parking lot of the Last Chance Animal Rescue site. Lacey had read about it online and had seen the pictures. She was deliriously happy. She would finally be able to rescue a dog and cat.

When Jake opened his car door, Lacey was suddenly seized with an overwhelming feeling of sadness. She couldn't do it, she explained to Jake. She hated decisions and had been doing fairly well making them lately, but she knew this was one decision she could not make. She knew if she walked in that building, she'd walk out with every animal in there. It broke her heart that she couldn't rescue them all.

Jake understood when she explained her feelings to him. "Look, we can't rescue every needy animal. You know that. But, what we can do is at least give two of them a great home. Tell you what, you sit here and I'll go in and look around. Then before you know it, Bob's your uncle. You'll have a dog and cat."

Lacey smiled through her tears. He was truly a wonderful, kind man. The fact that he was drop dead gorgeous was merely the icing on the cake. "If they have any..."

"Yes, Lacey, hush. I know what you're going to say. If they have any older animals in need of a good home, they're the ones I'll look at. Now, let me go before I change my bloody mind. It bothers me too, you know."

Lacey sat in the car for what seemed like an hour. What could be taking him so long, she wondered? She wanted to go in and get him but knew that she couldn't. A minute later, she saw him come through the doors holding two leashes, not one, but two. At the end of each was a dog; each one swishing his tail happily and walking by Jake's side.

Walking alongside Jake was a shelter employee holding a cat carrier. Lacey could hear the meowing even with the car windows up. She couldn't wait to see her new family members. Tears rolled down her cheeks; she felt a mixture of happiness and sadness, but she'd have to deal with that. One way she could assuage her guilt was to donate money, and perhaps foster some animals. Who was she kidding, she mused. Any fostered animal under her care would never leave; she wouldn't let them. But she could help in other ways and she knew she would.

"Well, meet some new bludgers, Lacey. This one's an Australian shepherd. He's about 7, or 8, they reckon. This shy one is an Australian cattle dog, about the same age give or take a year. Jake took the cat carrier from the shelter employee. And this," Jake said, after handing the leashes to Lacey, "is Hoppy. She has four legs but only three feet. Nobody knows how she lost her foot; she was just dropped off at the shelter one night. They reckon she's about 8, or 9."

Lacey noticed that Jake's beautiful blue eyes looked moist. She didn't want to stare and embarrass him but it did her heart good to see a man so vulnerable when it came to animals. Her heart was filled with love for this wonderful, kind man.

"Before you accuse me of picking out these dogs because they're Australian, you'd be wrong. Well, half wrong. The Australian shepherd is not really Australian. They're actually Seppos! How'd ya like that? And this one here, the cattle dog, is what we call a blue heeler. Now she is indeed an Aussie dog. So, did I do right?"

"Jake, you bloody well did right. Righter than right. Just perfect. Two old dogs and one old three-footed cat. Now I ask you who wouldn't want such a group?" Lacey was experiencing such happiness, in between wiping dog drool off her face.

Jake opened the cat carrier and let the cat out. The cat moved quietly and softly out of the cage, and was immediately knocked over by the Australian shepherd. Much to Jake and Lacey's delight, the cat was not fazed at all.

"So, Jake. I think we'll have our hands full here. I think we should give them a day or two before giving them a name, don't you?"

Jake gave her a surprised look. "Well, they already have a name and after all these years, don't you think it might be a bit confusing to change their names now? It doesn't matter about Hoppy, I'm sure. She's a cat. Doesn't matter to her what you call her; just like Jingles. Look how many names he has, and he tends to ignore all of them, most of the time."

"Okay, so what are their names? I hope I like

them. But it doesn't really matter, does it? That's not what's important."

"Too right, Lacey. The important thing is that they've got a forever home now. See if you can guess this one's name," Jake said, pointing to the cattle dog, the blue heeler."

"Easy peasey, Jake. His name is Bluey. I'm sure of it. Oh wait, I'm assuming he was owned by an Aussie, but he probably wasn't, being here in America. So, I give up. What's his name?"

"Don't laugh. His previous owner, excuse me, his previous companion, had a good sense of humor. His name is *Moo*. Too bloody funny, if you ask me. Now, what's this girl's name, the Aussie shepherd?"

Lacey giggled so hard she almost choked. "I don't have a clue. Ozzie? I don't know."

"You silly bugger. Ozzie! How silly, although come to think of it, that's not a bad name. But her name's Tillie, it's short for Matilda." Jake laughed as hard as Lacey was laughing. "Matilda, because she's an Australian shepherd, as in Waltzing Matilda."

"I get it, I get it. So I've got Moo, Tillie, and Hoppy. Bloody perfect! Let's get them back to my place so we can get them settled in."

"Bloody well works for me." Jake managed to sneak a kiss in between the two dogs competing for attention. Hoppy had eased her way back into the carrier and was lying quietly.

"Jake, I have another favor to ask of you. It occurs to me now that I really do need my own car. Will you take me out tomorrow to find one? Not a new car, of course, not with these two hooligans. I think a nice 4-wheel drive or All Wheel Drive as I understand they're called would be good. If I could get one second-hand that would be great. I just try to buy American whenever possible and I don't want to buy a new car right off the lot. I've done my due diligence and I know it doesn't pay to do that."

"A Seppo car, eh? Figures. But whatever you desire, I'll make it a priority to find you one. In the meantime we'll use this car. I certainly don't mind. Uncle Alex won't mind either. The car will probably cost you big bikkies, but if you need help in that department I'll shout. And before you protest, Lacey, I've got the big bikkies; I'm not skiting about that, please don't get me wrong. I just want you to know that I'm not hurting for money and what good is money if you can't use it to help people?"

"You're the best thing that has ever happened to me, Jake. I love you. And, I love you for so many reasons, but I don't love you for your money. I know you know that. I'm not hurting either, thanks to two inheritances. I certainly couldn't support myself on my freelancing jobs, but they make me feel good, knowing that others appreciate my writing."

Before they knew it, they'd arrived at Lacey's manse. The dogs seemed to know that they were home. As soon as Lacey opened the front doors, they both barreled inside. "I forgot to tell you, Lacey.

They're very active dogs. It's in their breed.

"We'll have to play Frisbee with them and give them chores to do. They aren't the kind of dogs to just sit around. They need to be able to run; they need a lot of exercise every day! How would you feel about adding a fenced in area for them? Strewth. It would have to be a big area, at least an acre. Bloody hell, who's the boofhead now? I should have discussed this with you before picking these two. I'll build the fence, Lacey and I'll pay for it."

"I'll make a deal with you, Jake. I'll pay for it and pay you for your services too if you'll build the fence. In the meantime I'll keep an eye on them and won't let them run on their own. It'll be good exercise for me, too."

"Let's seal that with a kiss, as long as you get the silly notion out of your head that you'll pay me. I love you more than I ever thought could be possible." Jake kissed Lacey deeply and held her in his arms, hugging her, not wanting to ever let her go. A sudden meow reminded them that Hoppy wanted out of the carrier.

"Bloody sorry, Hoppy. Here, let's get you out of there and come see your new home; then some tucker, okay?"

Later that night, after Moo and Tillie had exhausted themselves and had run Jake and Lacey ragged they all relaxed in the great room. Lacey had fed them earlier. They looked like the perfect family. Hoppy chose to lie on the back of the sofa between Jake and Lacey. Moo and Tillie laid on the floor at their feet, completely relaxed and snoring. "TC should be here, Jake. I know he's Alex's cat, but I hope he'll be able to visit and get to know the new family."

After Jake squeezed Lacey's shoulder, he ran his hand down her arm, stroking her as one would a cat. The look on his face was one of unbridled happiness." Boofhead will be here quite often, I can guarantee you that. You know he won't let us exclude him from anything."

Jake called Uncle Alex and told him he'd be home within the hour to take Aunt Lois home if that met with his approval. He was surprised when Uncle Alex told him not to worry, that Lois would be spending the night there with him. She was still sore and having a little difficulty getting up from the chair. Uncle Alex and Jingles were going to nurse her and that was apples with Jake. "You're a cunning old bastard, Uncle Alex; all wool and a yard wide." Jake grinned.

The dogs were rejuvenated by now, and Jake took them out for a long run and play session. Lacey set up the litter box for Hoppy. She opened a can of cat food and set out a bowl of kibble for her on the kitchen table. She could reach it by first jumping on a chair and then onto the table. Lacey knew dogs well enough to know that no matter how well fed they were they would still steal Hoppy's food if they could reach it. She'd have to come up with a better arrangement in time, but for now this would have to do. She brought Hoppy in to the kitchen and showed her the chair that she had pulled out from the table. Hoppy sat down on the table in front of the food bowls. "There you go Hoppy, bog in."

Jake and the dogs returned from another exuberant outing. He showed them where their water bowl was and the two blankets where they were expected to sleep. Their former companions had apparently trained them very well because they were well-mannered dogs and very obedient. No use in making a bed for Hoppy as they both knew that she would sleep, and do, wherever and whatever she wanted. She was very much like an Australian, Lacey mused, although she was just being facetious. Alex would appreciate her thoughts.

Lacey and Jake sneaked toward the bedroom, hoping not to disturb the sleeping dogs or Hoppy. Judging by the loud snoring coming from the dogs, there was probably no fear of that. Hoppy was another matter, of course, but she was happily ensconced on the back of the sofa by now. She seemed quite content, most likely for the first time in a very long time.

Jake placed his hand in the small of Lacey's back and guided her into the bedroom. He nuzzled her neck with sweet, short kisses, making little murmuring sounds.

"Jake, a penny for your thoughts; I hope they're about me, sweetheart."

"Umm, you'll have to pay at least a zack for my

thoughts, Lacey and if you don't know what a zack is I guess you'll never find out. They're good thoughts too, worth much more than a zack. But if you must know, I was wondering what a beaut like you sees in me. Then again, I am a Greek god, right?"

"A fair dinkum Greek god, for sure, but don't get tickets on yourself about it." Lacey leaned over and kissed his incredibly soft, sexy lips. They were like velvet pouches drawing her lips into his. She enjoyed their lovemaking, and she also enjoyed just kissing him and anticipating their lovemaking. She thrilled at his touch especially when he looked into her eyes with his baby blues while lacing his fingers through her long hair. And his scent, oh my, did he smell great. Was it really cologne or was it his strong, masculine pheromones? Whatever. He set her olfactory senses on fire. Well, he set all her senses on fire. She wanted to hold him until she blended into him. How could she get enough of him? Lacey pulled him onto the bed.

*****

They awoke the next morning, sated and happy. Unable to move their legs, each of them had been pinned down by a large lump of dog. Seeing Lacey and Jake awake was apparently cause for celebration. Moo and Tillie rolled over on their backs. Rolling from side to side, they kicked their legs in the air with tails wagging.

"Well, so much for bloody sneaking in here last night," Jake teased, urging the dogs off the bed.

"Okay, kids, time for walkies and then brekkie." He kissed Lacey good morning for the second or third time. Stretching his muscular arms over his head he gave Lacey a splendid view of his rippling back muscles. She sighed, something she definitely seemed to be doing a lot of lately.

Lacey made the mistake of speaking to the dogs, which resulted in their jumping up and plopping down on each of their chests. This did not please Hoppy, who Lacey had just discovered, was sleeping at the head of the bed, between their pillows. Hoppy let out a loud meow and gave the dogs a disdainful look to which neither of them paid any attention.

"When the dogs and I return from our walkabout, there's something I think we should discuss."

"Is it about zacks?" Lacey asked, hopefully. She didn't like the sound of the *we need to talk* inference.

"What? You think I want to talk about a sixpence? A zack is a sixpence, Lacey, but really it's just a nickel." Jake shook his head and left the house leaving her to ponder that one.

Half an hour later, Lacey heard the now familiar sounds of paws scrabbling across the hardwood floors. Jake's voice rang out, calling them into the kitchen for brekkie. Lacey had already fed Hoppy on a shelf that she could reach without the dogs stealing her food.

"So, Jake, what's up?" Lacey said, with a nonchalant air when really, she felt anything but.

"First, you have to give me a pash. Then we'll talk."

Lacey was growing frustrated with Jake's constant use of Strine. Actually she was upset knowing that he took such delight in her ignorance of it. "I swear, I'll pash you alright, Jake! You'll be pashed like never before."

Jake pulled her to him and gave her a deep, passionate kiss. "Now, that's a pash, Lacey. And you're quite good at it too, I might add." Then he hugged her tight and gave her another kiss.

"You're a real larrikin, Jake Anderson. But I'm not complaining. That was a wonderful pash."

"I know. There's plenty more where that came from. But first, we need to talk." He obviously noticed the stricken look on Lacey's face so he jumped right into the subject at hand. "I think we need to take you out car shopping tomorrow and get that out of the way. Then we can start making serious plans, about turning this place into the B & B that you've been talking about."

"Do you mean that, Jake, do you really think we can do this? I think I'm going to cry."

"Aww, just like a bloody Sheila. You cry if you're happy. You cry if you're sad. You cry over good news. You cry over bad news. Is there anything you don't cry about?"

"Hmm, there are some things I don't cry over,

Jake," Lacey murmured, as she looked into his eyes. "I'm so excited about everything going on in my life right now, I can hardly stand it. But with you by my side, sweetheart, I think I can do anything."

"Lacey, sometimes I don't know what to say. I'm happier than I have any right to be. What we have feels so right. Just a few weeks ago we were at each other's throats and now look where we are."

"We're right here together, Jake, right where we belong."

"Well, love, let's share this happiness with Uncle Alex and Aunt Lois and of course, the king himself, Boofhead. I'll go pick them up and bring them over here. Does that sound bonzer to you?"

"It's bloody bonzer, Jake."

CHAPTER FORTY-ONE

In no time, Jake, Uncle Alex, Aunt Lois, and Jingles were in Lacey's great room. Moo and Tillie were beside themselves. Apparently, they'd never met a person they didn't like, and were running from person to person, tails held high and wagging. Hoppy was in her usual spot, claiming her place on the back of the sofa, lest Jingles get any ideas of usurping her. Jingles was not the least bit interested in doing anything as mundane as lying down. After sniffing Hoppy's nose and determining she was no threat to his position as the exalted king of the house, he turned his attention to the dogs. He was busy doing his happy dance and teasing them, running between their legs, jumping on the sofa and swatting their tails as they ran by.

Jake hugged Lacey. "Ahem! May I have everyone's attention, please? And yes, Boof, that includes you too." Jake announced that he and Lacey were going to turn her home into a B & B which was met with much enthusiasm by Alex and Aunt Lois.

"Purr, Purr." Jingles seemed to understand; well, of course he did.

They all talked excitedly about the B & B and the upcoming Christmas party at the café. Before they knew it, several hours had flown by. The dogs were finally exhausted from all the excitement. Jingles finished performing for everyone and had joined Hoppy on the back of the sofa. Deftly nudging her aside, he let her know who's boss. Uncle Alex and Aunt Lois were sitting contentedly on the sofa; Alex's arm around Aunt Lois's shoulder. Jake was sitting on a recliner with Lacey snuggled on his lap.

After hours of merriment, the house had gone quiet. The only sounds intruding on the solitude were the crackling of the fireplace. Two snoring contented dogs, competed with the purring of two happy cats.

Happiness, thy name is…well, happiness, thy name is every creature in Lacey's great room.

"Purr, purr. Purr, purr."

EPILOGUE

Thirteen Months Later

Lacey stared at the reflection of the happy woman looking back from the vanity mirror. She'd never seen such a contented look on her face. She even felt beautiful. Jake made her feel that way.

His June proposal, on her thirty-fifth birthday, had been shocking to say the least. The only times they had ever even skirted the idea of marriage was when Jake would casually mention that he couldn't marry again. He never really explained why not, and Lacey never pushed it. She was happy just being with him, and didn't need a legal certificate to prove her love for him.

It was quite a surprise when Lacey walked into the great room on her birthday and found a long florist box on the coffee table. Jake was waiting for her on the sofa. When she entered the room, he handed the box to her and waited expectantly for her to open it.

Lacey took the box and removed the top. Inside, there were a dozen long-stemmed red roses, her favorites. Lying on top of the roses was a black velvet box. She held her breath, savoring the moment. Slowly, she opened the lid. Inside, was a gold ring with a big, beautiful Australian opal in the center. Previously, she'd told Jake that she didn't fancy diamonds, and preferred rubies and emeralds instead. He'd asked her what she thought of opals and expressed his delight when she said she liked opals too. She realized now he had deliberately maneuvered the conversation toward precious metals. She grinned, thinking Jake is more precious than any gem.

Jake took the ring from the box, got down on one knee and took her left hand in his. "Lacey Belle Robertson, I love you with all my heart. Do you think you could marry an obnoxious Aussie?"

"Oh, Jake, I could absobloodylutely marry an obnoxious Aussie. I already feel half-Australian, thanks to you. Yes, Jake, I'll marry you. I guess it really *is* important to me. Who would have thought? I can't wait to be Mrs. Jake Anderson. And, I *am* taking your last name. Don't look so surprised. I've surprised myself too." He kissed her ring finger and then placed the ring on it. She smiled, and threw her arms around him, almost squeezing the breath out of him.

*****

A year had passed since Jake first began work on the makeover of Lacey's home. Jake had turned it into an inviting and comfortable B & B. The results were more than she could have hoped for. Even after seeing the architect's plans for the conversion, she still couldn't believe how magnificently it had turned out.

The first floor remained basically the same. The major exception was a large reception desk off the newly constructed foyer. This is where the guests would sign in. Jake had built the desk utilizing all his skills as a fine homebuilder and furniture maker. All the furniture gleamed and the room oozed warmth.

The second floor now featured a long hallway with six bedroom suites. There were three on each side. Each room was tastefully decorated by Lacey and Aunt Lois. They filled the rooms with furniture handmade by Jake with help from Uncle Alex.

Lacey had brass plaques made for each bedroom door with the names of the particular rooms engraved on them. With a touch of whimsy, one room was named after Ned Kelly. Kelly was the famous Irish-Australian outlaw who was a convicted cop killer. He was also a much admired folk hero. Alex would probably comment, "They're Australians."

Another room was named after Abby Maria Hemenway, a teacher, writer, and Vermont historian. Three other rooms were named after presidents.

Lacey had left one door unnamed for now. The plaque was already engraved, but it would wait for Christmas Day to be presented to Jake. Her heart felt light in the thought that Jake would be touched.

The third floor was reserved for Alex and Aunt Lois, now Mr. and Mrs. Alex Kelly. They had married last Valentine's Day in Aunt Lois's Hearth and Home café. It seemed all the village residents were crammed into the place, all wanting to witness the marriage of two of their favorite people. The café was now owned and run by Aunt Lois's niece, Lois, who had been graciously welcomed by the community.

Jake had had an elevator installed off the new

entrance hall for their guests. Alex and Aunt Lois found it quite convenient, as they had accepted Jake and Lacey's invitation to move in with them.

Jingles, of course, had the run of the place. He would often accompany the guests to their rooms, much to their delight. His favorite place was the reception desk where he would greet each guest, do his little happy dance, then sit and watch them sign in. Jingles had become quite the draw for the Mountain Paradise B & B. Lacey contemplated many names before finally deciding on Mountain Paradise. She didn't know which made her happier, the name, or the fact that she was able to decide on one.

Lacey's articles about TC, with accompanying pictures, were prominently displayed at the reception desk. Everyone enjoyed reading about his celebrity and insisted on having their picture taken with him. Hoppy was the shy little girl who preferred to remain in the background. She and Jingles had become fast friends. They were constantly grooming each other, and were quite often seen lying together in a sun patch inside the great room.

The dogs were friendly, walking up to the guests and licking their hands in greeting. It seemed their tails never stopped wagging.

Brochures clearly stated that the Mountain Paradise B & B was pet-friendly. Guests could bring their own pets, but expect to be greeted enthusiastically by the two housedogs. They were also kindly advised that Jingles was the real owner of the place; he would come and go as he pleased. Non-pet lovers need not apply, which of course, pleased the pet lovers. This useful information kept the Mountain Paradise fully booked.

The only dim light in Lacey's bright sky was the news Summer and Bradley had brought about Steve. She sighed, realizing how fortunate she was having dodged a bullet with Steve. Maybe even literally, she mused.

Just as Lacey had long suspected, Steve was mentally ill. His girlfriend, whom he'd met after Lacey rebuffed him, was stabbed and beaten by Steve. She required surgery and a lengthy hospital stay. Lacey was saddened by the update, but hopeful Steve would receive the treatment he desperately needed. At times, Lacey felt pangs of guilt. Could she have prevented what happened? Reassurances from Jake, Alex, and Aunt Lois, to the contrary, helped her through these episodes of doubt. Perhaps, one day she'd call him. Then again, maybe not. Steve was firmly in her past; she wished him well. Now, Jake was her present and her future.

Christmas Eve finally arrived. Lacey and Jake were busy trimming the tree. Getting the home ready for their Christmas Eve dinner, they placed garland around the fireplace. Jingles was into everything. He rolled over the floor, and chased errant Christmas balls that he'd knocked on the floor. In general, he was doing his best to unwrap presents, just having a good time. Hoppy merely watched his antics from the comfort of the sofa.

During the day, the dogs enjoyed several long romps outside with Jake and Lacey. They caught Frisbees, and balls, and enjoyed running around their fenced in acreage. Now, the dogs were lazing happily by the fire. Occasionally, their snoring sounds filled the air.

Uncle Alex and Aunt Lois joined in the last minute trimming of the tree. Christmas carols sweetened the air, while holly berry and pine scented candles glowed brightly inside the room. The presents, or prezzies, as Jake called them, were under the tree. Some of them were partially ripped open, as if some excited child got caught in the act.

"Meow? Meow?" Jingles vocalized, as he strutted back into the room, as if he knew the jig was up. Lacey swore he was trying to look innocent. The look of pure mischief had given him away.

For such festive occasions, they dined in the formal dining room. After dinner, they would retire to the great room. At midnight, they would open their gifts.

At 12:01, Lacey brought a large and small package into the room. Both were adorned with big red bows. She placed the big package on the floor in front of Jake. "I hope you don't mind, sweetheart. I wanted to do this for you. If it's painful, or you think it's not appropriate, no worries. I'll get you something else." She held her breath as he unwrapped the gift.

Jake's jaw dropped. He barely knew what to say. In his hands, he held a portrait of his late wife,

Shanna. Lacey had it painted from a photo that Jake had. The next package contained the brass plaque with 'Shanna's Room' engraved on it.

Jake's face reflected a mixture of happiness and sadness. The tears flowed easily without Jake bothering to hide them. Quiet sobs escaped his throat and he swallowed hard. For the moment, he was without words, and hugged Lacey harder than he'd ever hugged her. Lacey knew his heart was big enough Shanna, and her as well. She was glad they could both reside there comfortably, and forever.

It was Jake's turn to surprise Lacey now. She didn't quite know what to make of the note tucked inside the envelope that he had given her. *'Good for two round-trip tickets to Woop Woop.'* Jake laughed at the look on Lacey's face as she read the note aloud. "Where is Woop Woop? It sounds Australian. Jake, is this real?"

"I'm just taking the Mickey out of you, Lacey, my love. You're half right, though. The Woop Woops are just a fictitious remote part of Australia. Now look at the next envelope." Jake gave a knowing smile to Uncle Alex.

Lacey gasped when she opened the next envelope. Tucked inside were two round-trip first class tickets to Oz' for their honeymoon. She didn't even try to stem the tears; they flowed happily down her face. Aunt Lois rushed over to hug her, and then Jake.

"Australia? We're actually going to Oz? To

Tasmania, I hope? My passport is up to date, but how about a visa?"

Jake hugged and kissed her. "No worries on the Visa, love. We can do it online and you'll be good to go in less than 24 hours. We're only going if you don't tell people you're going to see the koala *bears*."

Uncle Alex cracked up and said, "No worries, Jake. I don't think our Lacey will ever make that mistake again."

They all took turns opening their Chrissie prezzies accompanied by a lot of oohs, and ahs. Jingles lived by the premise if it isn't tied down, it's a cat toy. He proceeded to dive into all of the packages; chasing the dogs if they dared to pick up something he thought was his. Mayhem was too mild a word to describe the utter chaos. Jake and Lacey looked at each other with adoring eyes.

It was a whirlwind week for all of them. They'd decided to marry on New Year's Eve. All of their good friends had been invited. Aunt Lois charged her niece, Lois, with setting up the banquet for the reception.

New Year's Eve arrived almost too soon. Lacey was an organized person, but she was still nervous that she hadn't covered all her bases.

Summer and Aunt Lois helped her dress. Lacey's voice choked. "I've been saving this wedding gown ever since my mother gave it to me on my twenty-fifth birthday. We were the same size. I'm thankful

I'm able to still fit into it. You know, I've often wondered if she knew she wouldn't be around for my wedding." It was a simple, straight line dress; floor length, and the top had off-set shoulder straps. It was the most exquisite gown Lacey had ever seen. She'd brought the gown with her to Vermont, *a tout hasard,* just in case.

Ellie Stuyvesant was quite a talented pianist, just like Nana had been. Lacey loved the old piano and was thrilled to have it available for Ellie to play. Lacey could play a little. At night, she'd often practice, which seemed to have a calming effect on Moo, Tillie and Hoppy. When Jingles was visiting, which was quite often, he would do his little happy dance, seemingly enjoying the piano accompaniment.

Ellie played, 'Es ist ein Ros' entsprungen (Lo, How a Rose E'er Bloometh)' by Johannes Brahms. Lacey loved 'Pachelbel's Canon', but wanted something not so commonly used at weddings because marrying a Greek god Aussie was anything but common.

Summer wore a pale pink, off the shoulder dress, of organza lace, and carried a small bouquet of pink and white orchids. She and Bradley preceded Lacey into the room, with Bradley holding Jingles on a leash. Jingles danced merrily in front of them, a red ribbon tied around his neck. Dangling from the ribbon was Lacey's and Jake's wedding rings.

Uncle Alex walked into the room with Lacey on his arm. He served as Father of the Bride, as well as

Jake's Best Man. A bouquet of blue orchids and white stephanotis rested in her arms.

Lacey eschewed the traditional face-covering veil. She had always been a mixture of traditional, contemporary, and avant garde. Her whimsical choice for the wedding bouquet was so, Lacey. Jake stared and grinned from ear to ear. His eyes grew moist as he wiped tears, not caring if anyone noticed.

Uncle Alex gave Lacey a kiss and then placed her hand in Jake's. He took Jingles' leash from Bradley. Then, Alex and Jingles stood by Jake.

Lacey's breath was taken by the vision of Jake all tarted-up in a tuxedo with a black silk shirt; she didn't think *tarted-up* was the proper term when describing a male. With Jake, who was never seen in anything but casual clothing, *tarted-up* seemed to apply. Then again, she was a Seppo.

The officiant, who was a friend of Uncle Alex's, performed the ceremony. Jake and Lacey had written their own simple but meaningful vows. Lacey gently suggested that Jake make his vows cussword-free—he did.

When it was time to exchange the rings, Jingles stood on his hind feet and pawed Jake's leg. He lifted his head to expose the ribbon with the wedding rings. He then did his happy dance and positioned himself between Jake and Lacey. His ring-bearer duties were carried out with great success. Everyone laughed and there was a chorus of oohs and ahs in the room.

"I now pronounce you husband and wife," were the sweetest words Lacey had ever heard. She was bubbling more than the finest champagne.

Jake had hired a professional photographer who'd been taking pictures and video throughout the day. He lined everyone up in front of the fireplace. Lacey and Jake were in the middle, with Summer and Aunt Lois to the left. Alex stood next to Jake, with Bradley standing next to Alex. Moo and Tillie lay down in front of everyone. Their heads were up, and their paws were stretched out before them. They looked right at the camera. Aunt Lois clasped Hoppy in her arms for the picture.

Posing front and center was Jingles, of course. At Lacey's suggestion, the photographer had sat him in front. The photographer was not from Ascot Vale. He was not familiar with Jingles or his reputation, therefore, he cautioned Jingles not to move. That gesture brought polite giggles from the assembled guests. They knew that nothing could make Jingles move from being the center of attention.

Marianne had given everyone champagne glasses in anticipation of the midnight hour.

At the stroke of midnight, the photographer snapped the picture as Jake pashed on Lacey. Everyone raised a glass of champagne and yelled, "*Happy New Year.*" Then one very special guy, knowing all eyes were upon him, did his happy dance. He then gracefully leapt into Lacey's arms, turned his boof head to the camera and smiled. That's how the villagers would recount the story of Jingles for years to come.

"Meow, Meow, Purr, Purr."

~THE END~

About the Author

Sheryl Letzgus McGinnis

Born in Queensland, Australia, Sheryl McGinnis is a proud Australian-American. She has authored four drug addiction books, and numerous other publications. A former radio disk jockey and television voice-over artist, Sheryl uses her talents to keep kids off drugs. Jack is her husband of 45 years, and she's a mother as well. Animals are also her passion; Sheryl is the Founder of a humane society in North Carolina. To learn more about Sheryl Letzgus McGinnis, visit her website: Sweet, Christian & Inspirational Romance.
www.sherylletzgusmcginnis.com, e-mail:
sherrymcg@cfl.rr.com, or
http://www.topazpublishingllc.com

GLOSSARY

The Australians (of which I'm proud to be one) speak English, well, sort of. Their slang is called, Strine and can be quite confusing to non-Australians. I've included many words and expressions in this book, most of which have been used by my family ever since I can remember and some that are new to me. As with all languages and slang, words come in and out of use and popularity.

With some exceptions, most Australians speak with the same tempo and idiom. Whereas in the US there are many accents (from a southern drawl to a New Englander sound and everything in between) it would take someone with a keen ear to discern the differences between a Tasmanian and a Queenslander, although slang words (Strine) may have different meanings in different parts of the country. I've appended this glossary to help you understand the richness and humor of the Aussie lingo as you read the book. Aussies also use rhyming slang just like their British counterparts. Have a go, mate!

Aces: Really good, excellent

Akubra: The great Australian iconic fur felt hat, an important part of the Australian culture

All wool and a yard wide: Authentic and totally trustworthy

Ambo: Ambulance

Ankle biter: Small child

Apples: She'll be apples, it'll be alright

Argy-bargy: An argument. Actually an Ulster-Scots word that I discovered in a wonderful book by the Irish physician and author of "An Irish Country Doctor," Dr. Patrick Taylor. I've used it in my story because I'm sure some Australians of Irish ancestry would use it and mostly because I like it.

Arvo: Afternoon

As cross as a frog in a sock: Very angry

As cunning as the rats under the porch: Very cunning, shrewd

As flash as a rat with a gold tooth: Ostentatious

Away with the pixies: Day dreaming, in another world

Bastard: Often used among men as a term of endearment for one another

Beaut: Great, wonderful

Best bib and tucker: Your best clothes

Big bikkies: Expensive. It'll cost you big bikkies

Big noting yourself: Blowing your own horn, boasting

Bloke: A male

Bloody: The Great Australian Adjective (the more polite term is ruddy. Ruddy is to bloody as heck is to hell.

Bludger: Lazy person, someone who relies on others to do things for him, a layabout

Blue: A fight, argument, "they got into a blue."

Bluey: A redhead

Bob's your uncle: There you have it, there you go. "Just do this and Bob's your uncle."

Bonzer: Excellent

Boofhead: Person or animal with a large head, stupid

Bollocks: Man's testicles

Brekkie: Breakfast

Buckley's chance: Slim chance or no chance

Bugger: A variety of meanings and used in many ways, from the original meaning for sodomy, to meaning exasperation, annoyance, an exclamation, used as a verb and a noun, "bugger off," "I'll be buggered," "the silly bugger."

Captain cook, take a captain cook: Take a look

Cark it: To die

Cheek: Nerve. What a bloody cheek, what a nerve.

Cheers big ears; same goes big nose: An Australian toast

Chook: Chicken

Chuck a sickie: Calling in sick to work when you aren't sick

Come a gutser: To fall, while walking or running. Also to fail as a result of pride.

Crack a tinny: Open a cold beer

Crack onto someone: Hit on someone, I think he's cracking onto me

Crook: Feeling ill, sick. To "go crook" on someone, however, is to get angry with them.

Cunning as a dunny rat: Shrewd as an outhouse rat

Dill: An idiot

Dinky-di: True blue, genuine

Doing his block: Getting angry

Drongo: Dopey, a stupid person

Dunny rat: Outhouse rat

Earbasher, Earbashing: Talking someone's ears off

Earwigging: Eavesdropping

Fair dinkum: Genuine, real

Fat date: Your arse (your bum) Get off your fat date and do something

Feeling clucky: Feeling maternal toward someone

G'day: The Great Australian Greeting. "G'day, Mate. Ow's it going?"

Get up yourself: Having a high opinion of yourself

Ginger Meggs: Legs

Gobsmacked: Really surprised, amazed

Googies: Eggs

Good oil: Useful information, the truth

Grinning like a shot fox: Very happy, smugly satisfied

Ham and eggs: Legs

Happy as Larry: Very happy

Having a lend of someone: Taking advantage of a

gullible person

Hooroo: Goodbye

It's a goer: Something that will definitely happen

Kangaroos loose in the top paddock: Intellectually inferior, "not the sharpest knife in the drawer."

Kiwi: New Zealander, also a bird.

Knickers: Pants, underwear

Knock your block off: Punch someone in the head

Lair: A brash and vulgar flashily dressed young man

Larrikin: Good time Charlie, harmless prankster

London to a brick: Absolute certainty. "It's London to a brick that prices will go up"

Mad as a cut snake: Insane, mad

Mod cons: Modern conveniences

Moggy: A cat

No worries: Not a problem, don't worry about it

Ooroo: Same as Hooroo, goodbye

Pash: A long passionate, sexy kiss

Piker: Someone who doesn't like to fit in socially, apt to leave parties early

Pikkies: Pictures

Prang: In a car accident, bash up the car

Prezzy or pressie: A present

Pull your head in: Shut up, showing annoyance with what another person is saying

Ratbag: A rascal, a rogue, outlandish, strange person, an insulting term

Ridgy-didge: Genuine, the truth

Ring you: I'll ring you; I'll call you on the phone

Seppo: An American, a Yank. Septic tank = yank, shortened to Seppo

Sheila: A girl

Shout: Treat, It's my shout (my treat)

Silly as a two bob watch: Bob = a shilling in the old money, worth about 12 cents

Silly buggers: Behaving in a silly way, messing around

Skite: Brag, boast

Sling off: Unkindly criticizing someone

Spag bol: Spaghetti bolognese

Spit the dummy: To lose your temper, not able to be pacified

Strewth: Exclamation

Strine: Australian slang originating from how Aussies pronounce Australian - Au-strine

Ta: Thanks, thank you

Taking the Mickey out of: To tease, make fun of, ridicule

Tarted up: All dressed up

Taswegian: Nickname for someone from Tasmania

Tickets on yourself: Think highly of yourself. She's got tickets on herself.

Too right: Darn right or damn right

Tucker: Food, dinner

Tucker, beaut tucker: Really good food. That's

beaut tucker, mate

Up yourself: Person with a large ego - You're really up yourself

Vegemite: The Great Australian spread for toast, bread, etc.

Wakeup to you: I'm a wakeup to you, I'm on to you, I'm wise to you.

Walkabout: Gone for an extended walk in the bush (Aboriginal)

Walkies: A walk, take the dog for walkies

Waltzing Matilda: The Great Australian unofficial national anthem

Weetbix: Whole grain breakfast biscuits (crackers)

Wacker: Crazy person

Whinge: Whine, complain

Within cooee: Very close; almost; he came within cooee of beating his old record

Yobbo: A lout, ill-mannered oaf

Zack: Six pence in the old money, worth about five cents today

www.ingramcontent.com/pod-product-compliance
Lightning Source LLC
Chambersburg PA
CBHW021504240626
47154CB00002B/491

* 9 7 8 0 6 1 5 7 4 2 7 4 8 *